JUPITER

John Carney

Published by Key & Candle, Inc.
Jupiter, Florida
keyandcandle.com

ISBN:
978-1-953666-02-4

eBook ISBN:
978-1-953666-03-1

Book design and illustrations by John Carney.
Leaf illustrations adapted from Gustave Dore.

I wrote the story that was in my heart,
and I dedicate it to the one who put it there.

– *JC* –

The mind is its own place, and in itself
Can make a Heav'n of Hell, a Hell of Heav'n.

John Milton, *Paradise Lost*

Table of Contents

Chapter o

"*P*eccato!"

Giovanni swore aloud as he opened his eyes. He grabbed his cell phone from his bedside table to check the time, but all he could make out between his fingers were zeros. He snatched his battered glasses from the windowsill near his bed and watched the glowing numbers come into focus as he slid the frames in place before his eyes. The instinctive sense of unease with which he awoke was immediately confirmed by his first clear sight of those diabolical numbers — he was late.

Giovanni sat up in his bed, stretched his arms and back, and tussled his short, brown hair. He reluctantly unlocked his phone to check it for messages. There were none. He didn't expect any, but he couldn't shake the nagging feeling which plagued him every morning until he looked. Invariably, he thought of Her when he reenacted this daily ritual. Pushing the thought aside, he pulled on a dingy pair of cotton shorts and a well-worn football jersey before shuffling across the hall to the bathroom.

Standing in front of a dirty mirror, Giovanni brushed his teeth and tweezered unwanted hair from his face. Then he perched on the hard, plastic toilet seat and evacuated his bowels and bladder. Every morning it was the same — toothbrush, tweezers, toilet. While he sat, he stared vacantly at a framed painting hanging on the opposite wall. It was a painting of a boat — a long, wooden trireme that ended in a hull-smashing beak in the front and a tail that curled up in the back. A striped sail was held aloft by a single mast, and circular shields decorated the railing that ran along the ship's exposed deck. A small, brass placard set into the frame read *"La Nave di Teseo."*

While staring at the painting, Giovanni finished his task at hand, then flushed away his body's refuse, thus completing his morning routine.

In the apartment's small, galley kitchen, Giovanni made a quick break-fast of a bowl of granola and a glass of orange juice, then left his apartment and hurried to his car — a boxy black and white affair so covered by dust that it appeared colorless. When Giovanni opened the car door, a wave of heat escaped from within and encircled him, arresting him in his haste. He spent the first few minutes in the car delicately balancing himself to keep from touching any of his exposed skin against the scalding interior while he waited for the air conditioner to start blowing cold air. This ritual over, he navigated to the nearest highway onramp and joined the din of traffic.

The sun gently warming the left side of his face, Giovanni sped down the highway. A smile flitted across his face as he basked in the simple pleasure of the moment — the brisk zephyr running through his hair from the coastal breeze, the warm tingle in his cheek from the sun's gentle emissions, the exhilaration in his heart from the momentum of the car rushing toward the park. However, once he turned toward the rising sun, these pleasant sensations were cast aside, replaced by a painfully overwhelming glare: the heat of the sun had long since baked the black out of the street's asphalt, and the faint grey road reflected the sun's rays directly into Giovanni's face, causing him to squint and shield his watery eyes. Irritated, he turned onto the northbound highway and breathed a sigh of relief as the sun shifted from his field of vision.

Several minutes later, he veered off the highway and turned west toward Jupiter, an interminable place where time moves in strange ways in the absence of seasons. Giovanni accelerated past the shopping plazas, past the grotesque maze of highway on and off ramps, past the tollbooth that guarded the entrance to the Turnpike — he drove past all the pedestrian attractions that marked his hometown — and turned into Riverbend Park, where Jerry and Thomas, his friends from college, awaited him.

Giovanni parked his car, killed the engine, and surveyed the park. Behind the nearly empty parking lot, a small, metal trailer bearing an advertisement for canoe rentals sat among uneven rows of trees — the first few layers of a dense and pervasive forest. The trees grew among one another indis-criminately: tall, dark pines still covered with needles stripped of color; sparse spurts of holly; twisting and bowing oaks, their serpentine boughs writhing in air; and palms of every size — from stubby, spiky saplings to stout, thickly armored pillars to smooth, towering giants with heads nodding in the wind above the rest.

The white, sandy gravel crunched as Giovanni jogged across the parking lot to where Jerry and Thomas sat in the cab of an immense, grey pickup truck. Each wore dark sunglasses and held slender phones before their faces. As he neared his friends, Giovanni held up his hands in a *mea culpa* gesture.

Thomas waved comically before jumping out of the passenger side of the truck.

"Sorry, guys — took me a little bit longer than I expected," Giovanni apologized as he shook hands with Thomas.

"Gio! Long time no see, man. How are you?" Jerry said as he exited the truck.

"Yeah, good to see you. Everything is good. How about you?"

"Working like crazy. I just closed a big deal yesterday, so the boss gave me an early weekend."

While Thomas went inside the trailer to pay for their canoe, Jerry pulled a grey cooler from the bed of the truck, and he and Giovanni set off along a winding path that led them out of the sun and toward the river.

"Are you going to the festival this weekend?" asked Giovanni.

"What festival?"

The two men stopped at a crossroads in the woods to wait for their friend. Jerry set down the cooler and sat down on it.

"You haven't seen the advertisements?" Giovanni continued.

Jerry shook his head and shrugged.

"The town is sponsoring a festival this weekend for Halloween," Giovanni explained.

"I haven't seen anything about that."

"Well, it should be fun. There's a poetry reading tonight, two plays tomorrow, and I heard something about a private brunch."

"Two plays?" Jerry asked incredulously.

"Yeah, I'm not really sure how it's going to work, but I'll be there."

"Let's get going, boys!" Thomas called out as he approached his two friends. "Gotta hurry so I can find an alligator to wrestle!"

Thomas crouched down and readied himself to pounce on an imaginary foe. Jerry reached out with an open hand and nudged Thomas' shoulder, un-balancing him and sending him tumbling sideways. While Thomas fell, he grabbed Jerry's outstretched hand and both men fell to the ground, giggling like children.

"Get it all out of your systems now: I don't think the river will be so forgiving," Giovanni said with an airy smile as he picked up the cooler. Jerry and Thomas gave up their playful wrestling, and the three men set off along the path to the river.

"Can you believe it's already been a year since we graduated?" Jerry asked as they walked down the shaded path. "Feels like it was just yesterday."

"Feels like an eternity ago," Giovanni countered. "You still in sales?"

"Still in sales," Jerry confirmed. "I'm selling tiles these days."

"Tiles of what?" Thomas asked.

"Just tiles, smart guy; it's not a front for anything."

"You like it?" Giovanni asked.

"Yeah, I do—"

"As much as selling weed?" Thomas interrupted.

"Maybe not that much," Jerry said with a wide smile, "but selling weed doesn't provide health insurance and a corner office. What about you, Gio? How's the life of a private tutor?"

"Eh, it's got its ups and downs."

"Like a seesaw?" Thomas asked.

"Anyway," Jerry steered the conversation around Thomas' attempted joke, "so you like it?"

"It's alright, but I'm trying to find a position with a private school."

"You think that'll be better than tutoring?" Jerry asked.

"It's either that or playing the lottery," Giovanni answered.

"I don't think that's much of a long-term plan," Jerry responded.

"Yeah, Gio, you know the odds of winning that thing?" Thomas added.

"No, sorry — 'playing the lottery' means teaching in a public school," Giovanni explained, "because any day you could win a lifetime supply of lead, if one of the hundreds of students for whom you're responsible starts gunning people down."

"Don't you think you're being a little dramatic?" Jerry asked. "And if you're so worried about it, why don't you get one of those new teacher carry permits that the Governor started issuing? Then you could carry a gun of your own to protect yourself at school."

"You know, I don't think I am being dramatic, and if I wanted to carry a gun around at work, then I'd reenlist in the military."

"Ya'll waitin' on a canoe?"

The voice came from the shadows of the forest where a teenage boy was reclining in a hammock strung up between two trees near the river. He wore a camouflage bucket hat pulled low over his eyes and a sleeveless T-shirt emblazoned with the words 'Kill 'em all!'

"We got one comin' down for ya now," he said without getting up or raising his hat. He waved his hand idly in the direction of a rack of equipment. "G'on and grab vests and paddles and wait down there."

"Which color?" Giovanni asked.

"Don't matter," the teen mumbled drowsily in return.

The three men selected the driest vests and newest paddles available and walked to the riverbank to await their canoe.

"Kill 'em all?" asked Jerry with a mocking glint in his eye. "I'll show *him* how to kill 'em all with my Glock!"

"How about something automatic?" joked Thomas while he used his paddle to mime hip-firing a machine gun.

"How about something rocket propelled?" countered Jerry.

"How about something incendiary?"

"How about something nuclear?"

Giovanni heard Jerry and Thomas' conversation only faintly, as though echoed down a long stairwell. He was distracted by the image of their reflection in the river: three men in football jerseys, each a different color — Thomas wore the blue and white of Abaluhya, Jerry the purple of Orlando, and Giovanni the red and gold of Roma. He tried to find his friends' eyes in the water, but their dark sunglasses kept them concealed.

A yelp of anguish from behind the three men interrupted Giovanni's abstraction. They turned to see the teenager in the bucket hat dancing in circles around the clearing, goaded into action by some stinging insect's harassment. The young man's cries of distress were soon intermingled with a mirthless laughter, like the sound of desiccated leaves blowing across an abandoned school yard. A slender, elderly man — the source of the laughter — paddled into view of the launch.

"Woe to you! Dreaming of angels and set upon by bees? Come on into the boat; I'll deliver you!"

"Oh, fuck you, Charlie, on your ancient old ass!" the teenager punctuated his invective by smacking at an insect on his neck.

"Hope you to see Heaven with a mouth like that? *Remember only thy last things and thou shalt not sin forever*." The boatman turned his attention to the three men on the riverbank. "Now, this your canoe I'm ferrying?"

"No, we ordered the deluxe model," Thomas said earnestly. "Where's the motor? Where's the flat-screen?"

They watched as Charlie untied the line with which their canoe was tethered to his.

"Don't sass me, boy. These boats ain't got no motors, and you have to bring your own mosquito screens."

"I hope this guy is our tour guide!" Thomas exclaimed with a snort of laughter.

"Guide? I'm no guide. I can lead you to t'other shore, but I'm not agoin' through the marsh hither and thither with you young bucks."

"... Goddamn swamp...bitten and stung...sons of bitches..." muttered the teen as he resumed his reclining position.

Giovanni, Jerry, and Thomas all piled into the canoe, stowed their cooler and their life vests, and pushed off into the river. Giovanni cast a backwards glance toward their point of departure and saw that the boatman had lifted his gaunt, skeletal face to the ascending sun. The fiery orb reflected in the lenses of his sunglasses, giving the man eyes that glowed like coals. Giovanni stared at this demonic visage until the bend of the river obscured his view.

As the gentle current carried the three men down the narrow river, the sounds of civilization receded, replaced by a chorus of birdsong. Thomas and Jerry were talking about some girls they had been seeing lately, but Giovanni wasn't listening; he was focused on his surroundings. New flora appeared as they floated along: willows on both banks leaned toward one another, providing an arched canopy of branches that sagged from the weight of their leaves; mangroves encroached as far as they dared and stretched their long, clawed arms deep into the water; gumbo limbo trees peeked through the rest, hidden and obscure but for the bark they shed like discarded snakeskin. As they drifted toward a shadowed swathe of river, the birdsong abated, replaced by the rhythmic rattling of cicada wings.

"Gio?" said Thomas.

"Yeah?"

"I asked if you were seeing anybody these days."

"Oh, no, not really."

Thomas paused a moment before asking his real question.

"Have you heard from her lately?"

Even the cicadas seemed to stop their noise to listen.

"No," Giovanni eventually replied.

"Ah, well, I saw her downtown last weekend," said Thomas.

Giovanni paddled in silence.

"She was asking about you," Thomas continued.

"We don't speak any longer."

"Oh. So what should I tell her if I see her again?"

"Tell Her whatever you like; just don't tell me about it."

"OK..." Thomas said. "Well, look, not to be insensitive, but you can do a lot better than her. I never understood what you saw in her in the first place. She's not very pretty, She said the dumbest things, and her family literally threatened to kill you."

"Wow, sounds like she was a real winner, Gio," Jerry chided. "No matter though — lots of other fish in the sea," he splashed his friends playfully.

"Yeah, you just have to get back out there," Thomas added. "Find someone better and you'll forget all about her."

"Yeah, maybe," Giovanni replied.

"No, definitely," Jerry corrected him.

"What did you ever see in her anyway?" Thomas pressed.

Giovanni let his paddle drag in the water, slicing through the calm surface beside the boat. A woodpecker set to hammering its beak against a tree trunk somewhere nearby.

"It's hard to explain," he finally responded. "Sometimes it felt like we were the same person, sharing the same thoughts, hopes, dreams — I don't know — everything really. Maybe I lost myself in that, maybe..."

Giovanni's voice trailed off. The sun had climbed to its zenith and all the inhabitants of the swamp quieted in reverie. Only the cicadas disobeyed the unspoken prohibitions as they once again filled the air with their rattling. The sound seemed to come directly from the sun — a monotonous tune to accompany the infernal heat.

The river's course veered sharply to the right, but a still pool had formed just outside the bend, and an enormous dead oak lay at the center of the pool. The tree had greyed with age, and it lay haphazardly jutting out of the water, reaching skyward like a crumbling staircase. The three friends pulled their canoe alongside the trunk of the fallen oak and looped an anchor rope around one of its branches. Giovanni climbed out of the canoe and walked along the slight incline to the uppermost portion of the trunk. Jerry followed suit and settled himself on the midsection of the trunk. Thomas remained in the canoe and passed a beer from the cooler to each of his friends. They all stretched out as best they could and let the sun envelope their bodies with warmth. Jerry pulled a joint from his pocket and lit it. The three friends passed it back and forth until the clearing was filled with smoke and laughter.

"It doesn't get much better than this," Thomas remarked through a mouthful of smoke.

"If only the girls didn't bail on us," Jerry added.

"What else is new? Did you tell Jerry about last night at *The Cellar*?" Giovanni asked Thomas, but he didn't wait for a response before telling the tale himself. "His friends pestered him all night long to come meet them at the bar, but once we got there, they spent the entire time on their phones inviting other people to the bar and ignoring us. They would have paid us more attention if we had stayed home!"

Jerry erupted in laughter, snorting smoke out of his nose.

"You're just not closers like me!"

"We'll see," Thomas retorted with a wink. He held his bottle of beer up to his eyes and swished the liquid back and forth before draining the remains into the river. "Anyone need another?"

Thomas had already pulled three new bottles from the cooler. Jerry and Giovanni each traded Thomas an empty bottle for a full one, then all three men settled back into reclining positions.

The beer in Giovanni's bottle was warm when he awoke. He nudged his friends until they too roused from their naps.

"Let's get out of here," Giovanni suggested. "The current is going against us on the way back, and I have to get downtown before five."

"What's going on downtown?" Thomas asked before bringing his bottle to his mouth and emptying its lukewarm contents in one long draught.

"Poetry reading at *Ray's*," Giovanni answered.

"Really?" Jerry replied with an impish smile. "So you want to be a poet these days?"

Giovanni hesitated.

"No," he finally said.

"But you're still writing poetry?" Jerry asked as he picked up the butt of his joint from its resting place between two branches and relit the tip.

"Just on the side, like. It's not as if I go around telling people I'm a poet."

"Well, hey, no offense, but that shit is *so* boring," Jerry said. "I mean, I'm sure your stuff isn't boring," he quickly recanted. "Just poetry in general."

"Yeah, and it's gotta be the only job that pays less than a teacher!" Thomas joked.

Jerry took a final exaggerated drag on the dying joint before pitching the faintly burning ember and ash into the river. He blew the smoke out in one gargantuan ring which immediately began drifting upstream.

"Can't let it die a virgin!" Thomas cried out.

"Someone get it!" said Jerry with a triumphant grin.

Jerry and Giovanni scrambled down the tree trunk and toward the canoe. Thomas resumed his post at the bow as Jerry hastily clambered off the tree and into the aft seat. Giovanni, last to enter the canoe, climbed down from the upper reaches of the ossified trunk. He put one foot into the small boat, a hand still gripping the tree for stability.

"Hurry up!" Jerry insisted. "It's getting away!"

In one fluid movement, Giovanni pushed the canoe off from the trunk, grasped the sides of the canoe, and sat himself down. He crouched into his seat in the middle of the boat just as the momentum from his maneuver sent the craft and her inhabitants toppling over into the river.

Chapter 1

"**D**ead. All dead."

Thomas sat on the edge of the bed of Jerry's truck. Before him, three waterlogged cell phones were arrayed on top of the cooler.

"Damnit. Sorry, guys," said Giovanni, toweling water from his hair.

"That was a team effort," Thomas reassured him.

"Yeah, don't worry about it," Jerry added.

"Three dead phones, and one lost pair of glasses," Giovanni said ruefully.

One of the phones' screens lit up with white light.

"Looks like we've got a survivor," said Thomas as he picked up the illuminated phone.

He tossed the phone to Giovanni. It buzzed erratically, then the light extinguished.

"Looks like you may have spoken too soon," Giovanni replied. "I can't tell. I can't see anything without my glasses."

The phone issued two beeps in response.

"Somebody start CPR," Jerry joked.

"He's a fighter," Thomas added.

"Yeah, well, I think this was his last fight," said Giovanni. "Either way, I've got to go. I still need to go home and stop at the library before heading downtown."

"Alright, Gio," Thomas said in farewell.

"See you soon," said Jerry.

The clock in the dashboard read 1:11 p.m. as Giovanni drove away from the park, but the rhythmic beeping of his slowly dying phone was marking time according to its own unusual meter. Eventually the beeping stopped, leaving behind an uncomfortable silence. Giovanni switched on the radio.

"Welcome back, Floaters! *Espero que todos estén disfrutando de su tarde de viernes.* Stay tuned 'cause I've got a Halloween track coming up next *para todos los Floradores que hay. Yo soy* DJ LP, and you're listening to W-A-K-E, The Wake!"

Giovanni nodded along with the music until he reached his apartment. Inside, he prepared for the evening in his small bathroom: he rinsed himself clean of the river water, shaved his face, combed his hair, and set contact lenses in his eyes to replace his sunken glasses. He crossed the hall to his bedroom and donned simple attire — black jeans and a black T-shirt. He halfheartedly searched his kitchen for something to eat, but his stomach had contorted itself so uncomfortably that the only fare he trusted was a baguette dipped in oil and vinegar. After a few mouthfuls, his nausea made the food unpalatable. He pushed the plate away angrily, frustrated at his inability to control his body.

Giovanni exhaled slowly as filled a glass with water, the one vessel emptying as the other filled. He drank his water then slipped his black sneakers onto his feet and walked out of his apartment. It was only as he was turning the key in the door lock that he realized he had forgotten something. He quickly unlocked the door, dashed inside, and grabbed a tan canvas bag full of books and two sheets of carefully folded paper from where they lay atop his desk. He slid the papers into the back pocket of his jeans as he exited the apartment. He tossed the bag into the backseat of his car, then drove across town to the library.

The library itself was a large, plain building of grey concrete that sat inside a circle of tall, shady oak trees. A grey, metal awning projected out from the building and was supported by a pair of matching circular columns. As he pulled into the library parking lot, Giovanni saw only one other car — old and grey and parked just outside the entrance. He parked near the old, grey car, but left a space between them. Grabbing his tan canvas bag from the backseat of his car, Giovanni walked into the library.

Two sliding glass doors parted as he neared the building's entrance, and cold air blew straight through his damp clothes once he crossed the threshold. The library was empty except for a young woman sitting in a cushioned chair behind a low counter. She had dark eyes and darker hair that fell just below her shoulders. She wore a simple white blouse and a black and grey scarf. From over the counter, Giovanni could see her shapely, crossed legs emerging from a black skirt.

Here is the prettiest woman who ever came to town, Giovanni thought to himself.

"Can I help you?" she asked.

She smiled at him, showing her brilliant white teeth and soft dimples, but her eyes told him that it wasn't the first time she had asked him the question while he had stood there transfixed by her beauty.

"Oh, sorry. I have some returns for you."

Giovanni emptied his bag of books on the countertop. He selected five books with plain jackets adorned with a simple round logo, stacked them, and slid the pile across the counter.

"Homer, Horace, Ovid, Lucan, Vergil," she read aloud while she scanned the black and white barcodes on the inside of the books.

"Know them?" Giovanni asked.

"I know of them."

"Ever read them?"

"No, they're all so old."

Giovanni forced a smile as he passed her a pile of paperbacks. One by one, she scanned their barcodes and set them aside, but not before inspecting each of their covers. One featured a profile of a hooded man with a stern face and an Aquiline nose; the next, a painting of a man in a bonnet dressing himself before a dog; the next, a black and white portrait of a young man with a strong jaw; the next, a young Roman with a petulant countenance; finally, a series of six differently colored panels. The librarian reached for the last remaining item on the counter: a small, black notebook that was banded shut. Giovanni saw her intended target and quickly snatched the book off the counter and tucked it away in his bag.

"Sorry, that one isn't for you," he mumbled in response to her puzzled visage.

"Is that all you have for me then?"

"Afraid so," Giovanni paused, "but maybe you have something for me?"

"Something for you? What's that? More books?"

"No, your name."

She flashed her dimpled smile.

"I'm Veronica, Veronica Shiro."

"It's a pleasure to meet you, Veronica Shiro. My name is Giovanni Alberto."

"Nice to meet you too," she said, still smiling. "I was just about to take a break. Would you like to sit with me?"

"I'd like that very much."

They exited the library together and sat on one of the benches that lined the sidewalk. The metal awning above them kept them shaded from the sun's brilliance. An advertisement for the following day's performances had been affixed to one of the columns supporting the awning. 'An Evening of Deceits and Disguises' was printed in large, bold letters across the top of the poster, followed by a date: 'Saturday, November 1.' Below that, a comic mask and a tragic mask set their diametric faces against one another.

"Are you from around here, Veronica?" Giovanni asked.

"Yeah, I went to high school right across the street. This place is a little piece of paradise. Are you from around here?"

"Yes, nearby."

"That's not a nearby accent."

"My family is from Italy. I lived there when I was younger."

"Wow, that's lucky," said Veronica. "What do you do now?"

"I'm a tutor."

"What do you tutor?"

"Oh, all kinds of things. Anything really."

"Do you like it?"

"Sure."

"That's not very convincing."

"Well, what about you? Do you like being a librarian?"

"No, not really. I have to do an internship for my degree program, and this seemed like the best one — it's inside, air conditioned, no hard labor involved, and I get to meet handsome strangers," she said, again flashing her dimpled smile.

Veronica retrieved an apple from within her bag.

"Would you care to split an apple with me?"

She punctuated her question with a crunch as her teeth broke through the apple's crisp skin.

"No, thanks."

"You don't like apples?" she asked with a smile. "Who doesn't like apples?"

"I like apples."

"I lo-o-o-ove apples. Oooh, and their blossoms too!" she cooed. "Gently folded petals, beautiful colors, and an amazing smell — I love to bury my face in them!"

"Yeah, they're very pretty."

"'Very pretty?' Is that all?" she teased. "Let me guess — you're a wedger, aren't you?"

"Excuse me?"

She laughed at his confusion.

"Do you cut your apples into wedges? Is that why you don't want any of mine?"

"No, when I eat an apple, I always start the same way," Giovanni explained. "I peel off the sticker, tear off the stem, and pick out the shriveled stuff from the obverse cavity — the little hole on the underside—"

"You mean the apple's asshole?" Veronica asked.

Giovanni grinned at the vulgar expression.

"If they could be said to have one," he agreed. "That little pinch of dried and brittle detritus is all that remains of your beautiful blossom, by the way. It was only there to attract some passerby — some passing bee. Then, having collected the necessary deposit, the flower's beauty fades, and we're left with the object of true value — the apple that nourishes us, rather than the flower that deceives."

"And you don't want any of that nourishment?" she smiled and offered the apple again.

"No, thank you."

Veronica finished her apple in one large bite, then deposited the core in a nearby bin. She stood before Giovanni.

"So what are you doing tonight?" she asked. "If you ask me nice enough, I may just let you take me out."

Giovanni gazed into Veronica's dark brown eyes and saw himself minutely in the moist reflection; he saw himself with her; he saw friendship, intimacy, and dedication; he watched them embrace, kiss, lie together; then he saw them learn to ignore one another, pretend not to care about one another, and, finally, grow to hate one another. She blinked, and the illusion disappeared. In his eyes, she saw only longing.

"Tonight?" Giovanni finally responded. "I can't tonight. I have a reading."

"What kind of reading?" Veronica raised one eyebrow as she asked.

"It's a, uh, a poetry reading."

"You're a poet?"

"No, I'm not a poet. I'm just reading a poem I wrote is all."

"I don't know," she said dubiously, "I'm pretty sure that makes you a poet. I didn't know there even were poets anymore. What does a poet do these days?"

"Oh, any number of things," Giovanni answered, "besides writing poetry of course. Nobody is very interested in that."

"Do you like it?"

"I like writing. I don't like trying to sell what I write."

"I get that. It must be hard. I mean, to be honest, I don't read poetry."

Veronica retrieved a small, white phone from her purse. The screen illuminated at the touch of her slender finger.

"OK, so how about you give me your number, and I can call you later?"

"My number? Funny thing about that — I don't have a phone."

"Who doesn't have a phone?"

"I mean, I have one, but I dropped it in the river today."

"You dropped your phone in a river?"

"Yeah, pretty dumb, huh?" Giovanni forced a self deprecating laugh.

"What about your home phone?"

"I, uh, I don't have a home phone."

"So what am I supposed to do — mail you a letter?" she said, stuffing her phone back into her purse. "If you don't want to go out with me, that's fine, but you don't have to make up stupid excuses. I've got to get back to work anyway."

Veronica spun away from him and hurried inside. Giovanni remained on the bench, his brow furrowed in confusion. He thought about pursuing her — returning to the cool shade of the library, explaining about the clearing and the canoe, following his friends' advice.

I don't read poetry, she had said.

Giovanni got in his car and sped away from the library.

Chapter 2

Giovanni fought to keep up with the highway traffic as he headed downtown. Pulling off the highway, double lines of innumerable red brake lights stretched down the street leading into the heart of the city. Giovanni slowed his car to the requisite crawl and joined one of the interminable lines. After what felt like an eternity, he pulled onto a side street, then into a concrete parking garage. The first two levels of the garage were full, but he found an open spot on the following floor, parked his car, and made his way to the stairwell.

The stairwell reeked of piss, and there were several puddles that each looked likely enough culprits in the glare from the halogen lights. Giovanni navigated around the larger puddles as he descended. He emerged onto the street and walked just a few paces before arriving at the entrance to his destination. Dark glass windows bearing the words *Ray's Downstairs* flanked an open doorway.

Giovanni paused before entering and cast his eyes northward, where the lighthouse erupted out of the ground, violently red like some demonic, cartoonish erection. The thing was much too far away to see, but he didn't need to see it to know what it looked like, what it was. He had grown up with that gargantuan pillar watching over him, watching over the town, its twin beams shining like searchlights across the water, across the land, across the water, across the land — never finding whatever it was they were chasing. Nevertheless, it stood there on its little promontory, a priapic eruption of stone red as a boiled lobster with a black, bulbous head full of glass and steel and light. Inside, a circular staircase wound its way around the building's cylindrical innards, stopping twice where a small rectangular window marked a resting spot on the journey upward along with illuminating the shaft during the day. Giovanni caught the scent of salt on the breeze and was momentarily transported to the tip of that edifice, where a narrow metal walkway ringed the beacon. Although he had been there many times during his life, he knew at once that this particular memory was from the most recent time he had visited the lighthouse — with Her. His face was set toward the ocean where the morning sun still hung in the air. The heat on his face offset the winds at that elevation, striking a soothingly dangerous balance. He knew, too, without looking, that She was nearby. That's the way it had been. The way it had to be, even now. Nothing he could do would change that. The sea breeze carried Her scent to him—

Giovanni's eyes snapped open as he shook the vision out of his head. He was still outside of Ray's, alone in the fluorescent light that escaped from the bar's dim windows. Pushing through the doorway, he found himself in a cramped, two-tone hallway of red and black that led to a wrought-iron circular staircase. He followed the staircase's spiral descent until he emerged into a large, smoke-filled room. Standing to the side of the staircase, he allowed his eyes several moments to adjust to the gloom. A glossy black bar top to his right ran the length of the narrow room. A neon sign behind the bar advertised to passersby on the street of the beer offered on tap. The words were indecipherable from the inside, but they cast a neon red glow throughout the room. To Giovanni's left, a stage faced the body of the room. It was set simply with a battered stool and microphone stand. There were a few tables and chairs in varying states of disrepair scattered throughout the room, but the audience seemed to prefer standing in front of the slightly raised stage. Behind the tables stood two columns that created a line of demarcation for each half of the bar. While performances took place in the forward half, conversation, clandestine commerce, amateur pharmacology, and the odd game of billiards dominated the rear. As the two billiard tables often went unused, however, they were often repurposed as bench seating for the imperturbable clientele.

Finally acclimatized to the darkness, Giovanni walked across the room. He walked past the stage to his left, past that poets' altar — there the shrieks and the whispers, the moaning and the gloating, the lamentation and the praise; there they blaspheme and there they pray. He walked through the room to the far end of the bar.

"Oi, Gio!" a voice called out from behind the bar.

He looked up and saw the bartender, his thick frame outlined in red, smoky light. As the large man came nearer and his face came into relief, Giovanni saw he wore a grin that spread to his eyes — a grin he recognized at once.

"Vere, good to see you! How are you?" Giovanni clasped his friend's hand.

"Oh, I'm pretty good, mate. You?"

"Yeah, same."

"What are you drinking?" Vere asked.

"Uh, tequila I guess."

"Dutch courage from Mexico?" Vere replied with a grin. "You ready?"

"I'll know after the tequila."

"Aw, c'mon — you're going to do great," said Vere while his hands worked swiftly behind the bar. First he picked up two small glasses, wet their rims and dipped them in salt, set them down and filled them with spirits — a double shot poured neat and topped with twists of lime — and the publican passed one of these over the wooden bar to where his friend stood with glistening eyes. When Giovanni had retrieved his glass, both men held them aloft, clinked them together, brought them to their lips, threw back their heads, and drew out all the liquid. The shots done, the tequila gone, they plunked down their glasses and no one's thirst went unsatisfied.

"Salute," said Giovanni.

"Salute. We're still on for tomorrow, right?" Vere asked, wiping down the bar top with a ragged cloth.

"Yeah. Do you mind driving?"

"No problem. What time should I pick you up?"

"The first play starts at four, so will you come by around two?"

"Sounds good."

Giovanni sat on a barstool and traced his finger around the rim of his empty shot glass, while Vere worked up and down the bar — taking orders, pouring drinks, closing tabs. A few seats down the bar, an old man with a horrific, grey beard called for Vere's attention. Vere grabbed a bottle from the wall, walked over to the old man, and poured him two shots. The old man took a shot, slapped the glass back on the bar, then spun around on his barstool. A moment later, he performed the entire ritual again: shot, slap, spin. Giovanni stopped tracing his miniature rings, entranced by the old man.

"What the hell is that all about?" Giovanni asked Vere when he returned to the end of the bar.

"What?"

"The spinning."

"Oh, Simon? Don't worry about him; he's harmless."

Giovanni raised one eyebrow.

"More like witless."

"I wouldn't judge him too harshly, mate. After all, he's the one judging you while you're up there," Vere nodded his head toward the stage.

Giovanni looked back at the old man. He had resumed spinning on his barstool, an idiotic grin plastered across his face.

"Him?"

"Him."

Giovanni sat in silence while Vere moved his rag in small circles.

"What's on your mind, Gio?" Vere asked, setting a bottle of beer in front of him.

"Cardinals," Giovanni replied, sipping from the bottle.

"Church kind or bird kind?"

"Bird kind."

"And what do you think about the bird kind of cardinals?"

"I like 'em."

Vere laughed.

"That's what you're sitting there thinking? 'I like cardinals?'"

Giovanni laughed as well.

"Yeah, well, there's a pair of them that live somewhere near my apartment. I watch them in the mornings when they perch on my windowsill and flit around outside the window. They're playful. One of them — I think it's the female — she's bright red with a little black mask, and the other one — the male, I guess — he's not as bright, but his wings have that same reddish glow and he's got a grey mask."

Vere listened with an appreciative smile.

"Got names for 'em?" he asked.

"No, they probably have names of their own already; I just couldn't pronounce them."

The two friends shared another laugh.

"You've got one thing wrong though," Vere added. "The bright one isn't the female; that's the male."

"I've got more wrong than that, I'm sure," Giovanni responded.

"You feeling alright, mate?"

"I don't know. I guess. It's just — everybody has—"

"Who's everybody?" Vere asked.

"Jerry, Thomas, Veronica—"

"Who's Veronica?"

"Nobody. Anyway, they all have some idea about what I'm supposed to be, and I don't want the burden of those expectations: I don't want to be their idea of me."

"You can't run away from things forever, mate. You need to start running toward something at some point, even if it happens to be toward somebody's expectations of you."

"It's not just that," Giovanni pressed on.

"What then?"

"Unease, I guess."

"About what?"

Giovanni laughed.

"Everything, man."

"That's a lot to be uneasy about."

"It's just — it always feels like everything is building toward something, but it never arrives."

Vere furrowed his eyebrows contemplatively.

Meanwhile, Giovanni turned his attention to the stage, where a woman stood in the spotlight. She was dressed simply in black jeans and a white T-shirt. Her tight curls of hair were swept back into an unruly ponytail, and the bright whites of her eyes stood out against her bronze skin. She spoke forcefully:

> *"From the ramparts of Troy,*
> *She said her goodbye —*
> *'Goodbye, my Astyanax, good boy.'*
> *Then, Neoptolemus took her by his side.*
> *Past a stain on a stair —*
> *Streaks of red turning brown,*
> *And strands of blonde hair —*
> *He led her back down.*
>
> *I'll not go there.*
> *Not to that place*
> *Where Cleopatra, Dido, Helen, and Semiramis*
> *Are made by men to mourn men*
> *Like Achilles, Tristan, and Paris."*

"Who's that?" Giovanni asked Vere.

"Britney Barkhourt," said Vere, flattening his dark hair with the palm of his hand. "'So I Say Goodbye.'"

"Excuse me?"

"The piece she just read, it's called 'So I Say Goodbye.' She's read it in here a few times before," said Vere. "It's death, by the way."

"What?" Giovanni asked.

"Death — that's the answer to your riddle, the thing that everything is building toward."

Giovanni sipped slowly from his bottle. He wondered who Britney wrote her poem about — herself probably, but if she was Andromache, then who

24

was her Pyrrhus? He thought about his own poem — thought about Her — and a wave of self pity washed over him. He stood and plodded to the back of the room. He removed the carefully folded papers from his back pocket and sat atop one of the billiard tables. He held the paper before his eyes as he let his vision slide from focus. He ran his free hand along the coarse red felt that lined his makeshift couch until his finger encountered a hole, the result of some cigarette raining fire and ash from its tip. He traced the edge of the hole with his finger — once, twice.

"D'you mind?"

Giovanni looked up from his paper. A blonde woman stood before him with a pool cue in one hand and some loose quarters in the other. The color of her tight dress matched the table's felt.

"Oh," Giovanni hopped off the table. "No, sorry."

Giovanni marched back across the room and resumed his seat at the end of the bar. He peered back at the blonde woman, who seemed to have doubled. Blinking, Giovanni realized that a second woman had joined the first; the two of them stood with their pool cues, looking toward the bar and whispering to each other behind their hands. Giovanni turned away from the two women and stared at the sticky bar top.

D'you mind? she had said.

Giovanni traced his finger along a syrupy circle.

D'you mind? her voice echoed unbidden in his head again.

"Ahem," someone in front of him cleared their throat loudly.

Giovanni raised his eyes and saw that Vere had returned to the end of the bar. He was looking at something over Giovanni's shoulder.

"Huh?" said Giovanni stupidly as he turned his head in the direction of Vere's gaze.

The woman from the stage stood behind the seat next to Giovanni at the bar. She laughed at his confusion.

"D'you mind if I sit?" she asked, apparently for the third time.

"Oh, no, sorry," Giovanni mumbled as his face flushed a violent shade of red.

"Gio, this is Britney; Britney, Gio," said Vere.

"Hi, Vere," she greeted the smiling bartender as she sat next to Giovanni. "Nice to meet you, Gio."

"Nice job up there," Vere said, passing Britney a bottle of beer.

"Thanks! I'm just glad to be done," she replied. She took a long pause to pour the cold liquid past her lips. "I've been reading that damned poem to myself all day."

"What about you, Gio? You spend all day practicing too?" Vere asked.

"No, I went canoeing with Jerry and Thomas."

"Oh, I'm sorry I missed that," said Vere.

"Don't be," Giovanni replied. "We tipped the canoe and all of our phones drowned in the river."

Britney stifled a laugh into her hand.

"How the hell'd you manage that?" Vere asked.

"*Non lo so.* I have no idea. One minute we were blowing smoke rings, the next we were all in the river."

"How far from the launch were you?"

"Pretty far. We went out to that colossal log in the clearing where the river bends."

"You visited a dead tree instead of practicing?" Britney asked.

"Hey, I'm just reading mine from the paper."

"The judges like it better when you recite it," Britney countered.

Giovanni raised an eyebrow at her.

"And I like it better this way."

"You don't want to win?" she asked before draining the last drops of beer from her bottle.

"What's the prize again?" Giovanni asked.

"Tickets to brunch," Britney answered.

"I can buy myself brunch, thanks."

"It's not just any brunch; it's the *Producer's* Brunch — you know, the festival wrap party," Britney explained. "Everyone will be there: obviously the producers, but also directors, actors, writers — even a poet. Although it sounds like that poet won't be you, since you don't need to spend all day memorizing your poetry."

Knock, knock.

Britney rapped her knuckles against the glossy bar top.

"Can I have a Woodpecker, Vere?" she asked.

"Coming right up."

Vere filled a highball glass with ice, poured a long draught of *blanco* tequila, then splashed a deep red liquid on top. He bombed a maraschino cherry into the drink, then slid the glass to Britney.

"My hero," she cooed, popping the cherry into her mouth.

Vere chuckled, then ambled down the bar. Britney turned back to Giovanni.

"So what's your story anyway?"

"My story?"

"Yeah, who are you — other than the second best poet at this end of the bar."

Giovanni chortled.

"Oh, I don't know; no one really. I was a student, then a soldier, then a student again — I just graduated last year actually."

"And now you're a poet?"

"I don't know about that."

"What do you mean?"

"Poetry doesn't pay my bills."

"And yet, here you are, performing at a poetry reading."

"Well, reading a poem anyway. I don't know if I'd call it performing—"

"You mean you wouldn't call yourself a poet? Wait a minute — now I remember you!" Britney exclaimed. "We met a couple years ago at a party you were hosting with -----."

"Oh, yeah, maybe."

"Come to think of it, was that a Halloween party?"

"It may have been. We used to do that every year."

"I haven't spoken to ----- in ages! How is she?"

"I wouldn't know."

"You're not still together?"

"Yeah, no," he though about the question. "I mean, yes."

"That's about as clear as coffee."

"Sorry. We're not together anymore. It's a little more complicated than that though."

"It usually is. So what happened?"

"What usually happens — things changed."

"That's still pretty vague."

"It's also true."

"So what changed?"

Giovanni began mechanically shredding a cocktail napkin.

"I don't know. Lots of things."

"Look, you don't have to tell me if you don't want to, but 'lots of things' is a pretty shitty answer."

"What do you want me to say?" Giovanni snapped. "I've never wanted anything as much as I thought She wanted me. That's what changed: She stopped wanting me."

"So you didn't want her at all then?"

"What?" Giovanni asked with his face as much as his voice.

"You didn't want her at all: you just wanted the way she made you feel about yourself."

"Maybe you didn't understand what I meant—"

"Maybe you don't understand," Britney interrupted. "Finding satisfaction in life is up to each of us. You can't base it on someone else."

"That's not what I meant."

"Well, that's what you said, and she might have heard it the same way I did. Communication is key, you know."

"You're getting things all mixed up. I did want Her — I still do."

His face flushed red again before he continued with a calmed voice.

"The look in Her eyes when I first told Her I loved Her was like an affirmation of faith."

"Sounds like a lot of responsibility," Britney stated.

"What?"

"Affirming your faith for you — that's a lot of responsibility to put on another person."

"This is hopeless."

"What's your sign? You're a Capricorn, aren't you? I bet you're a Capricorn."

Giovanni smirked, erasing the frustration in his face.

"You actually believe in that stuff?"

"Sure. You don't?"

"No."

"So what do you believe in?" Britney asked.

"Not much."

"Do you believe in karma?"

"Karma? I don't know — sure."

"Giovanni?" she asked.

"Yeah?"

"Isn't that you?"

"Yes," he said slowly, confused.

"...Giovanni? Giovanni?..."

His name echoed out of the speakers in the ceiling.

"Oh, here I am!" he called out as he rushed toward the stage, zigzagging past dilapidated tables and chairs. He saw Simon on his left, still spinning on his barstool and grinning like an idiot. Giovanni stepped on stage, took his place behind the microphone, and hastily removed the folded sheets of paper from his back pocket. He raked his hand through his hair several times before addressing the audience.

"*Buona sera*. Good evening. I'm going to read a short poem for you tonight."

Giovanni cleared his throat.

The Strawberry King, part one

The people have gathered, girding the street;
They're crowding to see the King's gilded feet.
Plain feet with ten toes, just like all the rest,
But since they're the King's, they must be the best.
These feet must be shielded and sheathed in gold.
The cost of his shoes could scarcely be told.
In a bowl in his hand, there the real sight,
A quivering pile, his dearest delight.

    Strawberries! Strawberries! Ripe and so red —
    Everyone stared at the juice that they bled.
    Strawberries! Strawberries! Not often seen,
    Yet e'er at hand since the death of his queen.

What of this Queen who will soon be forgot,
Cast aside like a plucked 'forget-me-not?'
Ere it was she who was one of the serfs,
Who eat their plain meals upon their plain hearths.
Does no one recall how they adored her?
So kind and caring, young Queen Moxmori.
But sorrowful days of mourning have passed,
And the King is coming to break his fast.

    Women! Such women! From far and from wide,
    All congregated to be his next bride.
    Women! Such women! See nothing amiss,
    They've all set their sights on marital bliss,
For what could go wrong on a day such as this?

The Strawberry King, part two

The women have come; they stand in a row.
They've been arrayed since before the cock's crow.
They wait in suspense, each sighing aloud,
Until a great cheer erupts from the crowd.
"The King!" "He's here!" His head bobs up and down.
Everyone stares at his Boeotian crown.
The King with his bowl, he sits and he grins.
The girls file past and he thinks of their sins.
    Strawberries! Strawberries! Scarlet and sweet,
    But sticky and soft, like pieces of meat.
    Strawberries! Strawberries! Stain his hands red,
    And increase his girth with each one he's fed.
He sees one he likes and stops the review.
Waves to come nearer, "My dear, who are you?"
She sits on his left. He pours her a drink.
She swallows it down with a deft little wink.
"My name is nobody," shrewdly she says.
Already he knows that she must be his.
The King will soon learn we reap what we've sown —
In the maid's hand sits a bowl of her own.
    Women! Such women! Beware of their scorn,
    Or else you will join the others they've shorn.
    Women! Such women! As the King's new madame,
    The girl who became Queen Elisiam,
Then disposed of the King like a paschal lamb.

Giovanni refolded his paper and slowly lifted his eyes; the audience stared at him and he stared back. He turned to leave the stage, but darkness clouded his vision and he began to topple over. The last thing he heard before losing consciousness was the distant hiss of static.

Chapter 3

"Welcome back," Britney said from somewhere vaguely above Giovanni.

As his vision slowly returned, Giovanni realized that he was sitting on the floor at the end of the bar.

"What happened? How'd I get here?"

"I helped you, mate," said Vere, kneeling nearby.

Giovanni stood shakily, bracing himself against the wall.

"What happened?" he repeated.

"You fainted," said Britney.

"I did what?" Giovanni asked as he resumed his seat at the bar, careful to maintain his balance.

"You fainted," Britney said again. "No big deal. What'd you think happened?"

"It felt like a nightmare," said Giovanni. "Everybody was staring at me like they didn't understand anything I was saying. I thought I might have spoken in the wrong language or something."

Vere chuckled as he returned to his post behind the bar.

"It was in the right language," he said, then shuffled down the bar.

"We clapped for you," Britney added.

"Thanks for that. Were you the only ones?"

"Don't be dramatic. You did well..." her voice trailed off.

"But?"

"Well, I was a bit shocked to see you go down like that. I think everybody was."

"This is so embarrassing."

"You ought to go home and rest after that," Britney insisted.

"Thanks, but I'm fine," said Giovanni, almost keeping the irritation from sounding in his voice.

Simon stood in the spotlight on stage. From between layers of his mangy, wiry beard, his pasted-on grin showed two uneven rows of discolored teeth. He pulled the microphone from its stand.

"Lorries and genle-oo's! Lend me yer 'ttentions pleece. Is time to 'nnounce yer winner!"

"Did you catch any of that?" Giovanni asked.

"He's announcing the winner. Ready to eat crow?" whispered Britney.

"Is that what they're serving at brunch?" Giovanni countered.

"The judge's scores've been 'rithmeticked," Simon continued. "N'yer winner is 'So I Says G'bye!'"

Applause briefly filled the bar. Britney smirked at Giovanni before sauntering to the stage. She deftly avoided Simon's attempt to kiss her cheek, but could not escape from his congratulatory embrace. Her smirk turned momentarily into a grimace, then a thin smile as she thanked Simon.

"Sorry, Gio," Vere consoled his friend.

Britney rejoined the two men at the bar.

"Congratulations," said Vere.

"Yeah, nice job," Giovanni added.

"Thanks!" Britney replied. "Are you guys staying for a drink?"

"I don't want to hang around here any longer," said Giovanni.

"I've actually got to go too," said Vere. "I'm meeting Kateryna's cousin in town for dinner. Do you want to come?" he asked Giovanni.

"Are you sure?"

"Yeah, it's fine," said Vere. "I'll just phone ahead and let them know. Can you drive?"

"*Certo*. Sure."

"Are you sure you're up to that?" asked Britney.

"I'm fine," said Giovanni.

Vere walked to the opposite end of the bar and held a brief conversation with the tall woman pouring drinks on that side. He returned, wiping his hands on his bar towel.

"Shall we then?" said Vere.

"Have fun, you two," said Britney.

"Bye, Britney," Vere replied.

"*Ciao*," Giovanni added.

Vere waved to the tall woman as he and Giovanni made their way out of the bar. They emerged onto the street, where long strands of lights had been hung running down the length of the road creating a brilliantly blazing canopy of minuscule stars against the dark night sky. When Vere and Giovanni reached the parking garage, they climbed the three flights of stairs to Giovanni's car. The garage was nearly full now, and small groups of men and women walked from their cars to the elevators. Once they reached the ground floor, they streamed out of the open doors and onto the street in search of libations. From his vantage point in the parking garage, Giovanni watched this parade of youth and glamour entering the bars, but his mind drifted into a strange vision of the near future when the crowd had drank their share and found their thirst unquenched; he saw the parade moving slowly in reverse, out of the bars and into the streets; he saw them hunched over like demons, stumbling and spitting, vomiting on themselves, falling over one another, rising to vent their violence upon their neighbor, and still celebrating in their own filth. He shook his head to clear the vision from his mind, then led the way to his car.

Giovanni drove them out of the garage and past a bustling cafe; past *Ray's* with its harsh, neon signs; past *Ocean's* where men and women in multicolored jerseys spilled onto the sidewalk; past *The Spectacle*, *Bonglords*, and *Lullaby's*; and through an intersection with sterile, grey government buildings on three of its corners. After a series of quick turns, they briefly joined the chaos of the city's main street, then pulled onto the highway.

The evening traffic rushed down the highway like a current, bearing Vere and Giovanni toward their destination. As the two men in the small car neared their exit, Giovanni checked his mirrors and saw that the car was surrounded by three huge, black trucks — one on either side, while the third followed closely from behind. The entire convoy raced along the highway across three lanes. Giovanni peered into the driver seats of the massive vehicles that flanked his car. He could not make out the features of their operators through the heavily tinted windows, but he noticed that each of the drivers traveled alone. Vere nudged Giovanni and pointed toward the upcoming exit. Giovanni depressed the gas pedal, sped away from the hulking escort, and veered into the exit lane.

Heavy rain poured down through the darksome air as Vere and Giovanni drove along the curving offramp to rejoin the din of city traffic. They arrived at a small plaza of stores a short way down the road. Giovanni parked the car, and he and Vere jumped out and hurried down the nearest of three sidewalks that led to the corner entrance of a trattoria. While Vere went inside, Giovanni waited for his friend just outside the entrance. To protect himself from the worsening storm, he stood under a tricolor awning that projected out from the building. The name of the restaurant, *Il Pomodoro del Ciacco*, was painted in a delicate script on the face of the awning. A Roman mosaic was inlaid on the ground before the entrance, and the tiles formed a picture of a large black dog, framed by the words 'CAVE CANEM.' The beast's head was obscured, however, by a trio of pumpkins that sat atop the mosaic just outside the heavy wooden doors. Each of the pumpkins had an elaborate design carved into the thick walls of the fruit and a small candle placed inside the hollow cavity. The first pumpkin featured the profile of a wolf; its head was thrown back, its ears lay flat, and its lips were slightly parted to allow a silent howl to escape its throat. The second pumpkin was tall and skinny and bore the shrieking face of a haggard witch; her eyelids were pulled so far back that her bulging eyes threatened to leap from their sockets and fall to the ground; her mouth was agape and several misshapen teeth jutted out at awkward angles. The horrific visage was framed by several tendrils of twisting ivy, now brown and brittle and dead. The final pumpkin was decorated with a painstakingly detailed skull; it had vicious eyes and an unnerving leer; however, the finely carved features of the skull had already begun to sag from rot. The candles cast an orange glow from behind the monstrous images borne by their repositories. The wind made the candlelight flicker, and the black dog appeared restless among the dancing shadows. Giovanni stood entranced by the ghastly illusion.

"Gio? You alright, mate?"

Giovanni tore his eyes away from the fierce and strange images. Vere had returned from inside the restaurant with an attractive woman by his side. She was dressed plainly in the restaurant's black uniform, but the simple attire did nothing to diminish her beauty.

"No, it's — it's nothing. Kateryna, how are you?" Giovanni asked as he and the woman in black greeted one another with a hug.

"I'm great, thanks! You?"

"I'm well."

"So I was going to say something to you sooner," Vere admitted, "but we went down to the courthouse yesterday and got married."

"What? You — what? Wow! I don't even know what to say," said Giovanni, a broad smile breaking out across his face. "Congratulations!"

"Thank you," they replied in unison, followed by a laugh and a quick but tender kiss.

Giovanni hugged each of his friends in turn.

"My shift already started, so I have to get back inside, but I'll see you guys in there after dinner," Kateryna said before returning to the shelter of the restaurant.

Vere and Giovanni turned away from the doors to face the road.

"That was fast," said Giovanni.

"Yeah, but we're happy together. We both want the same things; we just figured, why wait?"

"Good for you."

"Thanks."

"So what are you doing about your last names?"

"We hyphenated. I'm Mr. Reynolds-Giles now."

"Nice to meet you, Mr. Reynolds-Giles."

They stood together without speaking, surrounded by the percussive orchestra of millions of falling raindrops. Vere was taller and broader than Giovanni, with slightly darker hair as well; standing side-by-side in the inky darkness, Giovanni looked a diminished copy of his friend.

"What time is Kateryna's cousin supposed to be here?" Giovanni broke the silence.

"Nine, but Rex is never on time."

"Did you say, 'Rex?'" asked a voice from behind the two men.

Turning to face the speaker, they saw that two men stood behind them like shadows. The man to the left was small, thin, and wore a disinterested countenance; while the man to the right was taller and fuller, with an amused expression on his pleasantly symmetrical face.

"Are you friends of Rex?" asked the taller of the two men.

"Not more parasites, I hope," the shorter man sniffed loudly.

"Rex is my cousin," said Vere. "Who the hell are you?"

"Pyricles didn't mean anything by it," answered the taller man. "It's his idea of a joke."

"Ha ha," Vere said drily.

"Allow me to make the introductions," the taller man continued. "This is Pyricles Pogony, and I am Lucas Port. You said you're his cousins?"

"I am," Vere shook hands with Lucas. "Vere."

He extended his hand toward Pyricles.

"Charmed," the small man responded with a listless wave of his hand.

"This is a friend of mine, Giovanni," Vere completed the introductions.

"Splendid!" said Lucas while wringing Giovanni's hand. "And you don't know Rex yet, you said?"

Giovanni nodded.

"Well, we're all friends here already, so I'm sure you'll get on with Rex just fine — everybody does."

While Lucas spoke, a black limousine pulled up to the restaurant and stopped as close to the awning as the sidewalk permitted.

"I say, here he is!" Lucas called out before turning to Giovanni. "You're going to want to see this. Our host is terribly elegant, you know."

A chauffeur in a smart, navy uniform emerged from the driver's seat and brandished an umbrella against the rain. Hurrying around to the front of the car, he opened the rear door and held the umbrella aloft, shielding the short gap between the interior of the car and the safety of the awning. Their host, Reginald 'Rex' Reynolds III, swung his legs out of the limousine, gripped the doorway with both hands, and hefted his girthsome weight from inside the car. He wore a thoroughly obnoxious orange suit that was well-tailored but nevertheless failed to hide the extent of his circumference. Standing beneath the chauffeur's umbrella, Rex retrieved his phone from within his left breast pocket and tapped out a message on the device's brightly lit screen before replacing it in his pocket. He stepped onto the sidewalk under the awning, and a woman emerged behind him. A black evening dress clung tightly to her body. The bodice of the dress was adorned with an astonishingly complex pattern of diminutive crystals. Swirling whorls of black and white gemstones traced the curves of the woman's lithe young body, while three starbursts of garnets decorated the chest. After the young woman, another couple exited the rear of the limo. Both were short of height and slight of build, and both wore matching black suits, simple yet stylish, with a green and white striped scarf draped about each of their necks.

"Vere!" the man in the orange suit called in greeting. "How are you? I'm glad you could make it!"

"Rex, it's good to see you."

The two men embraced.

"Kateryna tells me we're officially cousins now!" Rex said before turning to the woman by his side. "Felicity, say hello to my cousin-by-marriage."

"*Ciao*," Felicity complied.

"And this is one of my closest friends, Giovanni Alberto. Gio, this is Reginald Reynolds the Third."

"Rex, please. Reginald was my father's name."

"And his father!" Lucas chimed in.

"A name so nice we've used it thrice!" said Rex. "Giovanni Alberto? Why does that name sound familiar?"

"He's one of the poets that read at the festival's commencement tonight," Vere answered.

"That's right! We meant to make it to that, you know," said Lucas.

Rex whacked Giovanni on the back in an attempt at a playful pat on the shoulder.

"No matter, you can tell us all about it over dinner."

Rex strolled through the thick wooden doors and straight to the bar. An enormous bar top of warm mahogany ran around the room in a lopsided circle. Above the bar, row upon row of gleaming wineglasses hung suspended by their feet. A dark figure sat behind a large piano in the shadows within the strangely shaped bar. While he played, a woman with a violin traveled around the room, serenading each table with an accompaniment to the piano. A short woman with carrot-colored hair stood behind the bar. She wore the same black uniform as Kateryna, and her name tag read 'Anna.'

"Hi! How are you?" she asked with a smile.

"Tequila!" Rex shouted back. "The oldest *reposado* you've got."

The bartender quickly set to work. First she picked up the small glasses, wet their rims and dipped them in salt, set them down and filled them with spirits — a double shot poured neat and topped with twists of lime — and the publican passed these over the wooden bar to where the revelers stood with glistening eyes. When they had retrieved their glasses, they held them aloft, clinked them together, brought them to their lips, threw back their heads, and drew out all the liquid. The shots done, the tequila gone, they plunked down their glasses and no one's thirst went unsatisfied.

"Let's have another one, honey," Rex said to the smiling bartender.

"Same thing?"

"Single shots this time," he replied.

While Anna worked behind the bar, Rex took a handkerchief from his inner breast pocket and wiped the water from his bald head. He returned the white linen to his pocket, then pulled a cigar from his outer breast pocket, followed by a matching cigar cutter and lighter. He set the lighter on the bar while he prepared to clip the tip from his cigar. The lighter, like the cutter, was made entirely of a strangely tinted rose gold.

Snip, snip, snip.

Rex toyed with the cutter in his hand, clipping at air.

Snip, snip, snip.

He noticed Giovanni staring at the lighter and the cutter.

"You like that?" he asked as he held the cutter before Giovanni's eyes. "Most gold cutters you see are low grade alloys, or merely coated, if you can believe it! Mine is one of the rare few that is made entirely of twenty-four karat gold — even the blades! Therefore, every sharpening costs me twice: once for the sommelier's services, and once again in the cost of the gold shavings themselves!"

Snip, snip, snip.

"You forgot the band," Giovanni said, pointing at the piece of paper wrapped around the cigar near its base.

Rex smiled — a hideous grin, more gums than teeth.

"Then no one would know what I'm smoking!"

Upon closer inspection, Giovanni saw the fine detail in the shiny, embossed paper. Three golden crowns were stamped across the copper-colored backing, framed on both sides by the word 'HABANA.'

"Shots on the bar," Anna said, pushing the twee glasses toward the revelers.

Everyone but Rex picked up their glasses and looked expectantly to their host. Rex returned his cigar, cutter, and lighter to their respective resting places. He reached into his inner breast pocket and retrieved his phone. While his jacket was momentarily opened, something caught Giovanni's eye — a gleam from that same rose tinged gold shone from the inside of Rex's jacket. The object was familiar to Giovanni, but he couldn't identify what it was.

"So, you're a writer?" Rex asked Giovanni. "That's just my luck — surrounded by artistic types! But don't worry; I can more than hold my own among such company. I've read all three of Homer's epics!" he declared proudly.

Rex grabbed the small glass before him and tossed the liquid down his throat.

"Let's eat, eh?" said Rex as the rest quickly followed his example and drank their shots. The bar-side ritual completed, the party made their way to a large rectangular table that had been covered with a black tablecloth. Nine place settings had been arrayed around the table, each consisting of a folded napkin of crisp, orange linen, a pristine set of silverware, and a wine glass with a golden-gilded stem and base. Three decanters had been set in a triangle in the middle of the table. The bases of these were gilded with silver, and their bellies were full of crimson liquid, each of a slightly different hue.

The celebrants filed into the three-sided booth until all were seated. Rex occupied the exit on one side, followed by Lucas and Pyricles; Giovanni sat to Pyricles' right, after the corner of the table; Vere sat to his right, followed by an empty seat, another corner, then Felicity, then the couple in matching black suits.

Rex had removed his jacket prior to entering the booth, and Giovanni thought that he looked far less like a pumpkin in his simple black shirt — no less grotesquely large, but at least no longer monotonously gourdian. Their host had barely taken his seat before he resumed the conversation from the bar.

"Shakespeare too I know: the feuding Montesquieus and Capulets, the Moor of Verona, but my favorite was always Titus Andronicus, Roman general and Volscian defector. Yes, I may not have any fancy degrees, but few know the Bard like I do."

As he spoke, Rex lazily waved his hand at Anna, who stood behind the bar. He pointed to one of the decanters and made a circular motion with his finger. Anna retrieved the decanter Rex had indicated and began filling the glasses, proceeding clockwise around the table.

"Excuse me, honey, you seem to have forgotten someone," said Rex as he proffered his glass.

"It's customary to serve the host last, sir," she replied.

"What's your name, honey?"

"Anna."

"Well, Anna, why don't we cheat, just this once, and you top me off?"

"*Tsk, tsk, tsk*," Vere scolded. "Ladies first."

"Who's paying here?" Rex furrowed his eyebrows before raising his hands in surrender. "A joke, cousin, just a joke."

"Can I bring you some salad or appetizers to begin?" Anna asked.

"Let's just start with the meal," said Rex. "Bring us out some platters to share."

"I'm so sorry, sir, but we don't offer group meals without prior arrangements."

"Most nights maybe. Not tonight. Just tell me the cost and we can end this conversation."

"It's not the cost, sir. Our chef has to prepare those meals in advance."

"We'll see about *that*," Rex barked in response as he shifted his great weight out of the booth. He walked straight to the manager of the restaurant, a small woman in a grey suit who smiled awkwardly while listening to Rex's demands.

"Rather harsh way to treat the girl," Giovanni muttered.

"Don't let the bad acting fool you," said Pyricles. "Rex has arranged everything already; he just likes to put on a show."

Giovanni turned to Vere for verification. He nodded, then shrugged and rolled his eyes. Rex returned to the table with a triumphant grin. As he resumed his seat, the kitchen doors swung open and a trio of waiters in black marched single file to the table. Each of the men carried a covered tray of gleaming silver which they set down and uncovered in unison. Thick, coral-colored salmon filets sat on charred planks of cedar; beneath the planks, small, golden potatoes had been roasted and gently crushed; vibrant carrot stakes were piled high on one side of each platter, along with ramekins of a fragrant mustard and dill sauce.

"That was fast," said Giovanni.

"What'd I just tell you?" Pyricles shot back.

Giovanni took another look at the woman in the grey suit. She was standing where Rex had left her, counting a small stack of hundred dollar bills as discretely as she could. She motioned Anna over to her and the two women held a hushed conversation. Giovanni watched as the woman in the grey suit peeled two bills away from the rest and handed them to Anna. Giovanni turned back to the table. Rex had his hand in his jacket, and a gleam from the rose tinged gold caught Giovanni's eye again. This time, Rex noticed his interest.

"You like what you see?" asked the rotund man.

"I'm sorry, there's a glare that keeps distracting me. What is that — a golden phone?"

Rex turned his chest toward Giovanni and opened his lapel. The brilliant gold handle of a semi automatic pistol shined from within its leather holster.

"You like guns, Gianni?" Rex asked.

"Not at the dinner table, no."

"I love guns. Don't know if I can trust a man that doesn't own a gun," Rex said with a smirk.

"Gio was a soldier," Vere interjected.

"You were?" asked Pyricles. "Were you deployed?"

"Yeah, for a while."

"Really?" Rex added. He drank a large gulp of wine. "You kill anyone?"

"That's a difficult question to answer," Giovanni said slowly.

"How's that?" asked Lucas.

"Well," Giovanni drew out the pronunciation of the word to consider his answer, "when a mortar falls on a man, who has killed him? The soldier who fired the shot? The officer who approved the strike? The scout who sent the coordinates?"

"Is this a riddle?" asked Rex. "I don't know; who?"

"I don't know either," said Giovanni.

"Well, that's a shitty riddle," Rex replied.

"So who were you," asked Lucas, "the artilleryman or the officer?"

"I was the one sending the coordinates."

"So 'no,' then," said Pyricles.

"No what?"

"No, you never killed anyone."

The table was again beset by silence but awkward and heavy this time.

"Those men that died," Giovanni finally replied, "I watched them, I tracked them — hell, maybe I chose them. Honestly, I don't know who killed them. I'd like to think you're right; I'd like to think it wasn't me, but maybe it was."

Nobody said anything for a moment. Rex stared into his glass of wine as he swirled the contents around the bulb.

"You know," he said, "my great uncle was a soldier — a major in the first world war."

Rex stuffed the thick brown shaft of his cigar into the corner of his mouth. The blunt, unlit head bobbed up and down with every word he spoke.

"Highly decorated too," he continued, his words muffled by his mouth's new obstacle. "Of course you're familiar with the *Orderi di Danilo*. No? Montenegro? Nicholas Rex? No? Well, no matter."

Rex continued speaking, but Giovanni wasn't listening. He was mesmerized by the wagging tip of Rex's cigar. It was as though Rex was conducting an unseen orchestra into a crescendo with the stubby baton. He must have finished his discourse, however, because the cigar's tip now dangled toward the floor, and Giovanni's previous impression of the thing's rigidity vanished, replaced with a new illusion: he expected it at any minute to crumble into foul and bulbous little pieces of filth.

"You will have to excuse me now. I had intended to smoke this before we sat down, but I forestalled my own pleasure for my guests' convenience," Rex claimed.

"Oh, good form, sir! You are too gracious," Lucas answered sincerely as Rex exited the booth from his left.

Giovanni turned skeptically to Pyricles, who stared blankly back at him for several uncomfortable moments before explaining.

"Lucas has known Rex for quite some time. He knows how to precipitate future invitations."

Giovanni looked to Lucas, who winked at him before draining his glass with a contented smile.

The kitchen doors again parted as Anna led the trio of waiters back to the table. She quickly cleared the remains from the first course, and the waiters set down the second. They removed the lids and released an aroma of garlic and basil. Grilled chicken breasts had been slathered in pesto and laid in slices atop a bed of curly cavatappi pasta. Cipollini onions and chunks of tomatoes dotted the pasta. Anna retrieved the second decanter, refilled the wine glasses, then followed the trio of waiters to the kitchen.

Rex returned to the table with a man wearing rich blue pants with a matching vest over a white shirt and an intricately patterned tie of yellow silk.

"Look who's arrived!" said Rex.

The table responded with a chorus of greetings and raised glasses. Vere, Felicity, and the matching couple at the end of the table rose to greet the newcomer.

"Cheers, I wouldn't say no to a glass," the man in the yellow tie said as he poured the remaining wine from the second decanter.

"Nonsense! Come to the bar and catch up on shots," Rex demanded.

While Rex led the standing group over to the bar, Giovanni remained seated with Pyricles and Lucas.

"Who's that?" Giovani whispered to Pyricles.

Pyricles sighed loudly.

"That's the director," he stated, turning only his eyes toward Giovanni.

"The director?" Giovanni asked.

"Abin Nash. He's directing Rex's production, *Aichmalotoi*," Pyricles explained.

"And who are those two?" Giovanni continued. "The ones who were sitting on the end there?"

"The Head and the Heel?"

"*The Head and the Heel*?" Giovanni repeated incredulously. "Why do you call them that?"

"Because they're terribly good friends of mine!" Pyricles hissed back. "And terribly good friends may address one another with such terms of endearment!"

"Yeah, but why those terms?" Giovanni pressed after a moment had passed.

Lucas leaned across Pyricles to join the conversation.

"Well, they always work together, you see, but everyone knows who's responsible for all their ideas."

"The Head?" said Giovanni.

"Precisely. Once upon a time, she directed plays on her own. She became quite famous in certain circles for a play about a werewolf, *Homo Homini Lupus*. Meanwhile, he produced plays on his own — failures, mostly. There was one, just after her *Homo*, it was some absolute nonsense about a witch and a boy turned to straw. Anyway, that's around the time they began working together. They remade some Ingmar Bergman flick, and then got married — which was the strangest part of all."

"Why's that?" said Giovanni.

"Well, I don't like to gossip," Lucas leaned closer, conspiratorially, "but they're cousins."

"Cousins?" Giovanni repeated.

"Oh, yes; it's very clever."

"In what way?"

"Most people react in the same manner you did when they hear that those two are married — they're so overwhelmed by the taboo nature of the thing that they look at nothing else."

Lucas refilled his glass from the third decanter.

"What else?"

"Well, I've known the two of them for years, and I've never seen any real display of intimacy between them."

"...And?"

"And? Just watch how intimate the Head is with Felicity."

"Isn't it obvious?" Pyricles rejoined the conversation. "Their marriage is a beard! She's part of Rex and Felicity's marriage — all three of them."

"All three of them," Lucas repeated tilting his head and raising his eyebrows. "With each other," he added, then took a long drink.

"Does that work out well?" said Giovanni.

"Hmph!" Pyricles snorted in laughter before resuming his silence.

"So?" Giovanni asked Lucas.

"Well," Lucas grinned as he spoke. "What do you call a man with an unhappy wife?"

"No idea," Giovanni answered.

"Cursed. What do you call a man with a happy wife?"

"Tell me."

"Blessed. What do you call a man with *two* happy wives?"

"What?"

"Imaginary."

The three men shared a laugh as the rest of the party returned to the table. Behind them, Anna and the three waiters also returned. As they set their dishes down, the woman in the grey suit approached the table. She had a quiet conversation with Rex, during which her smile appeared more forced than awkward. The waiters removed the covers from the dishes and revealed sliced filet mignon steaks set atop small mountains of fluffy mashed potatoes. The soft pink interior of the steak showed between slices. Crisp spears of asparagus lined the outside of the dish like a green schiltron.

As the waiters departed, Anna approached the table.

"Is everything perfect tonight?" she asked. "Can I offer you anything else at this time?"

"Everything looks as beautiful as you do," Rex replied with a wine-stained smile.

"Mmm," Felicity made a dissatisfied mewling sound.

"Is anything wrong?" Anna asked her.

"You can't imagine how stupid the whole world has grown nowadays," Felicity answered while staring intently across the table at Rex.

"However stupid a fool's words may be, they are sometimes enough to confound an intelligent man," said Anna before leaving the table.

Tap, tap, tap.

Someone was tapping a fingernail against the table.

Tap, tap, tap.

Nearby, a clock began to chime. The tapping fell in sync with the clock. 12 chimes, 12 taps, then the woman with the violin began to play. A somber string of notes issued from her instrument. Outside, palm trees thrashed in the dark and windy night. The man behind the piano began playing an accompaniment to the violin.

"I love this song!" Felicity cried.

She clumsily climbed over the Head and the Heel to exit the booth. Pulling the nearest waiter toward her, she began dancing erratically. The waiter's face instantly lost all color. The Head got up, tugged Rex out of his seat, and the two began to dance in small circles. Rex buried his face in her neck and hair. Behind them, Felicity and the white-faced waiter grew bolder; she clung tightly to him and welcomed his hands to explore her body. The man behind the piano attacked the keys with his fingers, punching out a *molto vivace* tune that seemed to encourage Felicity's overtures toward the waiter. The woman with the violin followed his lead. The dancers spun in tight circles as the song reached its climax. When the song ended, the Head spotted Felicity, who was now fondling her dance partner. She rushed over, tore the two apart, and dragged Felicity back to their table.

"What the hell's wrong with you?" the Head hissed angrily. "Who's this man that you let him touch you like that in front of your wife?"

"And your husband!" Rex added.

In the booth, the Heel had moved into Felicity's vacant seat; he whispered something to Abin and the two shared a private laugh.

"You two were busy," said Felicity plainly as she took her seat next to the Heel.

"You looked pretty busy yourself," Rex spat back at her as he regained his own seat next to Lucas, who slouching so low in his seat that he was little more than a disembodied head above the table.

"What do you care?" Felicity said, pulling her phone from her purse.

"Why would you say that, Felicity?" the Head asked as she sat down next to Rex.

"What the hell's next?" Rex asked the table. "Who was it took her off the stage? Who brought her down off the pole? Don't forget where I found you, *Felicity*!" he bellowed.

The Head crossed her arms and stared silently out the window. Rex gulped down the rest of his wine and refilled his glass. The woman in the grey suit was at his side again, but she didn't bother smiling this time — awkward, forced, or otherwise. She was admonishing Rex loudly enough for everybody at the table to hear, but only Vere and Giovanni paid her any attention. Felicity laid down in the booth and wedged her feet behind the Heel. Rex's eyes drooped and his head nodded as he struggled to stay awake.

The woman in the grey suit gave up attempting to chastise Rex and turned her attention to Felicity instead.

"Here is the bill. Your husband asked that it be presented."

She set the bill down on the table.

"What do I do with this?" Felicity asked petulantly as she sat up, but the manager had already left the table. "What do I do with this, Reginald? Reginald. *Reginald*!" Felicity screamed across the table.

"'At's mah fatha's name," Rex mumbled drunkenly.

"And *his* father!" Lucas piped up in response as his eyes snapped open.

"Are you blind? The *bill*, Reginald, it's right in front of you," Felicity insisted.

Rex loosened his tie and moved the knot to eye level before tightening it again in the fashion of a blindfold.

"Blind? Then call me Ulysseses, who purrout 'is own eyes when he discov'r'd 'at 'is fatha was the cyclops, Polygamus!"

Immediately after this declamation, Rex slumped incoherently against Lucas, who was similarly indisposed.

"Give me the damn thing," Felicity snapped at Pyricles, who passed the booklet to her.

She flipped it open and scanned the check, then scowled, snapped the booklet shut again, and tossed it onto the table.

"Doesn't it need a signature?" Vere asked.

"He's already paid," Felicity said over her shoulder as she tried to crawl out of the booth.

"Cheers to that," said Vere, and he and Giovanni lifted their glasses in mock salute.

Meanwhile, Felicity struggled to escape from the booth. The clasp on one of her shoes had caught the zipper on the cushioned seat of the booth. She tried to yank it loose, but couldn't. She put both hands on the edge of the table and pulled. Her shoe immediately broke free from the cushion and she began to topple backwards out of the booth. In a panic, she grabbed at the edge of the table again, but it did nothing to arrest her momentum. Instead, the entire thing went toppling over with her.

For an instant, everything hung suspended in air before Giovanni: Felicity clung to the table with her hands while her feet were kicked over her head; the table stood crookedly on two legs; plates hung above the table and the food hung above the plates; the gold-stemmed glasses and silver-bottomed decanters were primed to fall, but the liquids they contained remained oddly balanced. Then time caught up: Felicity tumbled onto the floor, the table tipped over completely, glasses smashed, platters shattered, and wine splashed onto the carpet. Silence fell across the restaurant. From the floor,

Felicity began to giggle uncontrollably. Rex and Lucas remained unconscious, slumped against one another.

Vere and Giovanni exchanged a cautionary look before they both rose from their seats and made for the rear exit.

"What the hell was that?" Giovanni asked once they were free from the chaos.

"That's why I don't accept any of his invitations. What a mess."

"Yeah, I feel bad for Kateryna; I can't imagine having to clean up after that."

"It'll be alright; Rex will pay for everything. I just wish I had been able to save another of those glasses. I know Kateryna would have liked a pair."

"Take mine," Giovanni offered. "Good thing I was holding it during all that."

"Are you sure? That's real gold."

"*Certo*. Of course," Giovanni said, proffering the glass.

"Thanks, Gio."

"Don't mention it—"

The yowl of sirens drowned out the rest of Giovanni's sentence. A moment later, three police cruisers rolled into the parking lot with their lights ablaze.

"I'm going to leave and avoid the show," Giovanni said, nodding toward the cops exiting their cars. "Do you need a ride home?"

"No, thanks. I'm going to stay and help Kateryna clean up."

"Tell her I said goodbye. Thanks again for the invite."

"Absolutely."

The two men exchanged a handshake, then a hug, then Giovanni got in his car and left.

Chapter 4

Giovanni awoke late again the following day. He didn't bother checking the time; the sun streaming down on his face through his westward-facing window told him that it was already well into the afternoon. He shielded his eyes from the sun.

Knock-knock, knock-knock.

Giovanni forced his eyes open as he recognized Vere's unique knock coming from the front door of his apartment. He leapt out of bed and hurried toward the door, stopped midway, ran back to his room and wrapped his bed sheet around his naked body; he scurried back to the door, nearly tripped on the edge of his sheet as he arrived at his destination, flung the door open, and discovered his friend in the doorway, fist poised to rap upon the door again.

"Hey, Vere," Giovanni greeted him as he stepped back from the doorway. "Come on in."

"Hey, Gio," Vere replied with a broad grin as he entered the apartment. "How you doing, mate?"

"Good, good. You?"

Vere sat on a small, beige sofa that bowed in the middle.

"Doing well," Vere grinned again as he tilted his head at Giovanni's bed sheet toga. "You ready to go?"

"Give me just a few minutes," Giovanni blinked to drive the sleep from his eyes, then dashed into the bathroom.

"Take your time," Vere called from the other room.

Giovanni rushed to complete a truncated version of his daily waste removal rituals, then crossed the hall to his bedroom, grabbed the previous night's outfit from its resting place on the floor, and quickly redressed himself. The two friends left the apartment and made their way to Vere's car. The interior had not yet heated to an unbearable degree, so they got right in. Vere turned his key in the car's ignition and a familiar voice projected out of his car stereo.

"*Bienvenido, los Flotadores*. It's a sunny Saturday afternoon, and I've got another classic track coming your way. *Yo soy* DJ LP, and you're listening to W-A-K-E, The Wake!"

A rock song began to play. Giovanni remembered he had forgotten to change his contact lenses. He leaned his head against the car window to check them in the side mirror; he frowned at the tired, bloodshot eyes that squinted back at him. As Vere drove slowly, conscientiously toward the coast, Giovanni tapped his feet and drummed the fingertips of his right hand against the window.

"You OK?" Vere asked.

"Yeah, yeah. Everything's fine."

"You want to give the percussion section the afternoon off then?"

Giovanni laughed and stopped his drumming and tapping.

"What's wrong?" Vere continued.

"Nothing really," said Giovanni. "I just can't get over last night."

"The fainting?"

"The losing."

"Losing? Just because you didn't win doesn't mean you lost."

"That's exactly what it means."

"Come on, you know what I'm trying to say. All that last night shows is that Simon chose Britney's poem."

Yeah, that's what I said: the judge chose a winner who wasn't me."

"So?" Vere asked.

"So what's the point?" Giovanni returned.

"*What's the point?*" Vere repeated. "Look, Gio, it's a shame that you didn't win, but what are you going to do? Give up? Stop writing?"

"I didn't say that."

"Sounded pretty damn close," Vere said. "I guess Britney was right too."

"About what?"

"About you memorizing your poem."

"Waste of time," Giovanni shrugged.

"Apparently not."

"Who even memorizes poems?"

"Oral poets," Vere remarked with a smirk.

"Yeah, well, oral poetry hasn't been much in demand the last thousand years or so."

"You never know, mate — the world's a crazy place. We may need oral poets again before too long."

Vere pulled into a large parking lot along the coast where hundreds of nearly identical cars sat in neat, uniform rows. He steered them into an empty parking spot.

Scrape.

The sound of the car's bumper grinding against the stone parking baulk sent a shiver up Giovanni's spine.

"Whoops," Vere muttered as he killed the car's engine.

The two men exited the car. Vere shouldered a black backpack from the backseat before they joined the procession crossing the street. After a brief walk, they descended a flight of stairs, then rounded a berm and emerged in the crowded orchestra of an outdoor amphitheater. Vere and Giovanni found an open spot at the back of the crowd, near the top of the hill, and stood together and surveyed their surroundings. The amphitheater was a simple affair — a stage set before a softly sloping, semicircular knoll. The sounds of the ocean could be heard from the hilltop where the evening's three judges shared a wooden picnic table under a portable awning. The awning shielded the three of them from the sun, just as their pseudonyms — Darkbloom, Daedalus, and Chinaski — shielded their identities. The true judges, however, sat on the hillside. Here, all manner of people congregated, and each small group established their space as best they could according to their supplies. The best outfitted arrived with an assortment of furniture resembling a full living room set, all of which conveniently folded into a set of small, nylon bags. The most frugal, on the other hand, had little more than a blanket to lay on the grass. At nearly every encampment, wine flowed into cheap plastic cups from bottles, boxes, and bags.

"I say, that can't be Vere and Giovanni?"

Giovanni looked toward the source of the voice, and his eyebrows lurched in surprise at the two men who stood before him: the taller of the two wore the leather skirt and bronze armor of a Greek soldier while the shorter man wore a Roman toga — white with a purple stripe. The taller man laughed at Giovanni's expression.

"Don't you recognize your two favorite actors?"

"Lucas?"

"One and the same! And Mr. Pyricles Pogony, at your service," said Lucas with a slight nod toward his counterpart.

"Speak for yourself," Pyricles muttered as he adjusted his sword belt.

"Good to see you, Lucas!" said Giovanni as he shook the man's hand. "Pyricles," he added.

Pyricles shrugged his eyebrows in response.

"Cheers," Vere greeted the actors.

"Can you believe this heat?" Lucas asked. "And me all done up in leather and metal! Calm down, boys," he grinned before adding, "at least Pyricles' toga might admit a bit of a breeze."

Vere and Giovanni laughed with Lucas. Pyricles remained aloof, his face betraying his dissatisfaction.

"Pyricles and I were just on our way to pick up a couple pints of not-yet-entirely-warm beer from the concessionaire when we saw you up here," Lucas explained. "Bit of a thespian tradition of ours — for luck. Would you care to join us?"

"You guys go. I'll hold down the fort here," Giovanni offered.

Vere, Lucas, and Pyricles ambled down the hill together while Giovanni made ready their site with the provisions in Vere's backpack. His attention was so absorbed by the unfolding and placing of a large, yellow blanket that he didn't notice the shadow that fell across him.

"Want a hand?" asked a voice that Giovanni vaguely recognized.

He looked up from his task, but the voice's owner stood in the blinding halo of the sun. Giovanni's hand leapt to his brow to shield his eyes from the painful light. He rose to his feet and sidestepped to escape the sun's directness. Britney, her hands in the back pockets of her olive shorts, stood next to the yellow blanket. She smiled and tucked a wild curl behind her ear before returning her hand to its pocket.

"Oh, hi."

"*Oh, hi* to you too," she replied. "Do you want a hand?" she asked again.

"I think I've got it. Thanks though."

"No problem. So how was dinner last night?"

"Don't remind me about last night."

"It can't have been that bad."

"It was. Let's just say, at least one of us got what we wanted — what *she* wanted."

"Who's that?"

"You."

"Me?"

She crossed her arms as her smile evaporated.

"Yeah, your poem won," said Giovanni. "You get to go to your fancy brunch."

"What? You want the tickets after all?"

"I already told you I don't care about the tickets."

"What then?"

"I — nothing, it's nothing."

"It's obviously not nothing."

"My poem was good."

"So was mine."

"Its — that was the best poem that I've ever written," Giovanni admitted. "I worked on it for weeks. It's damn near the best thing I've ever created in my life."

"So?"

"So it should have won!"

"*Simon* chose the winner, not me."

Britney started to say something more, but she was interrupted by the return of Vere and Lucas, each of whom carried a beer in either hand.

"Where's the third musketeer?" Giovanni asked as Vere handed him a flimsy plastic cup filled with frothy, pale yellow liquid.

"I think the appropriate term would be Centurion," Lucas replied with a grin. "He had to run for curtain call. Who's your friend?"

"I'm Britney," she responded.

"*Enchanté*, Britney," Lucas crooned. "Would you care to join us in a toast?" he asked, proffering one of his cups.

"Why not?" she answered, taking the cup. "Hi, Vere."

"Cheers, Britney," he raised his cup to hers.

The others followed Vere's lead, then the four drank their tepid brews.

"So you watching the play with us?" Vere asked Britney.

"Why not?" she smirked smugly at Giovanni for an instant before turning back to Vere. "I'm meeting a couple friends for the second play. Do you mind if they join?"

"Not at all!" Lucas answered. "There's plenty of room. Giovanni's done a hell of a job here! This is an excellent position. The fortifications, maybe, could be improved."

"Yeah, well, if any ne'er-do-wells come our way, you can always protect us with that sword of yours," said Giovanni. "Or is it just for show?"

Lucas flicked his eyebrows skyward, then made an exaggerated wink.

"You'll just have to wait and see!"

The four spectators took their seats on the blanket just as a voice boomed throughout the amphitheater.

"Ladies and gentlemen! Good afternoon, and welcome to An Evening of Deceits and Disguises brought to you by the Town of Jupiter. We'd like to take this opportunity to thank you for joining us, and to remind you to silence your phones and other electronic devices—"

"You hear that, Gio? Don't forget to silence your phone," Vere said with a grin.

"Very funny," Giovanni responded.

A man in a white tunic walked to the center of the stage. Black curtains fluttered behind him.

Aichmalatoi;

or

The Captives

Dramatis Personae

Marcus Antonius

*Cleopatra's consort & co-ruler
Former Triumvir of Rome*

Cleopatra VII

Pharaoh of Egypt

Ptolemy XV 'Caesarion'

*Pharaoh of Egypt, son of Cleopatra
and Caesar*

Alexander Helios

*Son of Cleopatra and M. Antonius,
twin of Selene*

Selene

*Daughter of Cleopatra and
M. Antonius, twin of A. Helios*

Turpio

Slave of Caesarion

Lanuvinus

Slave of M. Antonius

Timon

Peasant

Gaius Julius Caesar Octavianus

*Imperator of Rome,
Former Triumvir of Rome*

Marcus Vipsanius Agrippa

*Advisor to Octavian and
General in his army*

Gaius Cilnius Maecenas

Advisor to Octavian

Octavia Minor

*Sister of Octavian, ex-wife of
M. Antonius*

Marcus Aemilius Lepidus

*Pontifex Maximus, Former Triumvir
of Rome*

Gaius Sosius

Former General in M. Antonius' army

Prologue

The curtains remain drawn.

[Enter TURPIO, *center.]*

TURPIO

O, Divine Justice, take heed! I come before you as an emissary from our Poet. He stands faced with that all too familiar accusation: his critics claim that his work has been contaminated by those giants upon whose shoulders he perches. "Give us something new!" they clamor, all the while craving what they know — and what they know, they hate. Therefore, he will take what they know, and make of it something new, and they will hate it all the same. Judge for yourselves then whether our Poet deserves to continue his endeavors or be cast aside — for the same old words from the same old men mean little when weighed against your reception. Thus, I beseech you to pay heed to the pains our Poet has taken. Notice the careful manner in which He uses the characters that you well know to concoct this farce: the prodigal pimp, the greedy whore, the naïve youth, the clever slave, and the braggadocious captain. Our Poet tonight presents you a new production which He has named *Aichmalotoi*; or, The Captives. The facts stand as such: the two leading men of Rome have been engaged in an intermittent war for fifteen long years. In July of 30 B.C.E., Gaius Julius Caesar Octavianus, soon to be the Emperor Caesar Augustus, arrived in Alexandria to confront Marcus Antonius, soon to be deceased. Antonius had taken up with Caesar's mistress: Cleopatra VII, the great lady of perfection, excellent in counsel, the great one, sacred image of her father, beloved goddess, eminently beautiful and imminently deceased. They had been living in Cleopatra's Palace at Alexandria, and to that same palace the two lovers returned after their fleet was destroyed in the decisive Battle at Actium nearly a year prior to the young Caesar's arrival.

[Exit TURPIO, *center.]*

ACT I

*Inside Cleopatra's Palace at Alexandria. Two golden thrones sit on the stage,
centered near the rear.*

> *[Enter* ANTONIUS, *stage right. He wears Roman
> military attire with a sword at his side. He carries a
> large, golden cup full of wine.]*

ANTONIUS

Ah, Dionysus, your gift gives life! You've always been there for me,
waiting with a kiss that's cool in summer and warm in winter, strong in
the morning and soft in the evening. Where will you kiss me today?

> *[Enter* CLEOPATRA, *stage right. She wears a yellow
> dress and golden jewelry.]*

ANTONIUS

There she is, living image of Aphrodite, er, Isis — the goddess taken
form anyway—

CLEOPATRA

Is that the Falernian?

ANTONIUS

The wine? Of course it's the Falernian — the elixir of life!

CLEOPATRA

We hardly have any left, and you're spilling it everywhere! Do you
have any idea what an amphora costs these days?

ANTONIUS

We have plenty of Falernian left. Just look how full my cup is!

CLEOPATRA

A man should never be allowed to judge his own measures — what you
call full nearly always leaves the cup unfulfilled. Anyway, while you've
been drinking away the night, Octavian has nearly arrived.

ANTONIUS

Aye, Caesar's other son will be sailing in any moment now.

CLEOPATRA

Caesarion is Caesar's only true son.

ANTONIUS

No, according to Roman law—

CLEOPATRA

I don't favor that word.

ANTONIUS

Roman?

CLEOPATRA

No.

ANTONIUS

What then?

CLEOPATRA

No.

ANTONIUS

No?

CLEOPATRA

No! I don't favor it, and I won't stand for it! Now, what are you going to do?

ANTONIUS

Stick to yes, I should think.

CLEOPATRA

About the Roman!

ANTONIUS

I'm going to keep him out there, and us in here. We can go on for years in here feasting and drinking. My amphorae never run dry.

CLEOPATRA

Is that all?

ANTONIUS

Well, what are you going to do about him?

CLEOPATRA

Maybe we could bribe him.

ANTONIUS

Yes, maybe some of your jewels—

CLEOPATRA

The slaves. We could sell the slaves and—

ANTONIUS

Did you say we could geld the slaves?

CLEOPATRA

Geld the slaves? Holy Hathor, not this again—

ANTONIUS

It's brilliant! We'll geld them — all of them, all at once! Fetch my longest sword!

CLEOPATRA

[*Aside*] I'm sure it's not the one you carry.

ANTONIUS

What's that?

CLEOPATRA

Surely not all at once. Anyway, we haven't the time to geld all the slaves. Geld the ones that anger you if you wish — the cook should be able to handle the job easily enough. Then we'll sell them — eunuchs are fetching a good price this week.

ANTONIUS

Yes, tell the cook to geld them, and have him save the trimmings.

CLEOPATRA

There's a fine thought for once. The cook can reprise his recipe for pickled eels. We'll feed them to the remaining slaves and save a bit of the royal grain.

ANTONIUS

You can't feed them to the others — I need those trimmings! I'm going to rain them down on Octavian's head — and just you see if he doesn't try to slip a few inside his toga before he escapes to the rear for a bit of fun with his own.

CLEOPATRA

Gods of Egypt, save me from this drunken idiocy! I don't have any more patience for your nonsense. The Roman will be here soon, and your plans are all cock and no bull! Go on swilling wine then.

[Exit CLEOPATRA, stage right.]

ANTONIUS

Swilling wine? I'm embracing my divine role as a priest of Dionysus! Drunk!

[Enter CAESARION, stage right.]

ANTONIUS

There he is now, that young son of Caesar. Hail, Little Caesar!

CAESARION

That's not my name! It's Ptolemy XV, heir of the God who saves—

ANTONIUS

Heir of the goat who shaves—

CAESARION

Chosen of Ptah—

ANTONIUS

Chosen of blah—

CAESARION

Son of righteousness—

ANTONIUS

Son of lefteousness—

CAESARION

Address me properly! I'm the Pharaoh of Upper and—

ANTONIUS

    I'll address you with a proper fist about your head if you keep at it, boy.
    Your silly Egyptian names mean nothing to me. I rule here.

CAESARION

    Only until I wed.

ANTONIUS

    Who would ever marry you?

CAESARION

    Mother would.

ANTONIUS

    Mother wouldn't.

CAESARION

    It's tradition.

ANTONIUS

    You're not marrying your mother while I'm around, Oedipus. You'll
    have to find another tradition.

        [Enter HELIOS *and* SELENE *from opposite ends of the*
        stage. They crash into each other and fall to the ground.]

ANTONIUS (cont'd)

    What's this? Helios, Selene — go play elsewhere, little ones.

            [Exit HELIOS *and* SELENE *to opposite ends of the*
                            stage.]

ANTONIUS (cont'd)

    You're still here? What? What do you want?

CAESARION

    I want to know more about Aphrodite.

ANTONIUS

    Why?

CAESARION

    You said she's your Isis, like mother.

ANTONIUS

    Sure, she's our Isis. Anyway, Aphrodite needed a husband, so she inter-
    viewed all the Roman gods, from Ares, sacker of cities, to earth-moving
    Poseidon. All the gods vied for her affection, but she chose for her mate
    the lame blacksmith, pathetic little Vulcan.

CAESARION

    Was he handsome?

ANTONIUS

    Ugliest god there ever was.

CAESARION

    Was he brave?

ANTONIUS

Complete and total coward.

CAESARION

Was he clever?

ANTONIUS

That much could be said for the decrepit little mutant — he was a bit clever. Clever enough to convince Aphrodite to marry him.

CAESARION

But why would she choose him?

ANTONIUS

Because she knew that with a husband that weak, she could do whatever she wanted.

CAESARION

And what did she want?

ANTONIUS

She wanted a real man.

CAESARION

So what happened?

ANTONIUS

She married Vulcan, and ran off with Dionysus. Do you remember Dionysus?

CAESARION

The drunk god?

ANTONIUS

The god of wine, boy. He was generous, jovial, probably the most handsome of all the gods, definitely the most fun—

CAESARION

But Dionysus can't be the only one she ran off with.

ANTONIUS

What?

CAESARION

Well, if she would run off with Dionysus, then she's bound to run off with others.

ANTONIUS

That's not — there's nothing — that is — no more interruptions! You may be the Pharaoh and the heir and the chosen one — you may be the living image of Amun's holy cock — but I rule here. It's only fair — it's my turn, after all. Been my turn since Tarentum, but Octavian stole it from me.

CAESARION

Octavian stole your tarantula?

ANTONIUS

    No, idiot, he stole my throne! And he's on his way here now, from Brundisium of all places, on his way to do what he does best — stand himself between Maecenas and Agrippa and squeal like a skewered sow! Caesar he calls himself.

CAESARION

    But that's my name!

ANTONIUS

    Can you believe the gall of the brat? If he's Caesar, then call me Brutus and Cleopatra Cassius. We will be the new liberators! The brat means to cut short my turn at the helm, but I've still got Roman steel for him to taste — not the taste he takes of his generals' swords, but a proper impaling through the back of his head! And Roman wine for me. The vaults of Alexandria have been well stocked with Falernian for longer than I've yet lived. Let this new Caesar come then.

    [Enter LANUVINUS *and* TURPIO, *stage left.]*

LANUVINUS

    Hurry up — follow me. This is the throne room. It's not your place to be in here unless General Antonius calls for you, but he won't. If he needs anything from you, it'll come from me.

TURPIO

    What does the general plan to do about the Romans outside the palace?

LANUVINUS

    You just worry about watching over Caesarion. General Antonius'll take care of the Romans. And don't interrupt—

ANTONIUS

    Lanuvinus, what are you doing? Who's that with you?

LANUVINUS

    General Antonius, this is Caesarion's new slave, Turpio — another Egyptian. Palace is barely civilized as it is.

ANTONIUS

    A new slave for Little Caesar! What fun. You know, slave, I'm compiling a list for the cook. He's making pickled eels today for a treat, and I bet you could spare a few inches of meat.

TURPIO

    Thank you, General, but I have no right to be included. The quality of my ingredient is so far inferior to that of your own, and the quantity too, that it would be an insult to the House of Ptolemy and the cook. You should have the place of honor on your list.

LANUVINUS

Don't worry, General — I'll put you at the top of the list and myself as your number two. First in rank, first on the list!

ANTONIUS

Stay your hand, halfwit. Why does Caesarion need a new slave anyway? What happened to the other one?

CAESARION

He didn't survive your last recipe.

ANTONIUS

No matter — we'll get it right one of these days. Come with me, Lanuvinus. We will speak with the cook about his preparations.

[Exit ANTONIUS *and* LANUVINUS, *stage right.]*

TURPIO

[Aside] Did you see the look in the man's eyes? He won't outfox those Romans. The drunk god hasn't abandoned him yet, and by the time he reaches the cook, he won't remember why he left. I'll have to keep my time here brief to save my meat and spare your grief.

[Enter HELIOS *and* SELENE *from opposite ends of the stage. They crash into each other, fall to the ground, and exit to opposite ends of the stage.]*

CAESARION

Did you see that, slave? Did you see the two of them?

TURPIO

The two of whom? I see pairs all around me, little Pharaoh.

CAESARION

The twins, stupid! I saw them just now, one on either side, howling as they ran into each other and bouncing back by force of chests — they smote against, and then each wheeled round just there, shouting incomprehensibly. Only look, here they come again!

[Enter HELIOS *and* SELENE *from opposite ends of the stage. They crash into each other and fall to the ground.]*

CAESARION (cont'd)

There, see? That is what I want.

TURPIO

To play with your brother and sister?

[Exit HELIOS *and* SELENE *to opposite ends of the stage.]*

CAESARION

No, stupid! I want a twin of my own.

TURPIO

Ah, how ignorant of me, but why would you want such a thing?

CAESARION

Why? How dumb are you? I want a twin so I have what they have — a constant companion—

TURPIO

Yes.

CAESARION

Someone I can always talk to—

TURPIO

Indeed.

CAESARION

Who would help in any situation—

TURPIO

A true blessing.

CAESARION

Yes, I want a twin.

TURPIO

Of course you do.

CAESARION

Anyway, we Egyptians come in pairs. It's not just Helios and Selene. Look at Shu and Tefnut or Geb and Nut. Yes, I will have one of my own.

TURPIO

But how do you intend to procure this twin?

CAESARION

Money is no object for the Pharaoh of Upper and Lower—

TURPIO

Those Romans are posted right outside the palace doors. You cannot leave safely.

CAESARION

I will not let such a thing prevent my happiness! Those jackals have no authority here! I am the Pharaoh of Upper and Lower Egypt; Ptolemy—

TURPIO

Very well, little master, I will bring you what you seek.

CAESARION

You? How?

TURPIO

I shall have to keep ready for an opportunity and take advantage.

CAESARION

Yes, I suppose you had better. For that is the wish of the Pharaoh of Upper and Lower Egypt; Ptolemy XV Philopater; heir of—

TURPIO

> And your wish is my command. Now, go and make your room ready for your new twin.

> *[Exit CAESARION, stage right.]*

TURPIO (cont'd)

> I can see the beginning of a plot forming, emerging from darkness like the darting rays of Aten's disk cresting over the horizon. Antonius and Cleopatra have sealed their fates, and even the Romans wouldn't do violence to the little ones, but Caesarion is a threat. A Roman Caesar will not want an Egyptian Caesar contending for power, not want to return to Egypt in five years' time to quell another uprising, not want any Roman to remember the bastard son of Caesar. Naïve boy though he is, Caesarion doesn't deserve to die. I'll have to be clever to save the child from the Land of the Dead, while saving the length on my low-hanging head — you all heard what Antonius said!

> *[Exit TURPIO, stage left.]*

ACT II

*Outside Cleopatra's Palace at Alexandria. Octavian's ship is moored stage
left, and the mouth of the bay lies stage right.*
*[Enter OCTAVIAN, MAECENAS, and AGRIPPA, stage
left. Octavian wears Roman military attire with a sword
at his side that is so long it drags on the ground beside
him.]*

OCTAVIAN

Alexandria! At last.

MAECENAS

Alexandria.

AGRIPPA

At last.

OCTAVIAN

Let's go in then.

MAECENAS

Steady, Caesar. We've come for diplomacy.

AGRIPPA

Doors are probably locked anyway.

OCTAVIAN

I should offer him single combat and end this farce now.

MAECENAS

There's no need for that. We have him trapped.

OCTAVIAN

I don't want this to be another Mutina, where I graciously let the con-
suls lead the legions while I bravely oversaw the rear guard. Good thing
too because those two got themselves killed! Who knows what would
have happened if I hadn't been there to take over.

MAECENAS

Yes, few can match your power in battle, Caesar—

AGRIPPA

And in council you excel all men your age—

MAECENAS

So no one could doubt your strategy—

AGRIPPA

No one! Not in the whole army—

MAECENAS

But you mustn't forget our advice—

AGRIPPA

You must trust in us, Caesar—

MAECENAS

Yes, trust in us — after all, we've been bestowed with the benefits of age: wisdom and good sense.

OCTAVIAN

Benefits of age? I'll be thirty-three next month while Agrippa waits for three more months before his birthday! And what of you, Maecenas? A mere five years' difference separates us.

MAECENAS

Yes, Caesar, but together we're over twice your age. None would refuse the advice of one twice their age.

AGRIPPA

Just think what advice you might give a child of fifteen years.

OCTAVIAN

I suppose you're right. Why, even that child of fifteen might guide one of eight, er, seven — well, half-fifteen, anyway. Yes, now I remember your oily words, and their logic still confuses me! There is no surer sign of truth than that — what you say must be so.

MAECENAS

Exactly—

AGRIPPA

Precisely—

MAECENAS

The embassy then—

AGRIPPA

The embassy—

MAECENAS

Great Caesar, since you hold imperium over the whole Roman army—

AGRIPPA

Jupiter himself has chosen you to lead Rome—

MAECENAS

So you must listen to our counsel—

AGRIPPA

No one will offer you a better plan than ours—

MAECENAS

The plan we formed—

AGRIPPA

And still advise—

MAECENAS

Is to send in an embassy—

AGRIPPA

To talk to Antonius—

MAECENAS

To deliver him your terms for his surrender and the surrender of Alexandria—

AGRIPPA

After all, it may take the entire army to storm the palace.

OCTAVIAN

If he won't cede this city, then I'll give him — how many cities are in
Egypt?

MAECENAS

Seven, I believe.

OCTAVIAN

Then that's how many I'll burn! I'll give him seven cities burned to the
ground! Seven cities such as this, filled with his new people. I'll give
him ashes and dust!

MAECENAS

Brave Caesar, send in the embassy first. End this here and those same
cities are yours by morning.

AGRIPPA

Yes, and what if he should submit to you?

MAECENAS

Come — send the embassy. Old Lepidus first — Jupiter loves the man,
so let him lead the way — then Gaius Sosius and clever Octavia.

AGRIPPA

I've outfitted her in the disguise of a Centurion to get her past Cleopatra.

OCTAVIAN

Why don't we just send her in there with a sword?

AGRIPPA

Shamelessness!

MAECENAS

She goes with the rest under the banner of truce sanctified by Jupiter
himself!

OCTAVIAN

He won't mind.

MAECENAS

You need not bring shame upon yourself over Antonius. The embassy
will do the job.

OCTAVIAN

Oh, very well — send in the embassy.

[Maecenas claps his hands to signal the embassy.
Agrippa misunderstands and begins enthusiastically
applauding Octavian. Maecenas considers Agrippa;
Octavian considers Maecenas; Maecenas realizes he is
under inspection and joins Agrippa's applause.]
[Enter OCTAVIA, LEPIDUS, and SOSIUS, stage left.
Octavia takes center stage and curtsies in response to
the applause.]

OCTAVIAN

Now, let's have a look at each of you. Octavia, dear sister, use your cunning words to move Antonius' heart.

OCTAVIA

Sure you don't want to send me in there with a sword? I'll be certain to move his heart with that.

OCTAVIAN

Shamelessness! You go under the banner of truce sanctified by Jupiter himself!

OCTAVIA

There's no shame in treating a beast as a beast, but I wouldn't kill Antonius. I would just have some fun with him, or make him have some fun with me.

OCTAVIAN

You'll have no sword, but you can tell Antonius that I'll burn the palace down around him if I must. Lepidus, the Egyptian witch might yet surrender — she took flight quickly enough at Actium. After you've each made your case to Antonius, take Cleopatra aside and make her an offer of her own. Let her know that she may survive so long as Antonius does not.

LEPIDUS

And what of her children by Antonius, Caesar?

OCTAVIAN

Tell her what she needs to hear.

LEPIDUS

And what of her child by your uncle, Caesar?

OCTAVIAN

Whatever you like — there's nothing more worthless than promises made to the vanquished. Sosius, that eldest bastard is your responsibility. You've seen the little vulture before — make sure he's still there. I want to end this mess once and for all.

SOSIUS

I remember the look of the boy, Caesar.

OCTAVIAN

Good. Now, go and make ready for your task.

[Exit OCTAVIAN, MAECENAS, AGRIPPA,
OCTAVIA, LEPIDUS, *and* SOSIUS, *stage left.]*

ACT III

Inside Cleopatra's Palace.
[Enter ANTONIUS, CLEOPATRA, and LANUVINUS,
stage right.]

CLEOPATRA

Is that cup empty again already? I can't tell if you've wasted more through drinking or spilling.

ANTONIUS

Is't spilling or swilling? Anyway, go easy on me. It's hard work I've been doing with the cook. There's a lot of preparation that goes into pickled eels.

CLEOPATRA

Are you still wasting your time worrying about that?

LANUVINUS

It's alright — I've been helping.

[Enter TURPIO, stage left.]

CLEOPATRA

So you're both wasting your time on that?

LANUVINUS

No, we—

CLEOPATRA

I don't favor that word! I've heard it enough times today, and I'll not suffer it again!

TURPIO

Lanuvinus, have you just farted?

LANUVINUS

Done what?

TURPIO

Farted. You've farted in the throne room. We all heard it.

CLEOPATRA

Is that true? Have you farted in my throne room?

LANUVINUS

No!

CLEOPATRA

Was I unclear when I told you not to use that word in my presence?

TURPIO

Answer the question, slave! Have you farted?

LANUVINUS

But it was not—

CLEOPATRA

Not is a cousin of no, and I'll host neither today.

LANUVINUS

I mean, my lady, that I believe the sound came from a chair—

TURPIO

You blame your fart on the Pharaoh of Egypt?

LANUVINUS

I—

CLEOPATRA

You.

TURPIO

Which is it then, slave? Have you farted and blamed it on the the Great Lady, Cleopatra?

LANUVINUS

You bend your words like a snake through reeds!

TURPIO

You rend your shorts with a wind in the weave!

CLEOPATRA

Enough, slaves. You, why are you here? What's your business in the throne room?

TURPIO

Masters, and the lesser member of the palace who nevertheless finds himself in the throne room—

LANUVINUS

You insolent—

TURPIO

There is an embassy of Romans at the doors.

ANTONIUS

Romans! Is the coward Octavian with them?

TURPIO

They appear to be two soldiers and a priest.

ANTONIUS

So, two soldiers and a priest walk into the palace in Alexandria. Show them in — let's hear what these Romans have to say.

[Exit TURPIO, *stage left]*

CLEOPATRA

Remember, husband, these are our enemies.

ANTONIUS

Enemies? They're Romans!

[Enter LEPIDUS, SOSIUS, *and* OCTAVIA, *stage left.*
Octavia is disguised as a Roman soldier.]

ANTONIUS

Welcome, Romans! Look, wife, dear friends have come our way — my dearest friends in all the world! Lepidus, is that really you? Exile has not been so unkind as the stories we've heard then. Gaius Sosius, have they returned you to me? I have missed you dearly in this land of tricks and deceits. This one I don't recall, but he's a handsome lad. He looks like a true Roman soldier, and he travels in the best company. Cups! Cups for each of my friends!

LANUVINUS

Yes, General. Three cups brimming with wine.

ANTONIUS

Roman wine — the Falernian, elixir of life. And you had better make it four cups — mine is nearly dry.

CLEOPATRA

I'll go. You both mix your wine as though everyday is a feast.

[Exit CLEOPATRA *and* LANUVINUS, *stage right.]*

OCTAVIA

Your health, Antonius!

ANTONIUS

I like this fellow, but wait for the wine, friend.

OCTAVIA

Hail, Antonius, we all know your amphorae never run dry. We can toast here to our hearts' content, while Octavian, in all his pomp, rages outside. He has vowed to set fire to your city, and make havoc of all the Egyptians in their confusion.

ANTONIUS

You can't trust his vows!

OCTAVIA

And what of your vows?

ANTONIUS

Who is this Centurion? The young man has such a striking look. I'd like to see more of him. Just a peek under the skirt then, eh, lad?

OCTAVIA

Do you not recognize me? You seek a peek between my knees? Will I be recognizable to you from such a view? Come, do my Roman vestments really hide me so well that you don't see the curve of my hip, my thin arms and swollen breasts?

ANTONIUS

Who—

OCTAVIA

Oh, husband, how I've missed your touch!

ANTONIUS

Octavia?

OCTAVIA

None other! Now bring me those strong, rough hands — I want to feel them upon my body again! Show me how you've missed me, and I'll wear the bark right off your tree!

[Octavia grabs at Antonius' skirt.]

ANTONIUS

Octavia, control yourself!

OCTAVIA

You're in no place to make demands.

ANTONIUS

Gentlemen, help!

OCTAVIA

Just look at what you've been missing.

[Octavia begins to strip away her disguise.]

ANTONIUS

Stop that! Stop that before—

OCTAVIA

Before what? I need you Antonius, and you need me. Cleopatra is no match for me between the sheets!

ANTONIUS

Lepidus, Sosius — deliver me from this lustful woman! Save me from this Bacchanalia!

[Antonius hides behind Lepidus and Sosius.]

OCTAVIA

Very well, Antonius, you're safe for now, but surely your father, Creticus, urged you to set yourself always for the good of Rome. Put aside your quarreling with Octavian. Cede to him, and the Romans old and young will respect you more for doing so. Octavian will make amends if you will. He may even annul our divorce.

ANTONIUS

Royal sister of Octavian, the great betrayer, allow me to say what I have to say. Octavian will never win me over, not for all the wine in the world. No, I've seen before the weight of his promises. Countless cities of men I've stormed and sacked, and from all I took my legal plunder, hauled it away and sent it to Rome. Now, Octavian has seized that same city, Rome, the city that I have suckled with my victories as the she-wolf suckled Romulus!

OCTAVIA

I'll be your she-wolf. Just give me that little Roman sword of yours.

ANTONIUS

Octavian will make no amends now that he has nothing to gain from me, so I will make no pacts with him. Tell him to sail home now.

LEPIDUS

Sail home? Is that what you think he will do?

ANTONIUS

Well, it's quite a long walk.

LEPIDUS

Your judgement has been overpowered by some force. Look at me, Antonius. Aged though I am, I was your colleague too. Take me as your example, and cede now to Octavian. Don't suffer as I did at Sicily.

ANTONIUS

What happened at Sicily?

LEPIDUS

You ate an apple suspiciously?

ANTONIUS

You said you suffered at Sicily.

LEPIDUS

I did! When I put down that revolt led by Pompey's son. I defeated those traitors, with my legions at my back. Octavian asked me to step down then, to take my legions back. He offered me rewards for my victory — a good share of the plunder taken from Sextus Pompey and a place of honor in his Ovation. I wouldn't have it. I wanted the Ovation for myself. At the least, he could have named me as his partner-in-arms and shared the Ovation.

ANTONIUS

Lepidus, old friend, you won those battles — those lands were yours by right, as was the Ovation! Octavian should have done the honorable thing and hailed you in your triumph. And what about your legions?

LEPIDUS

I don't have any lesions, Antonius, but my plug has sprung a leak in old age — I've already dribbled all over your stage!

ANTONIUS

The men, Lepidus.

LEPIDUS

The men were behind me all the way! Just until they defected to Octavian. Then I had my just rewards—

ANTONIUS

You had ostracization!

LEPIDUS

No, I've never been to Ostrich Nation. No, Antonius, I had to fall on my knees and beg of Octavian that which he now offers you — exile, a life of sober solitude.

ANTONIUS

Ah, Lepidus, my old, old friend, you should not have stepped down at Sicily.

LEPIDUS

And you, glorious General Antonius, you have earned your rest, paid for it in blood across this vast empire. Fire this war anew, and your flame will flag, and no longer will Romans honor you.

ANTONIUS

I say my honor lies here, in the kingdom of Egypt. Another thing — it degrades you to serve Octavian's pleasure, that cowardly son of Caesar! It would do you proud to stand by me now.

LEPIDUS

How can I stand by a minnow? Swim perhaps.

ANTONIUS

I said—

SOSIUS

Ready, friends? Come, away we go now. There's no achieving our mission here. Best to return to Octavian and give our report at once — Antonius will not yield. He will not pay the price for this truce that his friends so desire. The gods have planted a fury in your chest, Antonius — they have made you cruel and relentless, and all for a title. Show respect for your own city! Here we are, sent from Rome, your closest, dearest friends. We long for you to set aside your grievances and make peace with Octavian.

ANTONIUS

Gaius Sosius, general of my armies, well said. But my heart still burns with anger and hatred whenever I remember his arrogance — and also when I eat the little black olives stuffed with garlic. But Octavian, he usurped me before all of Rome! That ersatz son of Caesar treated me like some outcast. You go back to him and relay my message — he'll not take this palace while I yet draw breath. I'll defend it to the hilt!

OCTAVIA

You can rear-end me to the hilt!

[Enter CAESARION, stage right.]

CAESARION

What's this? Ambassadors from Rome? Why was I not summoned?

ANTONIUS

> Now you're all in for an earful. You should have left when Sosius suggested it.

LEPIDUS

> Caesarion, is that you?

CAESARION

> Who's this old man?

LEPIDUS

> My name is Marcus Aemilius Lepidus.

CAESARION

> What do you want, old man Lepidus?

LEPIDUS

> I was a friend of your father. Do you not recognize me, child?

CAESARION

> I do not, and you may address me as Pharaoh Ptolemy XV.

ANTONIUS

> You see what I mean?

> > *[Enter* CLEOPATRA *and* LANUVINUS, *stage right.*
> > *Lanuvinus bears four cups. He distributes them to the*
> > *embassy and Antonius.]*

LANUVINUS

> Cups! Four cups of the best wine that—

ANTONIUS

> What took you so long?

LANUVINUS

> We would have been back sooner, but the great lady made me add more water four times! An eel could live in each of those cups.

CLEOPATRA

> You're mistaken, slave. Eels don't belong in cups — they get pickled in the kitchen. And I know just where to find an extra one, shriveled and peculiar though it may be.

ANTONIUS

> You'd better get moving, Lanuvinus, before she takes your little penis.

> > *[Exit* LANUVINUS, *stage right.]*

> *[The six remaining actors split into pairs: Octavia and*
> *Antonius, stage right; Cleopatra and Lepidus, center;*
> *and Caesarion and Sosius, stage left.]*

OCTAVIA

> Antonius, speak with me.

ANTONIUS

You need to go! Put this uniform back on before Cleopatra realizes who you are.

OCTAVIA

You should really be worrying about yourself. I'm maybe the only person in the world who could keep my brother from killing you. I could persuade him to let you live. That is, I could persuade him to let my husband live. Just promise to give me what you have under those skirts every night. I need you, Antonius! I want to feel you in my—

LEPIDUS

But, Cleopatra, think of your children.

CLEOPATRA

What about them?

LEPIDUS

Caesar has mercy to match his generosity. He is willing to let them live if you help him end this siege.

CLEOPATRA

At what price? I'll not be held to ransom.

LEPIDUS

He is willing to let you keep your ransoms.

CLEOPATRA

No ransom? I keep my gold, my jewels?

LEPIDUS

You may keep your gold, your jewels, whatever you like. What need has Caesar of any of this? As long as you continue to pay tribute to Rome, you will keep it all.

CLEOPATRA

Can the new Caesar be trusted?

LEPIDUS

He can be trusted to—

SOSIUS

Twist my auger! It's Little Caesar!

CAESARION

Address me properly, soldier.

SOSIUS

Look at that — same Little Caesar.

CAESARION

That's not my name!

SOSIUS

Just the same. How are you, Little Caesar?

CAESARION

I'm not Little Caesar! I'm the Pharaoh of Egypt!

SOSIUS

But Romans have no Pharaoh, so you are nothing to me, nobody.

CAESARION

Am too!

SOSIUS

Are not, Little Caesar Nobody.

CAESARION

Say that again and—

CLEOPATRA

I'll yield. What does he ask of me?

LEPIDUS

Remarkably little, Pharaoh. Caesar asks only that you keep Antonius' cup filled and the doors unlocked. Do this and he will guarantee your throne with just rewards as well.

CLEOPATRA

Antonius' amphorae never run dry — and my purse is never full — but to be the Egyptian Sinon?

LEPIDUS

Were your ancestors not themselves Greek?

CLEOPATRA

Not the type of Greeks to turn their city over to some—

ANTONIUS

Sex-crazed woman! Stop it! Stop it, I said! That's an order!

OCTAVIA

That's not the type of order I'll take from you! Now, report to the bedroom and assume the position!

ANTONIUS

I am a Roman General!

OCTAVIA

You're no Roman, and I'm no soldier. You'll just have to make me obey, husband.

ANTONIUS

[to all] Enough! I've heard enough — Octavian won't win me over. Now, out with you!

SOSIUS

Remember what we have said, General Antonius.

LEPIDUS

And you, Cleopatra. Farewell, Antonius.

ANTONIUS

Farewell, Romans.

OCTAVIA

Farewell, Egyptians.

SOSIUS

Bye-bye, Little Caesar Nobody!

[Exit OCTAVIA, LEPIDUS, and SOSIUS, stage left.]

CLEOPATRA

So, two soldiers and a priest walk out of the palace in Alexandria. Well, what now?

ANTONIUS

What now?

CLEOPATRA

When will you surrender?

ANTONIUS

Surrender? Why would we surrender?

CLEOPATRA

You heard what the Romans said! What if they burn down the palace?

ANTONIUS

Then we won't have to surrender.

CLEOPATRA

You act cavalierly enough with your own life, but you would waste mine too?

ANTONIUS

You would cling so greedily to life as to suffer the shame of surrender?

CAESARION

Never mind that — who was that Roman you were talking to?

ANTONIUS

Just another Roman.

CLEOPATRA

Not just another Roman — a Roman soldier. What did he want?

ANTONIUS

To remember past engagements. What about Lepidus? What did he have to say?

CLEOPATRA

Nothing. Just that Octavian is a liar.

ANTONIUS

And a coward!

CLEOPATRA

We can't trust anything that comes from that one.

ANTONIUS

    What about Sosius? I miss that man around here. What did he have to say?

CAESARION

    Sosius is a brute! He called me Little Caesar Nobody! I want him killed.

ANTONIUS

    Do you? Here's my sword—

CLEOPATRA

    [*Aside*] Fitted perfectly for a child's hand.

ANTONIUS

    Sosius is just outside now. Go and kill him.

CAESARION

    The Pharaoh does not take care of such things for himself!

ANTONIUS

    A Roman does.

CLEOPATRA

    A Roman takes care of all manner of things for himself.

ANTONIUS

    And an Egyptian cares for herself above all else.

                [Exit CLEOPATRA, *followed by* ANTONIUS, *stage*

                                        right.]

CAESARION

    What do I care what a Roman does? Anyway, I have slaves for such things.

    [Enter TURPIO, *stage left. He collects Octavia's*

    vestments.]

TURPIO

    What's all this? A discarded disguise to aid my endeavor?

CAESARION

    You! Where have you been?

TURPIO

    Waiting to serve — it's the greatest pleasure in my life. Where did all this come from?

CAESARION

    The usurper, Octavian, sent his underlings in to try to scare us off. Now, where's my twin?

TURPIO

    Patience, young master. I will bring you what you need.

CAESARION

You'd better! Because I heard Antonius say the cook is making something special for dinner tonight — pickled eels from a secret recipe! If you don't get my twin, then you can't have any.

TURPIO

It would be a shame to miss such a delectable dish.

[Exit CAESARION, *stage right.]*

TURPIO (cont'd)

Great gods of Egypt, Aten has finally risen — I see the light! Caesarion's twin will be his escape. I'll slip into town for a matching jackanapes. 'Tis better to stay away for now as well, lest Antonius should make good on his japes and take away all the length that hangs past my grapes!

[Exit TURPIO, *stage left.]*

ACT IV

Outside Cleopatra's Palace.
[Enter OCTAVIA, LEPIDUS, and SOSIUS, center.]

SOSIUS

That was him alright — arrogant little pyramid builder.

LEPIDUS

That's the son of deified Caesar.

SOSIUS

His son by Cleopatra, the witch of Egypt. Anyway, new Caesar says the boy's a demon.

LEPIDUS

Nonsense. He just needs a bit of learning.

SOSIUS

He needs a bit of caning.

OCTAVIA

I know what Antonius needs! Everyone could see it.

SOSIUS

I've never seen General Antonius so angry. I thought his head was going to explode.

OCTAVIA

I'll make his head explode alright.

LEPIDUS

Enough, woman! Antonius doesn't want you.

OCTAVIA

How can you say that? Of course he wants me!

SOSIUS

You're lucky you didn't ruin the whole thing, Pasiphaë!
[Enter MAECENAS and AGRIPPA, stage left.]

MAECENAS

At last! How did it go, friends?

OCTAVIA

Poorly.

AGRIPPA

Octavia, what happened to your disguise?

OCTAVIA

I had to show Antonius the Roman hills he's been missing, and he would have succumbed to me if these two had only let me get my hands on him!

MAECENAS

Dear lady, what if Cleopatra had recognized you? She would have had you executed on the spot.

OCTAVIA

Antonius would never have let her do such a thing. The man is still mad for me.

LEPIDUS

Cleopatra was far too distracted by Caesar's offer to take any notice of Octavia's antics.

AGRIPPA

She accepted then? She'll end it?

LEPIDUS

Yes, at daybreak tomorrow.

MAECENAS

Then the end of this farce is near, and Rome awaits our return. We'll fetch Caesar now, and share the good news! Come, Agrippa

AGRIPPA

To Caesar!

[Exit MAECENAS *and* AGRIPPA, *stage left.]*

LEPIDUS

Ah, but, Maecenas, the farce is never ending. Fortune never tires of interfering with human affairs. Low men are brought hight, high men are brought low. Finally, we all end in a shallow furrow.

OCTAVIA

I'd let Antonius end in my furrow.

[Enter OCTAVIAN, *stage left.]*

OCTAVIAN

Well? What happened? Tell me, dear sister, pride of Rome — will he save the palace from burning, or did he refuse? Is he coming out?

OCTAVIA

Most noble son of Caesar, Antonius will not come! He spurned me and my gifts, and bade you to sail home.

OCTAVIAN

The most wasteful scoundrel in all of Rome! And Cleopatra? What did she say?

LEPIDUS

The lady Cleopatra was amenable to your overture.

OCTAVIAN

Huh?

LEPIDUS

She affirmed your proposition.

OCTAVIAN

Speak sense, old man!

LEPIDUS

She said yes.

OCTAVIAN

Then the drunken fiend is mine! I will tell Agrippa to ready the cohort.

LEPIDUS

Steady, Caesar — you must be patient. The lady stated your terms will be met by sunset.

OCTAVIAN

Why not now? Who knows what kind of schedule these Egyptians keep their sun on.

LEPIDUS

It will take quite a bit more wine to subdue Antonius. Give the man some time to drink his last cups.

OCTAVIAN

Very well. What of the demon, Sosius, was it there?

SOSIUS

Aye, he was there.

OCTAVIAN

And?

SOSIUS

And...

OCTAVIAN

Did it have scales? How long was its tail? How many horns did it have?

SOSIUS

No scales, Caesar, nor tail nor horns that I saw.

OCTAVIAN

The little imp must have been hiding it all. These Egyptians do marvelous things with their makeup. It doesn't matter. The creature is already as good as dead! I want you to deal with it when the time comes, Sosius.

SOSIUS

Aye, Caesar.

OCTAVIAN

Yes, you, Sosius. Now, you may await my return to the ship.

[Exit OCTAVIA, LEPIDUS, *and* SOSIUS, *stage left.]*
[Enter TURPIO, *center. He wears Octavia's discarded disguise.]*

OCTAVIAN

Where'd you come from, soldier?

TURPIO

From the palace, sir.

OCTAVIAN

What were you doing in the palace?

TURPIO

Caesar commanded it, sir.

OCTAVIAN

I commanded? I sent only three inside!

TURPIO

Yes, sir, er, Caesar, three went into the palace, while you remained here as the fourth.

OCTAVIAN

With Maecenas and Agrippa — don't forget them.

TURPIO

Right, three went into the palace, while you remained here as the fourth, with Maecenas and Agrippa making five and six.

OCTAVIAN

But they only count as one.

TURPIO

One?

OCTAVIAN

One.

TURPIO

How one?

OCTAVIAN

They combined their ages, see, so it's just the one of them.

TURPIO

Right, so three went into the palace, while you remained here as the fourth, with Maecenas and Agrippa making five. But if Maecenas and Agrippa are each less than one person, then it stands to reason that neither should be counted, for how can you count a person as whole who is half? So four is the number.

OCTAVIAN

Four! That's right!

TURPIO

And four have exited the palace — Octavia, Lepidus, Sosius, and a soldier whose name does not bear mentioning — while you have remained here with Maecenas and Agrippa, none of whom should be counted.

OCTAVIAN

Well, four have exited, and I have remained here... Carry on then, soldier!

[Exit OCTAVIAN, *stage left.]*

TURPIO

This Caesar's more stupid than I had imagined, but he's found an apt rival in Antonius inebriated and impassioned. Now a fool and a drunk hold the city at bay, but who'll write that truth of this silly play? Though I trust you'll remember what you saw here today whenever you see a straw man burned away.

[Exit TURPIO, *stage right.]*

ACT V

Inside Cleopatra's Palace.
[Enter CLEOPATRA, stage right.]

CLEOPATRA

I suppose there's no chance of escape now — no simple ruse will fool those soldiers outside. I'll have to do as Lepidus bids me and take Octavian's offer. How else can I keep my palace, my gold, my jewels? This is the very history of Egypt, and only I am Egyptian enough to keep it all. Antonius is doomed anyway — why should I waste everything for him?

[Cleopatra unlocks the door to the throne room.]

CLEOPATRA (cont'd)

That's twice now I've rendered Egypt unto Caesar.

[Enter ANTONIUS and LANUVINUS, stage right.]

ANTONIUS

Cleopatra, my beauty, is it time for bed?

CLEOPATRA

It is for me, but I fear something will keep you away from me all night.

ANTONIUS

What?

CLEOPATRA

I don't particularly care, so long as it is effective.

ANTONIUS

Do you ever tire of your games?

CLEOPATRA

Do you ever tire of your shames?

ANTONIUS

What's this? Insults from a Greek pretending to be an Egyptian?

CLEOPATRA

Better than a Roman who thinks he's Greek pretending to be an Egyptian!

ANTONIUS

That's right — Roman to the hilt!

CLEOPATRA

The blade hasn't got far to go if it's your sword!

ANTONIUS

The Roman sword is a soldier's prize!

CLEOPATRA

Pity it isn't known for its size! And if you're so Roman, why are you fighting against Rome? You should surrender now, and save yourself some humiliation!

[Exit CLEOPATRA, stage right.]

ANTONIUS

Come, Lanuvinus — there are decisions to be made tonight. Cleopatra would have me surrender the palace and fall on Roman mercy, but I've never known Octavian to be merciful.

LANUVINUS

Perhaps the boy has developed mercy with age.

ANTONIUS

And perhaps a porcupine will develop feathers, a seagull will develop a trunk, and you will develop a new cock when the cook hacks yours off! No, only one thing is sure to develop with age — go and fetch me some more of the Falernian.

LANUVINUS

Yes, master. A cup of Falernian.

ANTONIUS

Better make it a bowl. It's going to be a long night.

[Exit LANUVINUS, stage left.]

ANTONIUS

What I do now, I do for the good of all of Rome. I must fight on. I must ensure that this scheming coward doesn't destroy everything that I have helped to build here and in Rome. No, I'll not surrender, and we can hold out here for months, years maybe.

[Enter LANUVINUS, stage left.]

LANUVINUS

There's none left, General.

ANTONIUS

Of course there is.

LANUVINUS

It appears there isn't, master.

ANTONIUS

No, there must be more down there. I've never run out before. Go and take another look, and if you can't find some more, then report to the cook!

LANUVINUS

Away with me then to search every nook!

[Exit LANUVINUS, stage left.]

ANTONIUS

> Rest easy, Lanuvinus, I'll forfeit my life before I let these Egyptians take a sword from a Roman, even a little paring knife from a slave like yourself.
>
> *[Enter LANUVINUS, stage left.]*

LANUVINUS

> Master Antonius, regretfully I must report that there is not a drop of Falernian left in all the storerooms.

ANTONIUS

> Do you mean to tell me that this is the end? The last cup of Falernian in the palace?

LANUVINUS

> General, your amphorae have run dry.

ANTONIUS

> Abandoned by Dionysus. Very well, I know what I must do.
>
> *[Antonius draws his sword from his scabbard with a flourish. It's length is underwhelming — it's clear that the blade filled less than half the scabbard's length.]*

LANUVINUS

> Master, no!
>
> *[Antonius stabs himself in the chest.]*

LANUVINUS (cont'd)

> Antonius, what have you done?

ANTONIUS

> Go and tell the coward he will find the King of Egypt in the throne room.
>
> *[Antonius dies.]*

LANUVINUS

> Antonius, son of Rome, I'll see that Charon gets his due. Oh, you stab so deep you hit my own heart too! For what now of me? What of the last Roman in Cleopatra's Palace? Maybe if I let in those Roman soldiers outside, then they would let me return home with them. They'll know a Roman when they see one, and we're all brothers again now that Antonius is dead. Better to try my luck with them than stay with Cleopatra. She'll have my head once she sees Antonius dead — although, at least she's only after one of my heads. She would never waste a slave with such games as Antonius. Yes, at least I'm safe from the cook. Hey, that's right! My tip won't be clipped! My cock is safe from the cook's chopping block! My dangling container is no longer endangered!

[Enter TURPIO *and* TIMON, *center. Turpio still wears
Octavia's Centurion disguise. Timon resembles
Caesarion, but the former is a full head shorter than the
latter.]*

LANUVINUS

Who's that? Praise Jupiter, a fellow Roman! Look here, General Antonius is dead.

TURPIO

Antonius dead? Osiris beware — a trickster is in your midst. This one's not as clever as Set, but keep a close eye on Isis and Nepthys.

LANUVINUS

Osiris, Set, Isis, Nepthys? That's no Roman — Turpio? What are you doing in those soldier's clothes?

TURPIO

Never mind that — Antonius is dead! How did he die?

LANUVINUS

He fell on his sword — an honorable Roman death for an honorable Roman warrior.

TURPIO

You Romans are a bit funny — shouldn't a warrior fall in battle?

LANUVINUS

What do you know of Rome?

TURPIO

I know that the death of a general is a solemn occasion.

LANUVINUS

That's true, at least.

TURPIO

And I know that words are traditionally said over the body of the deceased.

LANUVINUS

Aye, fancy-type words, but I'm not one who knows such.

TURPIO

I know some appropriate words to say for somber occasions.

LANUVINUS

You'd do that for General Antonius?

TURPIO

No, Lanuvinus, I'd do it for you.

LANUVINUS

Thank you, Turpio. Maybe not all Egyptians are uneducated, uncivilized simpletons.

TURPIO

So a man walks into the library at Alexandria and asks the librarian for a scroll about suicide.

LANUVINUS

This is no time for jokes!

TURPIO

You're supposed to ask what the librarian said.

LANUVINUS

I don't care what the librarian said!

TURPIO

No, dummy, she calls back — Fuck off! You won't return it.

LANUVINUS

I already told you, this is no time for jokes!

TURPIO

It's always time for jokes. What is life but a joke to which you never learn the punchline?

LANUVINUS

Where'd you hear such nonsense?

TURPIO

Timon told me.

LANUVINUS

Who's Timon?

TIMON

I'm Timon.

LANUVINUS

Who's that?

TURPIO

That's Timon.

LANUVINUS

Who's Timon?

TURPIO

He's a misanthropist.

LANUVINUS

A misanthra-what?

[Enter CAESARION, stage right.]

CAESARION

Who's that?

TURPIO

That's Timon.

CAESARION

Who's Timon?

LANUVINUS

    Don't go near him, young master! He's a rapist from Misanth!

TURPIO

    This is your twin.

CAESARION

    My twin?

LANUVINUS

    Caesarion has a twin from Misanth?

CAESARION

    This is not my twin.

TURPIO

    Not yet.

CAESARION

    Not ever! He's supposed to be a girl, stupid!

TURPIO

    A girl? Not all twins are like your brother and sister.

CAESARION

    This is all wrong! It's supposed to be a girl!

TURPIO

    Look, this is the twin I've found you. What's wrong with him anyway?

CAESARION

    I told you — I want a twin like Helios and Selene, like Geb and Nut. A
    twin to wed, stupid! I can't very well wed a man!

TURPIO

    Perhaps you could. Just give him a chance — you might like him.

CAESARION

    Like him? What's to like?

TURPIO

    What's to like? Look at him! He looks just like you!

CAESARION

    He doesn't look like me! With those dirty hands and suntanned arms?
    Wearing those rags that scarcely cover his broad shoulders and strong
    chest? That rich crown of hair and those kind eyes; that heroic brow and
    perfect nose; those soft lips, gentle hips, and fine legs.

TURPIO

    Indeed, what's to like about any of that? I'll remove him from the pal-
    ace immediately.

CAESARION

    Don't be hasty.

TURPIO

    No, no — you're right. I've gotten it all wrong, and this one won't do.

CAESARION

Well, look, I suppose you have already found him. Where did you find him anyway?

TURPIO

I bought him from a slaver near the Timonium.

TIMON

And him no worse for the transaction. Men are made of the very filth that they float down the Nile — excrement borne of excrement.

CAESARION

Does he smile.

TIMON

He does not.

TURPIO

But he won't become your twin until you give me your word that you will follow my commands.

LANUVINUS

You? Command the Pharaoh?

TURPIO

It is the only way that I will release Timon from his bond to me.

TIMON

Bound to men, bound to life — but which of the two is the worse?

CAESARION

And why should I want a slave for a twin?

TURPIO

He won't be a slave any longer once he becomes your twin, and then you will have what you need.

CAESARION

Well — alright.

TURPIO

Your word, young master.

CAESARION

I give you my word as Ptolemy XV Philopater—

TURPIO

Save the rest — we're a bit short on time. And, to really make him feel like your twin, give Timon your jewels.

CAESARION

What?

TURPIO

You gave me your word, and twins share.

CAESARION

Oh, very well!

TURPIO

Now, something more valuable still.

CAESARION

More valuable than all my gold?

TURPIO

He needs your name. Timon, you are now Caesarion — Caesarion, you are now Timon.

TIMON

It's a sorrow to meet you. I hope the name does you no good, just as it did me.

CAESARION

Oh, well, I hope you like your name. There's more to it than that though. Caesarion is just my short name. My full name is—

TURPIO

You mean his full name.

CAESARION

You know what I mean! Anyway, it's Ptolemy XV Philopater; heir of the—

TIMON

That's too many names for me.

TURPIO

You can't very well be Timon any longer.

CAESARION

Why can't he?

TURPIO

Because that name is yours now.

CAESARION

He could have it back. I don't mind.

TURPIO

Don't be ridiculous — you can't just go trading names as you like.

CAESARION

But—

TIMON

What use have I of a name? Death lies in wait for all men around any corner, and my name will not be remembered. Even if my name should live on in inscriptions, I will not. Call me 'Nobody' and be done with it.

[Enter OCTAVIAN *and* SOSIUS, *center.]*

OCTAVIAN

Victory is mine! By my own sheer force of strength, I have defeated the whole of Antonius' armies. Come out here, you shameful drunk, so I can accept your surrender!

LANUVINUS

As I've been saying, Antonius is dead.

OCTAVIAN

Antonius dead? Sosius, check the body.

SOSIUS

Aye.

OCTAVIAN

You.

SOSIUS

No, 'aye' means 'yes.'

OCTAVIAN

That's poor conjugating, Sosius. You should say, 'I mean yes.'

SOSIUS

I mean, it's him, Caesar. He's the general. General Antonius, that is. Not me.

OCTAVIAN

And? Is he dead?

SOSIUS

Dead drunk by the smell of him! I've seen him like this afore — he can really put away his wine, Antonius can. Come on, General — up you get!

[Sosius stands astride Antonius and heaves his body up.]

SOSIUS

The general appears to be leaking, Caesar. Might be he spilled his wine.

LANUVINUS

It's his blood, you fool!

[Lanuvinus puts his hand to the ground, then brings it to his mouth.]

LANUVINUS

His blood tastes like his piss.

TURPIO

[to Lanuvinus] Can't you see the man is dead?

LANUVINUS

[to Sosius] Yeah, can't you see the man is dead?

[Sosius roughly drops Antonius' body.]

SOSIUS

Who's this one then?

TURPIO

Looks like one of the Egyptian palace slaves.

LANUVINUS

You filthy liar! I'm a Roman—

SOSIUS

Enough of that! You're profaning afore the highest man in all Rome.

OCTAVIAN

What do we do with him?

TURPIO

Send him to the kitchen. The cook will know what to do with him.

LANUVINUS

My cock!

[Sosius punches Lanuvinus in the stomach.]

SOSIUS

What did I tell you? No more talking from you, or I'll slice that tongue right out of your head.

OCTAVIAN

And this one? Who is he?

TIMON

I'm not anyone — I'm Nobody.

SOSIUS

That's Little Caesar! Just look at his jewels.

TIMON

That's not my name.

SOSIUS

That's him alright!

TURPIO

You should address him properly — that's Ptolemy XV Philopater, heir of the god who saves, chosen of Ptah, sun of righteousness, living image of Amun, the young Caesarion.

OCTAVIAN

Young Ptolemy, you die today!

TIMON

Don't do me any favors.

OCTAVIAN

Favors? I'll do you no damn favors, boy! I'm going to have you killed!

TIMON

Such a kind man to spare me a life of misery and disappointment.

OCTAVIAN

I'll spare you nothing! You'll suffer misery and disappointment when Sosius takes your head! The man is practiced. And all the worse for you since he used to serve this very house. You should never have crossed the great—

TIMON

Look, if I'm to die, let's hurry it along a bit. If you think of anything else clever to say, just tell everyone you said it.

OCTAVIAN

Get them out of my sight, Sosius!

LANUVINUS

Turpio, help!

[Exit SOSIUS, *leading* TIMON *and* LANUVINUS,

stage left.]

OCTAVIAN

Who's Turpio?

TURPIO

Must be one of their Egyptian gods — they have such strange names down here.

OCTAVIAN

What about this one?

TURPIO

Looks like another slave, Caesar.

OCTAVIAN

Another slave? How many is that?

TURPIO

It's—

OCTAVIAN

I know how to count! There was one, then two, then... What comes after two?

TURPIO

What?

OCTAVIAN

Right, what. There was one, two, what... What comes after what?

TURPIO

A question mark?

OCTAVIAN

Right, one, two, what, question mark — how many is that?

TURPIO

Too many, Caesar. I'll set him loose on the mainland.

OCTAVIAN

Yes, go, child, and tell all of your little Egyptian friends of Caesar's mercy to freemen. Now, get him out of here, so I can murder the demon.

[Exit TURPIO *and* CAESARION, *center.]*

OCTAVIAN (cont'd)

Victory! It's true what they say — victory is all the sweeter when it's
won on the battlefield. Antonius, well, he only killed himself for fear of
me, so that's even better than defeating him in combat. And the boy, I
can still kill the boy. We can have a battle too — I'll even give him a
sword...well, maybe a knife. Sosius!

[Enter SOSIUS, stage left.]

SOSIUS

Caesar?

OCTAVIAN

The boy, bring me the boy.

SOSIUS

It's already done, Caesar.

OCTAVIAN

The boy is dead then?

SOSIUS

Aye, I killed him myself.

OCTAVIAN

Yes, you-you killed him but at my command.

SOSIUS

Caesar?

OCTAVIAN

You-you killed him at my command, so it's rather more like I killed
him, wouldn't you-you say?

SOSIUS

Would I?

OCTAVIAN

You would. Just as I thought. So if anyone asks, I killed the boy. And he
had a knife. No! A sword — bigger than mine even. Well, no, not bigger
than mine. He attacked me with a sword that was almost as big as my
own, but I killed him.

SOSIUS

As you say, Caesar. No stranger than what the cook wanted to do with
him.

OCTAVIAN

What do you mean?

SOSIUS

Well, he had the other one, the slave, he had him walk right up to the
table, remove his little bald man from his tunic, and set it right across
the table in front of him. Then he brought out the biggest knife I've ever
seen in my whole life. Bit mean pulling out a knife that big for a thing

SOSIUS (cont'd)

    that small. Anyway, his hand dropped with a chop, and the little thing
    fell off! But I don't think he was very practiced because the slave is
    bleeding everywhere. What should I do with him?

OCTAVIAN

    What do I care if some Egyptian lost his staff? The boy is dead, Ant-
    onius is dead, and I killed them both. I heroically faced down Antonius
    and the little Pharaoh at the same time! And they both had swords —
    big swords! — but not bigger than mine.

SOSIUS

    As you say, Caesar.

        [Enter CLEOPATRA*, stage right.]*

CLEOPATRA

    So this is the new Caesar?

OCTAVIAN

    And this the old Cleopatra.

CLEOPATRA

    It's done then?

SOSIUS

    Aye, like I was telling Caesar, I killed—

OCTAVIAN

    Sosius, go and wait in the kitchen. The lady and I need privacy.

                      [Exit SOSIUS*, stage left.]*

OCTAVIAN

    It's nearly done. Antonius is dead, Caesar's bastard is dead—

CLEOPATRA

    And my jewels?

OCTAVIAN

    Yes, I'll need those as well of course.

CLEOPATRA

    No! Lepidus gave me your word.

OCTAVIAN

    I don't favor that word. You won't use it again. And Lepidus only gave
    you his word, but don't worry, your children by Antonius pose no threat
    to Rome. No harm will come to them—

CLEOPATRA

    My effects are my own! You can't have my jewels!

OCTAVIAN

    Can't is a cousin of no, and both are unwelcome in my presence.

CLEOPATRA

I curse the day your mother spread her legs and let you claw your way from her poisonous womb!

OCTAVIAN

That's no way to begin our trip together!

CLEOPATRA

Trip? What trip?

OCTAVIAN

You'll have to return to Rome if you want to stay near your children.

CLEOPATRA

No. My life is mine alone, and I'd sooner die than return to Rome.

[Exit CLEOPATRA, *stage right.]*

OCTAVIAN

Women — always making overblown threats that they have no intention of fulfilling. Anyway, she can't die yet — I haven't commanded it.

[Exit OCTAVIAN, *stage right.]*

ACT VI

Outside Cleopatra's Palace.
[Enter TURPIO *and* CAESARION, *center.]*

TURPIO

So, two slaves walk out of a palace in Alexandria.

CAESARION

What now?

TURPIO

Now, it's time to depart while I have a head start — before Caesar gets smart, or the plot falls apart!

[Exit TURPIO, *followed by* CAESARION, *stage right.]*

Chapter 5

The black curtains swept shut across the stage to the sound of applause.

The man in the white tunic — Giovanni now recognized him as the actor who played Turpio — returned to the center of the stage.

"Thank you, ladies and gentlemen," his voice reverberated through the amphitheater's speakers. "Please enjoy a brief intermission while your players prepare for the next production."

"Delightful, just delightful," Lucas commented.

"Bit dark for a comedy, no?" asked Britney.

"The best ones always are," Lucas countered as he stood and adjusted his sword. "Cheers, my dears, but I must *adieu*," he stated with a small bow and a flourish of his hand. "I will see you, I hope, after the performance."

Lucas turned conspicuously toward Britney, smiled, then spun on his heel and marched to the side of the stage.

"Anybody want a beer?" Giovanni asked. "I'm going to run to the concession."

"No need, mate."

Vere rummaged through his backpack, withdrew a green glass bottle, and rolled it across the blanket to Giovanni.

"Ah, holding out on us I see," Britney said with a smile.

Vere chuckled and passed her a bottle, then retrieved one for himself.

"Hey, Britney!" a high-pitched voice trilled.

Two nearly identical blonde women stood at the foot of the blanket, their eyes guarded by sunglasses with emerald lenses.

"Lisa! Tracee!" Britney exclaimed. "I'm so glad you both came! Vere, Gio, this is Lisa and Tracee."

"We know Vere!" Lisa squealed.

"What? How?" asked Britney.

"Everyone knows Vere," said Tracee.

"Nice to see you again," said Vere. "Will you join us?"

The two women removed their sunglasses as they sat on the blanket next to Britney.

"How do *you* know L and T?" Vere asked Britney.

"We met last night at the reading," Britney responded. "They hustled me on the pool table," she continued with a smirk.

"We'd never," Tracee responded, mocking dignified outrage.

"Anyway," Lisa squeaked, "we had already made more than enough by the time you came along."

The five of them laughed together.

"Have you been here long?" Tracee asked Britney.

"Not too long, a couple hours."

"A couple *hours*?" Tracee repeated.

"Yeah, well, we watched the first play too," Britney explained.

"Two plays in one sitting?" asked Lisa. "I don't think I could do that."

"Hey, Vere," Tracee crooned, "I don't suppose you have anything to drink in that bag of yours?"

Vere smiled and handed two bottles to Tracee, who passed one in turn to Lisa.

"You're the best," Lisa said as she twisted off the cap. "So how do y'all know each other?"

"Oh, well, *everyone knows Vere*," Britney quoted Tracee, then laughed, "and I met Gio last night; he did a reading too."

"You're a poet too then?" asked Tracee.

"Something like that," Giovanni replied.

"So, you're not?" Lisa pressed.

"No, I just play one on TV," Giovanni quipped.

"Ugh, you're an actor?" asked Lisa.

"Huh? No," said Giovanni.

"He's a poet," said Vere.

"Better than an actor anyway," Lisa commented.

"What do you have against actors?" Vere asked.

"Yeah, what's wrong with actors?" added Britney.

"What's right with them?" Lisa replied. "I dated an actor once."

"You did?" asked Tracee.

"Sure, in college. I wouldn't do it again."

"Why not?" said Tracee.

"Vain creatures. You can't trust anything that comes out of their mouths."

"Maybe it was just the particular actor," Britney suggested.

"Maybe," said Lisa, "but I'll never know."

"I don't know," Britney replied vaguely. "I could see myself dating an actor."

"Hey, it's your rodeo, cowgirl," Lisa conceded.

"Ladies and gentlemen," a voice from the speakers boomed as the stage lights extinguished, "please take your seats."

A solitary spotlight flashed on against the fluttering, black curtains.

The Atlantiad

Dramatis Personae

Theodosius
King of Atlantis

Korinna
Queen of Olympus

Sosigenes
*Eldest daughter of Theodosius &
Korinna*

Irenaea
*Youngest daughter of Theodosius &
Korinna*

Doulos
Slave of Theodosius

Androcles
Son of Theodosius & Korinna

Achilles
*Achaea's greatest warrior, Leader of
the Myrmidon army*

Zeus
*God of thunder, lightning, and the skies;
King of Olympus*

Hera
*Goddess of women, marriage, and family;
Queen of Olympus*

Artemis
*Goddess of the hunt, wilderness, and
innocence*

Hermes
*God of trade, tricks, and thieves;
Messenger of the Gods*

Poseidon
*God of the seas, storms, and earthquakes;
King of the mortal realm*

Eris
Goddess of discord

Proem

[Enter THEODOSIUS, *stage left. He is blind, stooped
over, supported by a walking stick, and dressed in rags.]*

THEODOSIUS

O, you muses, fill me once more with your song. Support me so that I
might tell my story and not be crushed by the weight of it. Calliope with
your tablet and stylus in hand, select the words that I shall speak;
inscribe them in wax and set them before my mind. Erato and Euterpe,
take up your cithara and aulos and strike a tune to match my suffering
— as discordant a cacophony as your Apollonian tools permit. You,
Urania, spin your globe until Atlantis surfaces before you — allow your
compass to point intrepid voyagers toward the place where the island
once sat in the great sea. Polyhymnia behind your veil, chant and I will
let the reverie of your chorus reinforce my resolve and my recollection.
Terpsichore with your lyre and Thalia behind your comic mask, lend
your charms to my tale and temper my despair. Clio, unfurl your endless scroll on which you have recorded every flutter of butterfly wings
leading to my nadir. Finally, Melpomene, prepare your tragic mask — it
will mirror what I have felt through my betrayals, and when my pain is
too great I might hide my face behind it. You nine Olympian muses, aid
me in telling my tale and then give my spirit rest!

[Theodosius paces across the stage.]

THEODOSIUS (cont'd)

Zeus, son of Kronos, to you I dedicate this story — supreme and most
high ruler, you watcher of the heavens and giver of signs, you of the
golden sword and the furious, boisterous orders. I thought to entrust
everything to your hands, hands that couldn't be dissuaded even from
snatching at your own daughter — that most serene apogee of beauty,
Aphrodite. Barely was she born of the surf before you descended upon
her with those hands, flawless ivory palms and long elegant fingers
never betraying sinister desires. Following your own father's custom,
long had you lain with your sisters before you turned your attention to
your own creations. First, your daughters borne you by fellow gods, but
no sooner had you created man than you decided that their daughters
should not be denied you either — they too should be included in your
harem of missing, mutated, and massacred wives.

[Theodosius stops pacing; centerstage.]

THEODOSIUS (cont'd)

One thing only remains — my story.

[Exit THEODOSIUS, *stage right.]*

ACT I
Scene I

The agora at Atlantis. Stage right: an apple tree marks the path to Theodosius' house. Center: a set of steps descend from the facade of a temple. Stage left: a pair of gates leads to the island's port and shore.
[Enter THEODOSIUS and SOSIGENES, stage right.]

SOSIGENES

Father, slow down!

THEODOSIUS

Quickly, Sosigenes — we must hurry.

SOSIGENES

But why? Where are we going?

THEODOSIUS

What? Nowhere.

SOSIGENES

How does one go nowhere?

THEODOSIUS

What? Don't worry, child — it's nothing.

SOSIGENES

It's not nothing. Why did you wake me so early and rush me out in such a state? Tell me.

THEODOSIUS

On account of the deathless gods. One of them came to me last night! He came as a bull wearing a crown of laurel, and he plucked a blossom from the bough of an apple tree. It was almighty Zeus himself delivering a message of salvation! He showed me how we — you and I — can ensure safety for all of Atlantis.

SOSIGENES

I thought that's why you betrothed me to god-like Achilles, sacker of cities.

THEODOSIUS

Achilles! I'll tell you his wedding offer, daughter — 'a son or a conqueror,' he said, offering me an olive branch with one hand while brandishing his spear with the other.

SOSIGENES

But, father, the gods sanctioned my marriage to swift-footed Achilles — who are we to interrupt their will?

THEODOSIUS

Yes, as you say daughter: who are we to interrupt the will of Zeus? Come, I will tell you more of my dream.

[Exit THEODOSIUS *and* SOSIGENES, *stage left.]*

[Enter DOULOS, *stage right.]*

DOULOS

How many years will Doulos — wretched slave that he is — spend toiling in Atlantis? First his master sends him this way, then that, then back again — like a chained bird flittering about. Why, Fortune, do you smile always on Theodosius while you spit on Doulos? Other men suffer and triumph in equal share — their wealths and healths do wax and wane — yet never Theodosius. Ah, well, if Doulos must be a slave, best to be slave of Zeus' favorite suppliant. 'Tis better to be born a slave who enjoys the prosperity of Zeus' bounty than to be born free and suffer like Iapetos' son, who took on mighty Zeus, master of the fates of men and gods.

[Enter KORINNA *and* IRENAEA, *stage right. Korinna wears a green ribbon in her hair. Irenaea skips over to the temple and hides behind a column.]*

KORINNA

Doulos, I thought I might find you here. My husband keeps you up again? I'm afraid you must serve as our seawall, absorbing the interminable might of Poseidon's crashing waves — or is it Zeus' thunder? So much noise, and yet—

DOULOS

This one could not say, my lady — 'tis not a slave's place.

KORINNA

Well, aren't you philosophical this morning? Tell me — where is Theodosius? Where is Sosigenes? I awoke to a nearly empty house.

DOULOS

The master left with Sosigenes before this one had awoken.

KORINNA

And where have they gone, you stubborn man?

DOULOS

You might try the shore, my lady. The master has been spending much of his time there these last days. He is eager for the return of his son.

KORINNA

Androcles took his place among our fighting men at sea because such is the duty of young men of Atlantis — they must venture into the world to seize the prosperity that Zeus allots them. They grow into men of strength and character as they see the lands of distant gods and men, along

KORINNA (cont'd)

with the cities and homes of our allies. Spartan mothers may claim that only they birth real men, but the sons of Atlantis grow into men capable of more than wanton butchery. Our men are poets, philosophers, orators — they can negotiate peace with words, and guarantee that peace with sword and spear only when necessary.

DOULOS

You blaspheme against the nature of the gods. They care not for Atlantis or her sons. The gods are indifferent to the lives of men.

KORINNA

That's enough, Doulos. Take your sacrilege and your anger away from this place.

DOULOS

As my lady commands.

[Exit DOULOS, *stage right.]*

KORINNA

I'll not let that old grump ruin my day — today is a day for my daughter — today Sosigenes will wed! On some lesser island she would have already been a mother by now, but we don't let our girls fall prey to lecherous abduction on Atlantis. Now, Sosigenes is ready. Irenaea will benefit from seeing what she too might achieve as a woman of Atlantis. Although, she still has plenty of time before her own marriage — time to visit nearby cities and study in the gardens of the nymphs, time to learn the tales of heroic mortals and deathless gods, time to fill her lungs with the breath of the muses. What man would not want such a learned wife as that, with whom he might discuss matters both trivial and lofty? Surely any man would prize such a wife beyond all else.

[Enter THEODOSIUS, *stage left.]*

KORINNA (cont'd)

There you are. I feared the worst when I awoke to an empty bed this morning. Had Zeus taken yet another son of Tros for his cupbearer?

THEODOSIUS

Oh, very funny, dearest wife.

KORINNA

Dearest wife? Have you others then? Is that why you rush off in the small hours of the morning? I think even Phaeton was yet asleep, dreaming of his father's chariot. Where is Sosigenes? I must begin preparing her for her wedding.

THEODOSIUS

Oh, she was on the shore with me. I've hardly had a minute to spend with the girl these past years, and now we will share far less.

KORINNA

So that's your ploy? You take her in secret to whisper in her ear? About what, sly one? Tell me — should Achilles have courted you instead of her?

THEODOSIUS

Enough about Sosigenes. Where is Irenaea? Did you bring her with you? I see her not about the agora.

[Irenaea sings out from behind a column.]

IRENAEA

Mother, mother of the bride,

Easy to be recognized

On Atlantis, far and wide.

Mother, mother of the bride,

Known by all for what she wears —

A long green ribbon in her hair!

THEODOSIUS

That's enough, Irenaea. You're too old for childish games.

IRENAEA

Childish games? I was just playing hide and seek with the god of this temple. She's winning though — I can't seem to find her anywhere!

THEODOSIUS

Do not mock the gods, child.

IRENAEA

No, father, not I — not the daughter of Theodosius, most reverent of all men — who am I to question the plans of the gods?

THEODOSIUS

You know as much of the gods' plans for us as our apples know of our plans for them.

IRENAEA

Are we then merely the food of the gods? Are we all waiting to be sown, plucked, or reaped?

THEODOSIUS

That's enough, Irenaea.

IRENAEA

I'll go help Sosigenes prepare for her wedding too then.

THEODOSIUS

You have no need of your sister, and your sister has no need of you — she is a woman now and can tend to herself.

KORINNA

Nonsense, husband. Sosigenes has need of both Irenaea and myself, just as I had my own mother and sisters prepare me before our wedding.

THEODOSIUS

Sosigenes needs no preparations.

KORINNA

How can that be? Where is she?

THEODOSIUS

Listen, Korinna — the Lord of the Thundercloud came to me himself just last night.

KORINNA

Zeus came to you last night and you didn't think to wake me?

THEODOSIUS

There was no time! You must obey when Zeus commands!

KORINNA

Command? What command?

THEODOSIUS

The blossom—

KORINNA

What blossom?

THEODOSIUS

From the apple tree—

KORINNA

Apple tree? What are you talking about? And what have you done with Sosigenes?

THEODOSIUS

Yes, well, you see—

KORINNA

Where is my daughter?

IRENAEA

Where's Sosigenes?

KORINNA

What have you done with my daughter?

IRENAEA

Where is she?

THEODOSIUS

I've given her to Zeus! That's what he commanded, and I obeyed.

KORINNA

You've done what? You've given my daughter away?

THEODOSIUS

To Zeus! She will be his wife, a queen, more exalted than any other!

KORINNA

And what of Achilles?

THEODOSIUS

Achilles came here — to our home — and demanded a union of our houses. He would steal my daughter with no thought of just compensation!

KORINNA

So it's about money!

THEODOSIUS

It's about safety! An alliance with Zeus will keep us safe!

KORINNA

And how will Sosigenes stay safe?

THEODOSIUS

This is why the dispassionate sex must rule. I'm guaranteeing safety for all of Olympus, not just my own family.

KORINNA

Safer than an alliance with Achilles?

THEODOSIUS

A marriage to Achilles brings us an alliance with the Myrmidons. A marriage to Zeus brings us an alliance with the Olympians!

KORINNA

No, it brings only an alliance with Zeus, and even that cannot be trusted. The other Olympians will hound our daughter unto her death!

THEODOSIUS

He promised us safety! And glory for our son. Atlantis will even grow to her former stature. Don't you see? We're all saved!

IRENAEA

And Sosigenes? My sister? How is she to be saved?

THEODOSIUS

Saved from what? Don't you understand? She is to wed Zeus. She will have the most prominent marriage any woman could ask for.

KORINNA

The only marriage a woman might want less would be to you, Theodosius. Would that I had cast myself from the cliffs of Scyros that day my father gave me to you. Oh, gods, I am the most miserable of all Lycomedes' daughters!

THEODOSIUS

How can you say such a thing to me?

KORINNA

You have delivered my child unto her death — you may as well have killed her while she slept and me with her!

IRENAEA

And me!

THEODOSIUS

What is this nonsense? Who would not want Zeus as a husband?

KORINNA

His wife foremost, Hera, who has suffered his countless betrayals. But not only does Zeus offend his natural wife, he abandons his mistresses to whatever fates they should be forced to endure! They are the lost women of the Mediterranean! And what of Achilles? He will be here today, Theodosius! He is expecting to find Sosigenes ready to wed him.

THEODOSIUS

He is expecting a daughter of Atlantis — a daughter of Theodosius — nothing more.

KORINNA

What then, Irenaea? Absolutely not.

THEODOSIUS

Achilles will never know the difference.

KORINNA

Achilles is expecting a woman, not a child! And who are you to sell my children like this?

THEODOSIUS

It is not for you to say when Irenaea might marry. That decision is mine to make by the laws of gods and men.

IRENAEA

And what of the laws of women?

THEODOSIUS

It's my right, divinely prescribed by Zeus!

KORINNA

How fortunate for you that Zeus should make such pronouncements — each and every time supporting your position! And how else should it be since you are the one interpreting the declarations?

THEODOSIUS

I'll not remain to listen to this…this…this blasphemy! You will both offend our savior!

IRENAEA

And who will be Sosigenes' savior?

[Exit THEODOSIUS, *stage right.]*

IRENAEA (cont'd)

Who will be Sosigenes' savior?

KORINNA

Savior? Surely you realize there's no saving her now — your wise and lordly father has traded her away like a sack of apples!

IRENAEA

Then who shall be her redeemer?

KORINNA

Redeemer? No, Irenaea, we mustn't think like that — this is a time for prayer and offerings. Your father was right about one thing — the will of the gods cannot be questioned by mortals.

IRENAEA

And what about my will?

KORINNA

Our protectresses will not have forgotten us. If there is a goddess among Olympus who will aid us in our quest for justice, let her hear our prayers. Surely Hera will help us, and perhaps others — Artemis, Aphrodite, Persephone, or any other of the white-armed goddesses on high. We will beseech them all. Come, Irenaea.

[Exit KORINNA, temple.]

IRENAEA

Bow down before those who allowed this atrocity to occur in the first place? Never — these gods of my parents will never be mine. My sister was stolen from me! If the gods truly existed, they would not have asked my father to make such a sacrosanct offering as that. Either they don't exist, or they care nothing for mortals. Whichever may be the case, it hardly matters to me now. No, the gods will not help me, so I will help myself — now is the time to do as I will. My sister is gone forever, and the gods will never receive libations from me. As for my father, he must bear the blame for the horror of my sister's fate. I swear by her name that I will raze his beloved city to the ground — this city for which he sacrifices one daughter, and then immediately offers up the other. I will see the walls crumble like ridges of sand falling into the sea. I will watch the temples burn, their altars and idols engulfed in flames. I will paint my face black with the ashes of this city and be the grim hound that haunts her even in death!

[Exit IRENAEA, stage left.]

ACT I

Scene II

[Enter ZEUS *and* SOSIGENES, *stage left.]*

SOSIGENES

Where are we? This looks just the same as the agora at Atlantis.

ZEUS

This is the agora at Atlantis, but we walk among the Olympian plane rather than that of the mortals.

SOSIGENES

How do I walk among the Olympian plane?

ZEUS

Olympians such as I can cross at will.

SOSIGENES

And I?

ZEUS

You are here because I have brought you here. Now hurry, my dear — the wedding must take place shortly.

SOSIGENES

How does Zeus know of my wedding? And where is Achilles? Should we not wait?

ZEUS

Wait? We have no time to wait.

SOSIGENES

We have to wait for the groom at least. Achilles should be here any moment — that's why my father brought me to the beach so early.

ZEUS

The groom is already here, silly girl. Now, let's get on with it.

SOSIGENES

Achilles is here? But where? Is he hiding?

ZEUS

You are not to wed Achilles. I am to be your husband.

SOSIGENES

You — you are, my lord?

ZEUS

This displeases you?

SOSIGENES

It's only — I have always looked to you as a protector, like my father.

ZEUS

You will learn to see me as much more than that.

SOSIGENES

And Achilles?

ZEUS

He is of no further concern to you. You will forget him. Now, we must finish this wedding quickly — before the other gods arrive.

SOSIGENES

Should we not wait for them? Won't they attend the marriage?

ZEUS

Why would I want to wait for them? Should my wife watch while I wed you? And my brothers and children, what of them? Think what they would say if they sought to wed a mortal of their own — they'd say: 'Zeus did it, so too might I.' No, we do this now. Alone.

SOSIGENES

So I'm to be your secret wife? Tell me — will I be a prisoner of some high tower or an exile on some distant island?

ZEUS

You will be a wife of Zeus. Your children will be demigods, blessed beyond all other mortals.

SOSIGENES

And hated beyond all others too. The other mortals will begrudge them their gifts from jealousy while the other gods will spite them from pride. And what of Hera? Will she not hound them across the world until she sees them suffer and die?

ZEUS

And who are you to interrupt my will? We will be wed or you will fall dead. This is my decree. Come over here and lie down. Quickly, before the others arrive!

SOSIGENES

Y-y-yes, my lord. Only, wh-h-h-y are the others coming if n-n-not for a m-m-marriage?

ZEUS

They are coming for a marriage — that of Achilles and Irenaea. Now lie down!

SOSIGENES

I am to be your secret whore while Achilles marries my little sister?

ZEUS

Very well, I'll do it your way.

> *[Zeus grabs Sosigenes and pins her against the apple tree.]*

SOSIGENES

No! Stop!

[Whistling sounds offstage.]

ZEUS

Damnit! One of the other Olympians must be approaching! I'll keep you somewhere safe for now.

[Zeus forces Sosigenes behind the tree. When she disappears, a green apple appears on the bough.]

ZEUS (cont'd)

There — an apple for later.

[Exit ZEUS, stage right.]

[Enter HERMES and ARTEMIS, stage left. Hermes whistles as he enters.]

HERMES

What boredom reigns today. I say, Artemis, give me a bit of sport — come have a duel with me! The morning is threatening to run in reverse if I don't find some amusement.

ARTEMIS

I'll not be hacking off any of your limbs today, brother.

HERMES

Just one quick stroke, I beg you! My neck is your canvas — paint with that enormous brush of yours, that sleek javelin!

ARTEMIS

Immortality doesn't suit you. Better you were born mortal — maybe a son of Daedalus?

HERMES

Ah, but at least his story lives on, while the fallen hero rests.

ARTEMIS

You've missed the point of his story if you think Icarus is the hero. And he doesn't rest brother — he's dead. He did not die well, plummeting toward Earth engulfed in flames.

HERMES

It's you who has missed the point, sister. Always so dire! Icarus may be dead, but consider how he lived. He dared to reach out and touch the stars.

ARTEMIS

Small consolation.

HERMES

Don't you see? He flew when no other mortals could!

ARTEMIS

What about the artificer himself?

HERMES

What might we gods then do if we only try? Is almighty Zeus the only one of us who might wield the lightning bolt and marshal the thundercloud? Why not us? Sometimes, sister, I feel a fire inside me, coursing through my veins like mercury! I can create — inspire love, art, and harmony; or I can destroy — raze cities, kill men, sink ships! Why should I be denied my machinations? Why should any of us? Why prostrate ourselves before Zeus? 'He of the Storm Cloud?' More like 'He of the Shepherds' Daughters!'

ARTEMIS

You ought to watch where you say such things. Those loose lips of yours are bound to sink something. Look — here comes Hera. Do you intend to enthrall her with your egalitarianism?

HERMES

No, I daresay I have a better tale with which to entertain her. Perhaps you would like to stay and listen. I think she will be requiring your assistance before the act is done.

ARTEMIS

What are you up to now, little Psychopompus? Icarus' fate is too boring for you, so you crave Prometheus' eagle?

[Enter HERA, stage left.]

HERA

Good morning, Artemis, Hermes. I hope I find you both well.

HERMES

What a day! The Queen of all Olympus! I should say you do find us well, very well now that you've graced us with your divine presence.

HERA

What brings you both to spectate the mortal plane of Atlantis so early in the day?

HERMES

Should the hours of man dictate those of the gods? Why, I know some gods who make great use of the time mortals spend asleep.

HERA

Artemis, you come today to attend Achilles' wedding?

HERMES

So astute, our queen! Truly does she see all. Perhaps we ought to call her 'Fore Sight,' eh, Artemis?

HERA

Of course you are, and rightly so.

HERMES

Sagacity, beauty, punctuality — it is little wonder that Zeus chose you for his wife.

HERA

And why are you here, Hermes? I doubt very much that Artemis requires your assistance.

ARTEMIS

What could I possibly need from him? He could neither lift my spear, nor draw my bowstring.

HERMES

You'd both be surprised by what aid I might lend here in Atlantis or even Olympus. I came here merely in the hopes of basking in your divine presence. After all, Zeus was just here, and rarely can devoted lovers like you two bear to be apart for long. I wonder what it was that he was watching though — or doing.

HERA

Zeus has much business of which I know little and you know less. It's not your place to question him.

HERMES

What? I question Zeus? Never! But, then, who do you await? You wait on Achilles?

HERA

I do not wait on him — I am not his handmaiden. Although I suppose I do wait for him. He is to wed Theodosius' daughter this morn — a lovely girl. Yes, she seems to prove that sometimes Zeus does give with both hands.

ARTEMIS

Who knows Zeus' greatness better than Hera?

HERMES

Oh, I daresay she knows all about Zeus' magnanimity to beautiful and pious young girls. Why, the girl seems to prove that sometimes Zeus does take with both hands!

HERA

Enough! I can listen to no more of your snide remarks! Go find yourself a willing audience, or, better yet, go and amuse yourself among the mortals — at least you'll be among your intellectual peers!

HERMES

Your wish shall be my command, oh one true wife of Zeus!

[Exit HERMES, *stage left.]*

HERA

The nerve of that impudent wretch!

ARTEMIS

Having seen your ire, I think he'll not bother us further.

HERA

I certainly hope we don't have to suffer through his presence any more.

ARTEMIS

Yet I can't celebrate his absence. Who knows the trouble he'll cause when left to his own devices.

HERA

What's this? Have you seen this, Artemis?

ARTEMIS

Seen what?

HERA

The apple. I've never seen such a fine specimen. I think it's the most perfect one of the season. This must be one of Theodosius' trees.

[Enter ZEUS, stage right.]

ZEUS

My dearest wife! And daughter! So good to see you both here. What brings you to Atlantis today?

HERA

Sosigenes is to wed Achilles today — how could I miss the ceremony? How could Artemis? Is this not what brings you here as well?

ZEUS

Of course. Who should sanction the joining if not I?

HERA

Yes, no one respects the sanctity of marriage quite like you do.

ZEUS

And you, Artemis? You're obviously here for Irenaea. She'll be pleased.

ARTEMIS

Irenaea? I doubt she'll even notice my presence. She rarely visits my altar. I'm sure she will be much too preoccupied with Sosigenes to focus on anything else.

ZEUS

An impious daughter of Theodosius? I don't believe it. I've seen her sister — I know the type of girl that Theodosius produces.

ARTEMIS

Ah, but he doesn't make them all the same. No matter, we have the right one for today — Sosigenes will make an excellent wife for Achilles.

ZEUS

Yes, yes — although, it shouldn't make such a difference, should it? Which daughter, that is. Surely Irenaea will be just as worthy a wife

ZEUS (cont'd)

    with a bit of time. And she's the younger of the two. I think you and
    Hera will do Achilles a disservice, and the girls too.

HERA

    What matter is it to you? Why must you constantly scheme?

ZEUS

    I don't scheme.

HERA

    You do. Now, where is Sosigenes? I will go to her as a woman of Atl-
    antis and prepare her for her marriage.

ZEUS

    What a wonderful idea! Only, are you absolutely sure Achilles wouldn't
    prefer the younger sister? Tell me truthfully, Artemis — would Irenaea
    not be the perfect bride for Achilles?

HERA

    Yes, Artemis, be truthful. Don't lie to your lord Zeus. Who knows what
    plans he's conceiving.

ZEUS

    What would you know of my plans? Was it not my plan that set me atop
    the throne of lofty Olympus?

ARTEMIS

    I thought that was your mother, Rhea of the swaddled rock.

ZEUS

    Who are you to question me?

ARTEMIS

    Am I to understand that you have already decided the girls' fates? Does
    our say count for nothing?

ZEUS

    Enough, Artemis. What difference does it make to you which woman
    Achilles gets? He will get one, and he's not the type of man to fuss over
    names.

ARTEMIS

    As you command, my lord. Should someone tell the girls? Sosigenes
    will be dismayed to forfeit this honor.

ZEUS

    Why are you so obsessed with Sosigenes?

HERA

    Why are you?

ZEUS

    I? Obsessed?

HERA

Where is she, Zeus?

ZEUS

Not that it should concern you, but — I accepted the girl — as an offering.

HERA

An offering?

ZEUS

Yes, an offering. It's symbolic, dearest.

ARTEMIS

But — why? Achilles has been sailing for weeks already. Why would you do such a thing on the day that he will arrive?

ZEUS

Enough, Artemis.

HERA

Enough for her, perhaps. I'm not done here. Where is Sosigenes?

ZEUS

It's done, Hera. I've made my decision and given my command.

HERA

Command? And what command is that? That Theodosius give you his daughter? So where is she? Where is your offering?

ZEUS

I've put her somewhere safe.

ARTEMIS

And what about Achilles?

ZEUS

He'll be thankful that I have taken her away! Now that she has been offered the prospect of Zeus' companionship, how could Achilles compare?

HERA

Yes, what a tremendous lover and partner you are. Why, just look around to see the depth and glory of your harem!

ZEUS

I have no desire to remain here and be abused by you.

[Exit ZEUS, *stage right.]*

HERA

You may as well have killed the girl already, husband. You may yet get the chance to enjoy her — a nibble perhaps — but I will not let you keep her.

ARTEMIS

And what about Irenaea?

HERA

    Irenaea? What about her? You must realize that Zeus cares only for himself. And when is enough enough?

ARTEMIS

    Enough?

HERA

    Do we not have wills of our own? Should Zeus alone pluck the strings of fate?

ARTEMIS

    I've heard that tune before.

HERA

    I'll not forget about Sosigenes, nor Korinna, nor Irenaea, nor even Achilles. I know you feel the same, and together we will rescue our suppliants! I can hear Korinna calling to me now. I must comfort her with my divine presence.

[Exit HERA, temple.]

ARTEMIS

    What's Zeus started? He's stolen Sosigenes, Achilles' betrothed, and now he will have Irenaea, my suppliant, take her sister's place in Achilles' bed. And what am I to do? Am I expected to join in this battle — this ridiculously contrived fight? Oh, why can't Zeus control himself! And Hera, she will inflame this situation with her wrath. But should my altar suffer due to Zeus' actions? It's not as though Irenaea visits it, yet the child is dear to me. She has the spirit of a warrior in her soul and I will stand by her now — howsoever Irenaea might benefit here, that shall be my concern. Zeus can worry about the consequences.

[Exit ARTEMIS, stage left.]

ACT II
SCENE I

[Enter KORINNA, *temple. Her dress is lightly spattered with blood from a sacrifice.]*

KORINNA

Down, down, down. How many times have I walked down these same five steps? How many times did I bring Sosigenes and Irenaea here to make offerings when they were young? It is a strange path today.

[Korinna collapses at the foot of the steps.]

KORINNA (cont'd)

Oh, gods, won't you take pity on me? Spare me this shame and outrage! Sosigenes is gone. What horrible fate might she yet suffer? And now what of Irenaea? Is she to take her sister's place in Achilles marriage bed? And what of me? Am I to remain in Atlantis with the betrayer, the man who sold both my daughters on the same day? I can't stand the thought of it! How am I to share his home — his bed? And when he seeks to replant his seed — more apples for the marketplace — am I to brave this indignity too?

[Enter HERMES, *disguised as Doulos, stage left.]*

HERMES

Knife, hatred, tools, or fury?

KORINNA

Doulos?

HERMES

Sweet Korinna, why do you weep? Will your tears bring back Sosigenes or protect Irenaea? My dear woman, you have work to do!

KORINNA

I have work to do?

HERMES

Are there not plans you should be making?

KORINNA

What do you know of my plans?

HERMES

There's no time for questions. Where will that get us? If you truly want your plan to succeed, you must dedicate your mind to the problem at hand — do not let trivialities distract you until you have completed your endeavor.

KORINNA

It's fine for a slave to say such things, you who have so little to plan. All of your concerns are handled by us.

HERMES

Do not let pride cloud your senses, Korinna. I offer you aid when none else is forthcoming.

KORINNA

And why would you help me?

HERMES

I abhor what Theodosius did — delivering Sosigenes into the hands of Zeus whose smile hides a hideous mind full of wrath and insatiable lust. That brutish, conceited—

KORINNA

Doulos.

HERMES

Incompetent, moronic—

KORINNA

Doulos!

HERMES

Who? Er, yes, what is it?

KORINNA

Do not blaspheme. I don't know whether Zeus or Theodosius is most at fault here, but let's not flaunt our contempt lest we arouse suspicion.

HERMES

Of course. Your escape will speak louder than any epithets I can hurl at those despicable, scheming, overbearing—

KORINNA

Doulos!

HERMES

What?

KORINNA

Tell me your plan, so I may judge for myself its merits.

HERMES

As you wish. The young warrior Achilles sails here now. He expects to find a bride when he arrives. That much cannot be kept from the man. Let us use that to your advantage. After all, an alliance with Atlantis would serve Achilles well, but there is one which might yet serve him better.

KORINNA

With whom?

HERMES

Your father, King Lycomedes of Scyros.

KORINNA

You want me to marry Achilles?

HERMES

If he would have you. Otherwise, Irenaea.

KORINNA

No! Irenaea will not be sold off like her sister. If Achilles won't have me, then one of my sisters will stand in my stead.

HERMES

This can be no idle promise, lady.

KORINNA

And it won't be. Achilles shall have a daughter of Lycomedes rather than a daughter of Theodosius. But how am I to convince Achilles to abandon his alliance with Atlantis on the very day the deal is to be struck?

HERMES

He will need little convincing after the tongue lashing he receives from his host.

KORINNA

Theodosius will never disrespect Achilles to the man's face — he's much too cowardly for that.

HERMES

Then you must do it.

KORINNA

I? Why would Achilles listen to me?

HERMES

You must do it as Theodosius. Don his garb and affect his character. Go to the beach and welcome Achilles as I have counseled you. In his anger at Theodosius, Achilles will be quick to accept a marriage proposal from the elegant and beautiful lady of Atlantis, who will furthermore bear him a gift.

KORINNA

What gift?

HERMES

Pray to the gods, Korinna, that they might send you a symbol of their divine recognition of this course of action. An Olympian object will convince Achilles where words may fail.

KORINNA

And what of Theodosius?

HERMES

Where is your husband now?

KORINNA

Down in the orchard.

HERMES

I will see that he remains there long enough for you to explain every-thing to Irenaea. When he returns to the agora, I will arrange your disguise.

[Exit HERMES, stage right.]

KORINNA

How strange that man is acting today. I've never heard him speak like that before.

[Enter IRENAEA, her dress also bloody, stage left.]

KORINNA

Irenaea, good. I've just sent Doulos to keep your treacherous father occupied, but we haven't much time. Where have you been? And what's happened to your clothes?

IRENAEA

I took my ewe to the shore. I walked her into the shallows and we sat in the cool water. She rested her head on my lap and raised her eyes to mine. I took her by the chin and dragged a blade across her throat. I watched her blood run into the Great Sea and disappear.

KORINNA

Irenaea! You'd waste a fine sacrifice such as that when we need divine favor now more than ever?

IRENAEA

Have we not received our share of divine attention already? What more could the gods want from us? Sosigenes is already gone — am I to be next?

KORINNA

No. I'll die before I lose both my daughters on the same day.

IRENAEA

As though you have any say in the matter. Will your gods not act as they see fit, and always in their own self interest? Why should they help you? What can you offer them? Do you imagine they will starve without your burning the glistening fat and thigh bones of cows?

KORINNA

Hera has always looked after me. Consider the prosperity of our family and you will see the goddess' goodness.

IRENAEA

Hera didn't give father his orchard.

KORINNA

You have no way of knowing in what ways she has helped our family. Who are you to guess at the gods' actions?

IRENAEA

Who are you? You suppose the gods look after you because they have brought you to this point, but what if they have merely built you up to watch you fall? What if they led you here to watch you suffer — like Sosigenes, like my lamb?

KORINNA

Do not say such things! The gods will aid us, Irenaea. You will see the scope of their power and the depth of their compassion.

[Exit KORINNA, *temple.]*

IRENAEA

Will nothing shake her belief? Will she continue to recite her hymns with a mouth full of mud, covering herself in filth at the gods' whims? Not I. And not Sosigenes. Oh, sister, do you remember the adventures we created on this abominable island? We discovered lost cities, battled against great warriors, tested our wits before kings and queens, set sail on the greatest seas of the world. And now how do you suffer?

[Enter DOULOS, *stage right.]*

DOULOS

Every day it's the same — last five years — is Doulos not his own man?

IRENAEA

Where did you come from?

DOULOS

You're not supposed to be here. You're supposed to be at home, preparing. There is much to do, and who will be expected to do it all, eh? Doulos, that's who.

IRENAEA

So then you had better get to it. Go about your business and leave me to mine.

DOULOS

My business? Perhaps Doulos ought to be readying his own daughter for her wedding. But then, where is Doulos' wife? Where is his home, his orchard? Your family is the only business he has. Now, in your father's name, come along.

IRENAEA

Then now is as good a time as any to find some business of your own. I have matters that require my attention, so I don't have time to worry over your comings and goings.

DOULOS

You are like Doulos, girl — your only concerns are those of your father. How do you think he will react when he hears about your willfulness, your disobedience?

IRENAEA

And who am I to obey? You? My father? Zeus, your god of satyrs? Go then, and tell them of my actions, but stop pestering me.

[Exit DOULOS, *stage right.]*

IRENAEA (cont'd)

I am no slave, not to any man nor god! I can make a plan just as well as Doulos, Theodosius, and Zeus. My mother will have to seek escape on her own, for I'll not be a tool for her to use either. And where is Justice in all of this? If she won't mete out her judgement, then that shall be my final task. I will avenge Sosigenes — a revenge so terrible that even the gods will weep to behold it! I will hide in the shadows and wait for Theodosius, like a spider perched on the periphery of her web. He will feel the sting of my bite, and I will drag him down into death! I will be like Zeus, like Achilles, slayer of men. I will be the firebrand that curses this city to annihilation — I will sate my rage with my father's blood!

[Enter THEODOSIUS, *stage right.]*

THEODOSIUS

Irenaea! What are you doing here? Doulos said—

IRENAEA

Do not speak to me, murderer.

THEODOSIUS

Murderer? Doulos was right to alert me to your ravings. I'll have have no more of it. You ought to be at home preparing for your wedding.

IRENAEA

Don't you mean Sosigenes' wedding?

THEODOSIUS

Sosigenes is not your concern.

IRENAEA

How dare you speak her name? Why don't you call her what she was to you? Just another apple for the market.

THEODOSIUS

And now what is she? Nothing less than the wife of Zeus!

IRENAEA

And what of Hera in your daughter's grand new life? Will she not mind sharing her husband with a mortal?

THEODOSIUS

Don't be foolish, girl. Hera can do nothing against the will of Zeus.

IRENAEA

You would be surprised by what a goddess, or even a foolish girl, might accomplish against the will of Zeus. Goodbye, Theodosius.

[Exit IRENAEA, stage left.]

THEODOSIUS

Why can't these women see that what's good for the family, the city, the island is also good for them? Will my daughters not be safe wed to the most powerful men on Earth or Olympus? Sosigenes will be an Olympian queen, and Irenaea will be queen of Achilles' kingdom. What more could they want? One day they will see that my way is best. Until then, I will make their decisions for them.

[Enter HERMES as Doulos, stage right.]

THEODOSIUS (cont'd)

Doulos? Why aren't you at home? Have you prepared my vestments?

HERMES

Everything is in order.

THEODOSIUS

Good. And my wife?

HERMES

In the temple. She will be most displeased if you don't join her.

THEODOSIUS

I'll not let fear of a woman sway me. I'm no coward.

[Exit THEODOSIUS, stage right.]

HERMES

It is no cowardice to fear the havoc a woman's wrath may wreak.

[Hermes remains on stage.]

ACT II
SCENE II

[Enter ZEUS, *stage right.]*

HERMES

Is that Zeus I spy? Come back to Atlantis so soon?

ZEUS

Hermes? What's that you're wearing? And where have you been? I could have used you earlier.

HERMES

Used me?

ZEUS

Yes, you always know how to distract. Hmm. Well now. Ahem. Have you business here today then?

HERMES

Business? They say there is to be a wedding — I am merely here to observe. Have you business here today then?

ZEUS

No use trying to fool you, eh? It's the girl — I must have her!

HERMES

The girl?

ZEUS

Theodosius' girl, Sosigenes.

HERMES

Sosigenes? Is she not somewhere safe by now?

ZEUS

Safe enough. Who might harm her now it's just the two of us? You see, I transformed her! I nearly had her earlier, but some Olympians interrupted us. I only just had time to hide the girl before they would have discovered us!

HERMES

And which Olympians espied you?

ZEUS

Oh, they didn't see me, and neither did I see them. As I said, I only just had time to hide the girl and escape myself. But now I have plenty of time, and you're here to help. Stand guard for me — there, at the gates. I'll finally have the girl!

HERMES

> Do you mean she is here? What animal have you made her? Some kind of bird?

ZEUS

> A bird? Why would I give her wings? No, no more animals. I turned her into an apple — one of Theodosius' apples.

HERMES

> An apple? What are you going to do with an apple?

ZEUS

> I'm going to turn her back.

HERMES

> Turn her back?

ZEUS

> Yes, turn her back!

HERMES

> Dread majesty, Son of Cronus — what are you saying? A woman, a mere mortal, her doom sealed by you yourself? You'd set her free from all you commanded? Do as you please, Zeus — but none of the other deathless gods will ever praise you.

ZEUS

> Why shouldn't they?

HERMES

> What of the others then? The brides of Apollo forever in flight — Cassandra, Bolina, Daphne, Sinope, and Marpessa above all. You yourself sat in judgement of her case when she refused your son's advances; you allowed her to forsake Phoebus Apollo — morning dew fleeing the rising sun. Will you still deny to your own son that which you seek? If you return Sosigenes' form to her, all of your sons will demand you return their brides too — those daughters of rivers and streams, kings and queens. And if you comply and do this for your sons? The other gods have sons — yes, and daughters too. What will they say when they hear of what you've done?

ZEUS

> Why should it matter if they hear? I am Zeus and my very words are divine decree!

HERMES

> If only then it had not been you who transformed the girl. Had one of the other deathless gods changed her, then certainly you could change her back at the mere risk of incurring their wrath. However, since you changed the girl yourself, if you were to change her back you would be violating the ultimate and supreme decree of Zeus, our greatest god.

ZEUS

But I'm Zeus!

HERMES

I know who you are — you're the one whose words are divine decree. Although I suppose you should have been more careful with them then.

ZEUS

It's you who should be more careful. You and I are the only ones who know what I've done. Suppose I do turn the girl back? Suppose I do anything I like to her? What can one such as you do to obviate my will? Now move!

[Zeus shoves Hermes.]

[Enter ARTEMIS, *stage left.]*

ARTEMIS

Hello, Zeus, Hermes.

HERMES

Hello, Artemis. How good it is to see you again. Zeus was just expounding the benefits of a woman's company — how aptly they might apply their sweet words and the appeal of their form. But I must leave the two of you, much business remains.

[Exit HERMES, *stage left.]*

ARTEMIS

Your wife will be here shortly. Will you await her with me?

ZEUS

So you're upset with me too then, daughter?

ARTEMIS

I don't question your will, father, but what is to become of Irenaea? How is she to escape from this encounter without suffering?

ZEUS

Why should she suffer? Achilles is on his way to the island, is he not? She will wed him when he arrives and will never again need fear harm from anyone. Who would dare molest Achilles' woman?

ARTEMIS

Then you will look after the girl?

ZEUS

I have upheld my agreement with Theodosius thus far — I don't intend to cheat him.

ARTEMIS

No?

ZEUS

No — all the sons of Tros are dear to me. I have not forgotten their family. Assaracus had a son, Capys, who himself had two sons —

ZEUS (cont'd)

Anchises he sired with Themiste, but he also had a son with Nesea, Nereid of the island. That son is Theodosius of Atlantis, grandson of Assaracus.

ARTEMIS

All the gods know of your love for the sons of Tros. My only concern is how this affects Irenaea.

ZEUS

She'll be fine. Nothing will happen to her.

ARTEMIS

Nor for her. Is she nothing more than a hostage?

ZEUS

That is for Achilles to decide as her husband. Now, I too have affairs that need tending.

[Exit ZEUS, stage right.]

ARTEMIS

You can come out now, brother.

[Enter HERMES, stage left.]

HERMES

What a tyrant! Don't be fooled by his circuitous talk — he cares only for himself. Neither Theodosius nor Achilles' lives would make a bit of difference weighed against another opportunity to sate his lust. Tros, Assaracus, Capys, Theodosius — he pretends they are dear to him, but they are no more than a stable of studs from which the brood mares have been culled, one by one as his fancy takes him.

ARTEMIS

The studs are not safe either — Ganymede can attest to that.

HERMES

Too true, sister. What then will you do to protect Irenaea?

ARTEMIS

What can I do? She won't heed me.

HERMES

Perhaps she will heed another.

ARTEMIS

Who? She cares nothing for the gods.

HERMES

Not even your brother, Apollo?

ARTEMIS

Not even him.

HERMES

> She may not listen to shining Apollo, but Achilles will. The man is dear to the god, and the god is dear to the man. If Irenaea won't heed the god of truth and knowledge, then you can at least ensure that Achilles keeps to your plan. Otherwise the girl is doomed.

ARTEMIS

> Irenaea must not suffer for Zeus' passions. I will do as you counsel and disguise myself as my brother, but this plan still lacks certainty.

HERMES

> Perhaps another of the Olympians can help you.

ARTEMIS

> Who would risk incurring Zeus' wrath?

HERMES

> His wife.

ARTEMIS

> Hera? She will not aid me nor Irenaea. Even her suppliants she looks after only so long as they keep her altar.

HERMES

> Korinna has kept her altar sacred and weighted down with sacrifice. Hera will protect her. She merely needs to give her favor to a marriage between Achilles and Korinna. Korinna and Irenaea will get their escape, and Achilles will get a woman of Atlantis and a military alliance with her father, albeit a different woman and father than he was expecting.

ARTEMIS

> Very well — I will beseech Hera to aid Korinna and thus to protect Irenaea.

HERMES

> You are only doing as you must — Zeus has left you no other choice.

> > *[Exit* HERMES, *stage left.]*

ARTEMIS

> Yes, I see no other way to save Irenaea, trapped on Atlantis like a fly amidst a great, shimmering spider's web. And who else but Zeus might play the role of the spider, weaving hither and thither, leaving a sticky trap behind? None are safe from his desirous eyes! That hawkish gaze of his — perennially casting about in search of some new prey — there is no hiding from it! Yet I can still ensure that no harm befalls Irenaea. I will not let her be taken like her sister. And what of Hera? How can she let Zeus carouse like this?

> > *[Enter* HERA, *temple.]*

HERA

You seek to blame me for Zeus' outrages?

ARTEMIS

Hera, whence did you arrive?

HERA

I have been sequestered in the temple for the better part of the day, and I exit to hear you claim I am the cause of this new disgrace. I am the victim!

ARTEMIS

Sosigenes is the victim, and Irenaea may yet be as well.

HERA

You think I don't know that?

ARTEMIS

How then will you aid them?

HERA

Sosigenes is already doomed. It's just a matter of time until Zeus grows bored with the girl and lets down his defenses. Then I will find her. But it was Zeus who stole the girl — he created this situation! Any harm that befalls her now is his own doing.

ARTEMIS

And Irenaea, your suppliant's child?

HERA

What is she to me?

ARTEMIS

Do you think Korinna will abandon her? What mother would do such a thing?

HERA

Careful, daughter of Zeus.

ARTEMIS

It is Korinna and Irenaea who must now be careful. How will you aid them in their escape?

HERA

I? How will you?

ARTEMIS

I have a plan — a plan for Korinna and Irenaea to sail away from Atlantis.

HERA

What's this plan?

ARTEMIS

Irenaea will not wed Achilles. Instead, Korinna will wed him, and both mother and daughter will escape the island aboard Achilles sleek, black ships.

HERA

Why would Achilles agree to this plan?

ARTEMIS

He is a warrior. You must appeal to him as such. He will forsake an alliance with Atlantis for one with Korinna's father on Scyros.

HERA

He will not. Achilles is a man besides a warrior, and men always need something to sweeten their fare.

ARTEMIS

Then I will make a different plan. I will do whatever I must to protect my suppliant.

HERA

No. You will stay away from this island. Do you hear me, Artemis? Keep yourself away from Atlantis the rest of this day.

ARTEMIS

Will you keep all of Zeus' children at bay?

[Exit ARTEMIS, *stage left.]*

HERA

These daughters of Zeus are infuriating! I am his rightful wife by all the laws of Olympus, and still they seek always to aid him sneak around in the shadows. They play a dangerous game. Have they forgotten about Echo? Echo, who plotted to help you, son of Kronos. Well did she know of your proclivities among the Oreads — all of Olympus knows your weakness for nymphs. The girl was clever to distract me with her amusing stories while you dallied. It was the last clever thing she ever did.

[Enter HERMES, *stage left.]*

HERA (cont'd)

I thought we had finished with you already.

HERMES

Not quite, but why does the Queen of Olympus still brood on Atlantis?

HERA

Because my illustrious husband has forsaken me for an apple monger's daughter.

HERMES

It's hardly the first time.

HERA

A curse on your altar, Hermes!

HERMES

Why do you curse me, Hera? It is Zeus who wrongs you, not I.

HERA

And who is running about between the scenes, pulling strings and tipping blocks? Who is helping Zeus hide that wretched girl? I've been watching you, Hermes — the way you come and go.

HERMES

Do I do it so differently from the rest?

HERA

The rest may not knows your tricks, but I do.

HERMES

I have no need of tricks, but Korinna and Irenaea will need one from Achilles if they are to escape the island.

HERA

So that's your true purpose here? Artemis has sent you to argue for her plan?

HERMES

What matter whose plan if it's a good one?

HERA

I'd be inclined to agree with you if it was a good plan.

HERMES

What's wrong with it?

HERA

Have you not heard Irenaea? She's been raving quite openly about murdering her father and burning the city to the ground.

HERMES

We've all heard her ravings, but what can a young girl who has never held sword nor spear do to harm Theodosius, favorite of Zeus? The girl is merely upset. She will do as her mother bids her.

HERA

Perhaps you have a point. She is just a young girl — how much harm could she cause? And her mother has been a loyal suppliant of mine all her life. Very well, I will enlist Achilles in my plot and ensure he brings Korinna to safety, lest my altar suffers. But how to entice the man?

HERMES

A wedding gift from the Queen of Olympus should do the trick.

HERA

What kind of gift?

HERMES

It could be anything. Just apply some of your magic, give it the appeal of gold, and any object will aptly convey your intention.

[Exit HERMES, stage left.]

HERA

Anything, you say? Well, why not an apple? One of Theodosius' apples! I rather like the sound of that. And if Zeus can steal from Theodosius' orchard, then why mightn't I? Achilles shall have a golden apple!

[Hera plucks the apple, Sosigenes, from the bough of the apple tree.]

HERA (cont'd)

Ah, here's a ploy worthy even of Daedalus. Would that I had a servant such as you to build me a labyrinth or some other ingenious trap. Instead, Achilles will be my man. To think, a warrior who strikes fear into the hearts of men should be bought so cheaply. Yet why should I forever be the one to bear the cost of Zeus' games? Why do his brothers not reign him in? Can they be so satisfied with the drawing of lots? Where is Poseidon, who looks after the ships and sailors of Atlantis? Does neither this island nor its citizens concern him any longer? He too has a suppliant near.

[Exit HERA, temple.]

ACT III

Scene I

[Enter KORINNA, temple. She carries the Golden Apple.]

KORINNA

What a vision! If Hera sent the same dream to Achilles, he will certainly aid my cause. And no one will doubt the divinity of my plan when they see the goddess' gift — a solid gold apple! Even Irenaea will be convinced when I show her this.

[Exit KORINNA, stage left.]

[Enter THEODOSIUS, stage right.]

THEODOSIUS

Zeus, heavenly father, my offering has been made — Sosigenes sits by your side on Olympus. Now is the time to make good on your promises. Let the people of Atlantis see your will be done! What's this? Why is the agora not prepared for the wedding?

[Enter ANDROCLES, stage right. He carries a javelin and wears a sword belt with a sheathed sword.]

ANDROCLES

Did I hear there is to be a wedding?

THEODOSIUS

Yes, yes, my daughter — Androcles! Zeus be praised, you're here!

ANDROCLES

Father!

[Theodosius and Androcles embrace.]

THEODOSIUS

Come, my son, let me take a look at you. You know, I can still picture the day you left.

ANDROCLES

Has five years passed so quickly?

THEODOSIUS

Five years and still I remember as though it were yesterday. Those mighty triremes sailing under the green flags of Atlantis, they rowed all the way around the island in salute before turning to their course. Oh, what a beautiful thing to behold! But now, you are returned, and for the sight of you, I would forego all others!

ANDROCLES

You honor me, father. And my brother-to-be has arrived as well.

THEODOSIUS

He is here already?

ANDROCLES

His sleek, black ships clog the entire harbor.

THEODOSIUS

Were you able to dock?

ANDROCLES

Come, father — I am a son of Atlantis. I know the shores of this island as a clam knows the inside of its shell. My ship is just off the coast. I swam to the cliffs and scaled them like I did as a child. The house was deserted, so I thought to head to the agora. Where is the rest of the family — mother and my sisters?

THEODOSIUS

Oh, they must be preparing for the wedding with their retinue of friends — you know how women are. You'll see them all soon enough. First we must give thanks! Here, in the temple, we will thank Zeus for returning you to Atlantis.

> *[Androcles sets his sword and javelin down before the temple steps.]*

> > *[Exit ANDROCLES and THEODOSIUS, temple.]*

> *[Enter KORINNA and IRENAEA, stage left.]*

KORINNA

Irenaea, wait! You must hear of the vision that Hera has sent me.

IRENAEA

A vision? Really, mother, do you have any idea how ridiculous you sound?

KORINNA

See for yourself!

> *[Korinna proffers the Golden Apple to Irenaea.]*

IRENAEA

That?

KORINNA

It is our salvation!

IRENAEA

An unripened apple?

KORINNA

Unripened? It's gold, inside and out! Hera has shown me this and other things. She has sent me a plan — a way to escape!

IRENAEA

You are a fool if you still think the gods care for your problems. But go on, tell me your plan. How are you going to escape this pit of wretchedness?

KORINNA

I will wed Achilles.

IRENAEA

You will?

KORINNA

I will, and he will take us from here. We will go far from this island and the grasp of your father.

IRENAEA

I do not fear my father's grasp, and I will not run with you, mother, nor with Achilles.

KORINNA

But this is the only way I know to save you!

IRENAEA

I never asked you to save me! I will look after my own fate, and you would do best to look after your own.

KORINNA

My fate is nothing without you. I know you're angry, Irenaea, but you must be ready to leave when Achilles arrives. It is the only way.

[Exit KORINNA, *stage right.]*

IRENAEA

Still she remains loyal to her gods of filth and betrayal! I'll not participate in her absurd plot — I already have plans of my own. She may look after herself. Maybe her trinkets will be enough to secure her passage aboard Achilles' ship. That, then, is her chance for escape. Either way, her blood will not be on my hands. Oh, city of barbarians, city of false oaths, city of curses! Soon you will be a city of tombs.

[Irenaea retrieves Androcles' sword before the temple
steps.]

IRENAEA (cont'd)

What's this? Father's sword? It can't be, but it bears the apple blossom markings of his house. When was the last time he took this down? He must have spent all day cleaning the blade to restore its luster, fool that he is! Now it will be his undoing. That noise! Theodosius must be on his way to meet Achilles.

[Exit IRENAEA, *stage left.]*
[Enter KORINNA, *disguised as Theodosius, stage*
right.]

KORINNA

Oh, what a wretch I feel in this garb. Where has Irenaea gone to now? We don't have time for this — we have to get down to the beach. Perhaps she has already made her way down there.

[Exit KORINNA, *stage left.]*

[A scream pierces the silence.]
[Enter IRENAEA, *stage left.]*

IRENAEA

You are avenged! Do you hear me, sister? Theodosius is dead! Failed father and false prophet — he is fallen. At last, he is truly dead! And what kind of man screams so like a woman? I had to slit his throat just to stop that wailing. And the blood — so much blood. How can a man with no heart have so much blood? He was never a man at all. Oh, but that blood — how it stains my hands. Is he truly dead? Can it be? I will go and look upon his face once more.

[Exit IRENAEA, *stage left.]*

[Enter THEODOSIUS *and* ANDROCLES, *stage right.]*

THEODOSIUS

That is how you court the favor of Zeus, King of Olympus, master of the fates, and commander of the deathless gods!

ANDROCLES

Well done, father. Now, let us offer a prayer to Poseidon.

THEODOSIUS

Poseidon? He may look after you at sea, but you are back in Atlantis where Zeus reigns supreme.

ANDROCLES

Steady, father — we worshiped Zeus first, but we mustn't neglect the other gods.

THEODOSIUS

You mean the lesser gods, for none can compare with the might of Zeus. If those other gods have obligations here, then Zeus will see that they are performed in accordance with divine law. I do not beg their favor — I ask only for that of Zeus.

ANDROCLES

I know you mean well, father, but you are just as stubborn and implacable as ever. Very well. In honor of your wishes, Zeus will suffice for today.

THEODOSIUS

Ah, patronizing child, you will see my way is right — you will see how Zeus rewards his suppliants.

[Enter IRENAEA, *stage left. She holds Androcles' sword in one hand, and a golden apple with a piece of bloodied, green ribbon wrapped around its stem in the other.]*

THEODOSIUS

Who is that man? What has he got in his hands?

ANDROCLES

A green ribbon?

IRENAEA

A green ribbon — a green ribbon from Korinna's hair. Mother, mother of the bride—

THEODOSIUS

Korinna? My Korinna?

[Androcles brandishes his spear, charges toward Irenaea, and impales her upon it. Irenaea drops the apple and clings to her brother, sword still in her hand.]

IRENAEA

Androcles?

[Androcles recoils from the blade slicing his back.]

THEODOSIUS

Kill him! Kill that man who has murdered my wife, your mother!

[Exit IRENAEA, *stage left, pursued by* ANDROCLES.*]*

THEODOSIUS (cont'd)

How can this be? We were finally safe — she and the rest of Atlantis — safe from any threat from abroad! Who was that man and why would he kill Korinna of all people?

[Enter ACHILLES, *stage left.]*

ACHILLES

This is how you greet your son?

THEODOSIUS

Achilles? My son?

ACHILLES

Not now that you sent a warrior with spear in hand to attack me!

THEODOSIUS

My son — my Androcles — attack you?

ACHILLES

Great-hearted Androcles? You sent your own son out to kill me?

THEODOSIUS

No, you fool! He was not coming after you! He was attacking the man who murdered his mother!

ACHILLES

What trick is this? There was no other man out there — only a girl clutching a bit of ribbon. I arrived just in time to see that warrior strike her down, who can be none other than Irenaea.

THEODOSIUS

Irenaea? Why would she be on the beach? This is all a mistake.

ACHILLES

It is no mistake. The girl carried the very sign that Hera promised.

[Achilles proffers the Golden Apple to Theodosius.]

THEODOSIUS

Keep that accursed thing away from me! It's wrong — it's all wrong! The gods ordained this alliance. How has it gone wrong?

ACHILLES

The only reason for an alliance with Atlantis was Androcles' sword, and I would have had that when I took his mother to my bed. Now that both are dead, I have no need of a deceitful coward like you.

THEODOSIUS

Stay back, Achilles! Zeus will not allow you to kill me — not after all I've done for him, all I've sacrificed!

ACHILLES

Zeus does not care for you. He cares for no one but himself. Whatever you have done for him, whatever you have sacrificed, he will not save you.

[Achilles kicks Theodosius over, mounts his helpless body, and cuts out his eyes.]

ACHILLES (cont'd)

Suffer what Zeus has sent you, old man, and remember that he does not give happiness unwed to despair to mere mortals — every joy is tempered with grief. I know this well myself. You were forced to watch me kill your son, but I was forced to watch him wrench my own prize from my grasp — the deliverer of your misery suffers himself. Your life, at least, he has let you keep.

[Theodosius pushes himself into a seated position against the tree.]

THEODOSIUS

Achilles! Now is your time of glory — victory is yours. A gift of the son of Cronus, Zeus. He brought Androcles down with deathless ease. If twenty Myrmidons had charged against my son, they'd all have died here, laid low by his spear. No, deadly fate killed him, and from the ranks of men, Irenaea. You came third, and all you could do was finish off his life. One more thing — take it to heart, I urge you — you too

THEODOSIUS (cont'd)

won't live long, I swear. Already I see them looming up beside you — Death and the strong force of Fate, to bring you down at the hands of Priam's great royal son. Yes, you are in their grip already. Yet, Priam's son cannot claim the glory all for his own, for one of my own children will yet have their say in the matter.

ACHILLES

You truly are a fool, Theodosius. You have no children left to you.

THEODOSIUS

You will see all when the judge takes up his bow.

[Theodosius falls back to the ground, unconscious.]

[Exit ACHILLES, stage left.]

[Enter DOULOS, stage right.]

DOULOS

There's one task done, anyway — your clothes are ready, master. Master! What's happened to him? His face, oh that lordly and majestic face now covered in blood. His eyes — where are his eyes? Useless. Where are your gods now, master? Well, no life is left for Doulos on Atlantis, and no ship awaits him in the port. He must make for Androcles' ship where he saw it at anchor. Those men know Theodosius — they will allow both aboard, and so shall Theodosius finally serve Doulos. See if those gods will help Doulos carry Theodosius past the orchard, over the cliffs, and through the water. Up now, son of Capys, and take your last look at Atlantis!

[Exit DOULOS bearing THEODOSIUS, stage right.]

ACT III
Scene II

[Enter HERA, *temple.]*

HERA

Fool Irenaea! You've ruined it all, idiot girl! What's this? My gift, accursed thing, worthless now. Let it rest in the dust — I'll not sully my hands to touch it again. And what of Korinna? Where will be her resting place? I must go look upon her corpse at least.

[Exit HERA, *stage left.]*

[Enter ZEUS, *stage right.]*

ZEUS

At last — an empty agora. Finally, I will enjoy the fruit of my labor!

[Zeus searches the apple tree for Sosigenes.]

ZEUS (cont'd)

Where is she? What's this? My apple — my Sosigenes — shorn from your branch and left in the dust? Now the girl is dead for sure — she only remained alive so long as the apple remained on the branch. Who has subverted my will and wrought such horrors on this place? It can only have been Hera. Damn me for hiding the girl in plain sight! Oh, unhappy Fortune, even me you tease! Sosigenes was the fairest maiden of them all — anyone asked to judge her beauty would say the same!

[Enter HERA, *stage left.]*

HERA

So this is what comes of the best laid plans of Zeus — the annihilation of an entire family? I thought the sons of Tros were dear to you — although the daughters clearly weren't. I saw what became of Korinna, what became of Irenaea. And what of Sosigenes, husband? Has she too met her end, the poor girl? All that blood on your hands.

ZEUS

My hands? What have I to do with it? I promised Theodosius Achilles, and Achilles came. How am I to account for your deceit, your treachery? You are more at fault than anyone for the blood spilled here today!

HERA

You seek to lay those corpses at my feet?

ZEUS

You may lay their corpses wherever you like, along with your blame, but I'll not mourn those lifeless bodies lying in the surf. Does the sand

ZEUS (cont'd)

mourn them? Does the ocean? Then why would I, who am deathless too? Why would you?

HERA

So I should reserve myself to inaction while you steal the daughters of my suppliants? Those girls have two parents. Whatever arrangements you make with the fathers, the mothers come to me. They flock to my altar. They ask me why they must bear such punishments.

ZEUS

They're just humans! It matters little which of them dies or which of them lies with me.

HERA

And you're just an Olympian, one of many!

[Exit HERA, temple.]

ZEUS

Irrational woman! Do I complain when she curses and tortures my mortal children? And when she kills them, do I drag their corpses to her altar? It's absurd! They're just humans, after all.

[Enter POSEIDON and ARTEMIS, disguised as Apollo, stage left.]

POSEIDON

Brother, what has happened here? How come I to pass the expired body of Androcles, my suppliant?

ZEUS

Poseidon? You too seek to meddle in my affairs on Atlantis?

POSEIDON

Meddle? What concern is it of mine what affairs you conduct, here or elsewhere? I only ask about my suppliant.

ZEUS

And you, Apollo? What have you to say? What thin excuse brings you here of all places on today of all days?

POSEIDON

Do not ignore me, brother! What has happened to Androcles?

ZEUS

Ah, now it's clear — you both had a hand in this! This is no coincidence — it's a plot! An insurrection! Does this little coterie seek to dethrone me? You, Poseidon, you wish to redraw the lots? You wish to wield the flaming thundercloud? What would you have me do, brother? Answer me!

POSEIDON

There is no satisfactory answer that I can provide you. You have already made up your mind.

ZEUS

And you, Apollo? I take your silence as acknowledgement of your guilt, alongside Poseidon, in this absurd plan of Hera's, this failed rebellion! I curse you both! I cast you out — from the time the sun sets today, you both shall walk the mortal plane as exiles of Mount Olympus! Your disgrace will end when you have spent a full mortal year in servitude — only then will this insult have been repaid.

[Exit ZEUS, *stage right.]*

POSEIDON

One of my dearest suppliants has been murdered most treacherously, and now I'm cursed by Zeus and exiled from Olympus — how comes this to pass, Phoebus? Nay, stay your explanation. There is no profit to be had from wondering at such terrible knowledge. Zeus has made his declaration and now we must suffer, rightly or otherwise. For myself, there is only one mortal of which I know who deserves my divine aid — Laomedon, son of Ilus. He is building a wondrous city in the East. That is where I shall go.

[Enter HERA, *temple.]*

ARTEMIS

Look upon the cost of your proclamations, Queen of Olympus!

HERA

Artemis? You dare to defy my commands?

ARTEMIS

To save my suppliants, I would defy you across every realm of existence.

HERA

To what end? You have defied me — have you saved your suppliant?

ARTEMIS

That was more your fault than mine!

HERA

My fault? You are as dramatic and idealistic as ever.

ARTEMIS

And your sycophancy is only rivaled by your apathy! You too have a dead suppliant out there on the beach, her lifeblood leaking into the ocean. What did you do to save her?

HERA

Yours lies there too, daughter of Zeus, despite all your plans.

ARTEMIS

What would you have me do then?

HERA

Abide by the laws of Olympus!

ARTEMIS

The same ones that justify Zeus' actions? I would rather abide by the
laws of right than might. Uncle, if you go to Laomedon at Troy, my
brother will go there too. Misery is better endured with companionship.

POSEIDON

Yes, if serve we must, then let us serve in the furtherance of true greatness. Let us see what we can make of this Troy.

HERA

You would bestow such privilege on Ilium? Why not Athens—

POSEIDON

You know why I won't serve the Athenians!

HERA

What about Argos, Samos, or Sparta?

POSEIDON

Those are yours to guard, yours to improve.

ARTEMIS

I too will go to Troy.

HERA

You will?

ARTEMIS

That is, Apollo will go to Troy, but I will not be far off — ever at hand
should my brother need me, ever ready to remind him why he suffers.

[Exit ARTEMIS, stage left.]

HERA

Oh, a curse on the house of Tros! A curse on the sons of Ilus and Assaracus, Laomedon and Capys! Would that I could send them a gift —
Ganymede with his throat slit and his lifeblood emptied into the very
goblet he has borne for Zeus!

[Enter HERMES, stage left.]

HERMES

Just dump him on the beach when you do kill him — it's a mess out
there already.

HERA

I'm not murdering Ganymede! I'm just trying to make a point — do
you see the power that Zeus wields with such carelessness?

POSEIDON

Power which you might better wield?

HERA

The Olympians would never suffer a woman to rule them. No, I can never brandish the flaming thundercloud.

POSEIDON

Tell me — who then?

HERMES

Yes, my queen, tell us!

HERA

There are two of whom I can think who might sit atop the Olympian throne. You know of whom I speak, brother.

POSEIDON

You seek fruit from a barren tree, sister. The lots were fairly drawn, and I do not lust after my brothers' kingdoms nor their power. Zeus holds what is above, all that lies within the watery depths is mine, and everything below belongs to Hades. And while our kingdoms may lie below that of Zeus, they are not inferior, and neither are we. There, in the seas, I am the powerful one. It is I who wields the Silver Trident — I am the one who commands and controls all. You haven't the vaguest notion of the intrigues and occurrences of my court. Think then what you might know of Hades' kingdom, which lies beyond even the deepest reaches of my own — Hades whose gleaming helm permits him to travel unseen throughout all the realms, who guards his charges and his kingdom more voraciously than any other. Yet I do not look with jealousy at Hades nor at Zeus nor even at their consorts.

HERA

And what of your suppliants here in Zeus' realm? I saw one of yours out there in the sand. Tell me, what was his name?

POSEIDON

Androcles.

HERA

A fine name.

HERMES

Any name suits a corpse fine. What difference now what you call him?

POSEIDON

He was a fine man — honorable, pious, and the greatest warrior of all my suppliants.

HERA

He was the greatest warrior of all mortals! Only this young Achilles could defeat him, and not without the help of Zeus' ruse. But which other of our suppliants might Zeus decide to take? How will you stop

HERA (cont'd)

him when he comes for one of your own? This task falls to the two of us.

HERMES

Three of us.

HERA

Very well, the three of us. We must swear a pact of allegiance to one another.

POSEIDON

A pact?

HERA

A pact.

POSEIDON

As you wish, sister.

[Hera, Hermes, and Poseidon stand in a circle with clasped hands.]

HERA

To resist and oppose Zeus' will. To guard over the cities which are sacred to us each—

POSEIDON

To protect our suppliants.

HERA

To protect our suppliants and guide them to glory—

POSEIDON

Guide them to safety.

HERA

To see our altars piled high with sacrifice—

HERMES

To allay banality, ennui, and malaise.

POSEIDON

Let the pact be sworn then. I have little time left before I depart for Ilium.

HERA

You go to Ilium in the company of Apollo, whose sister is recently determined to oppose me? You violate our accord even before the words have finished being spoken!

POSEIDON

Our accord concerns Zeus. You'll not set me at odds with all the gods of Olympus — my brothers and sisters, nieces and nephews. I go to Ilium to serve my term of punishment, one which I have done nothing to deserve.

HERA

Yet we all know who is at fault for such an outcome!

[Exit HERA, stage left.]

POSEIDON

You and I both know that Zeus did not cause all that has occurred here today.

HERMES

Of course not. Hera and Artemis played their own roles also.

POSEIDON

And who, I wonder, choreographed their movements?

HERMES

They are deathless gods, two of the most powerful among us. I doubt very much whether any god could have so influenced them.

POSEIDON

Indeed. Which of the gods has such power? Perhaps we should look to the messenger.

HERMES

What could a simple messenger do to create such havoc as ensued today?

POSEIDON

That I hope never to discover. If I did, Androcles' death would require justice.

[Hermes begins to whistle.]

POSEIDON (cont'd)

Am I boring you, nephew? Go then and bring no further despair to this place.

[Exit HERMES, stage left.]

POSEIDON (cont'd)

Behold Atlantis — behold the souls of those who anger overcame. Some god knows the unholy deceit that has brought this island low, while the rest of us might only guess. And will the assigning of blame bring back the dead? There is one thing at least that I can do for this wretched island. I call to my subjects in every corner of my realm. I call on you all to listen to my words and see my will enacted, to cause the sea to rise and the earth to tremble, to take this island, forsaken by her gods. Take her gates, her temple, her orchard. Give them all to the sea. Take this barren tree and petrify it — let the thing sink and turn to stone. Most of all, take this accursed apple, foul and unholy as it is — take it to the bottom of the sea and there finally give calm to a tortured and wretched being.

[Exit POSEIDON, stage left.]

[Enter ERIS, *temple.]*

ERIS

Hear me now, you deathless gods. Another is come — another swells your ranks — I, who was formerly mortal but have been smiled upon by some power beyond even treacherous Zeus' control. Yes, I was a mortal born of mortal parents with famous names. I cast them aside with my own, cast them aside to the void from which I come. Born in blood and baptized in darkness, I emerge anew — Eris, daughter of night and bringer of discord!

[Eris retrieves the Golden Apple.]

ERIS (cont'd)

Come with me, sister, away from this sinking place.

[Exit ERIS, *stage right.]*

ACT IV

Scene I

[Enter THEODOSIUS, *stage right.]*

THEODOSIUS

Now you know my tragedy, or rather how it begins. You too know how my wrathful family tore itself apart like a many headed wolf — snarling and snapping at its own belly, chomping down on hunks of flesh and rending them from its body until nothing was left but a bloody mess amid bodiless heads. In such a way, the gods took my family from me. But now I must stop — I must not tell of further misery. Already every star is falling that was ascending when I began my tale, and to stay too long is not permitted.

[Exit THEODOSIUS, *stage left.]*

Chapter 6

The curtains swept shut across the stage to the sound of applause.

"Huh," Lisa muttered, "so that's what happened to Atlantis."

"What do you think happened to the old guy?" asked Britney.

Giovanni yawned, then stood and stretched his arms skyward. He stepped to the edge of the blanket.

"I'm going to go congratulate our friend Androcles," he said, turning toward the bottom of the hill.

He was halfway down the hill when he heard Britney's voice behind him.

"Gio, wait," she called.

He stopped abruptly and turned to face her, forcing her to check her own advance.

"What's up?" he asked, crossing his arms.

"Look, you don't have to take the tickets if you don't want them, but you're right — you deserved to win last night; your poem was better."

Giovanni blinked in surprise and confusion.

"To be honest, I knew I was going to win once I saw Simon was judging," Britney continued. "Did you see the way that creep kept touching me? I wasn't even going to accept that prize, but..."

"But?" Giovanni queried.

Britney shrugged.

"It was too much fun to mess with you."

She smiled, and both of them laughed.

"I still think you should keep the tickets," Giovanni stated as he uncrossed his arms. "You would have a better time at that Producer's Brunch than I would."

"What're you two laughing about?" asked Vere as he rejoined Britney and Giovanni.

"Britney just offered me her tickets to the brunch tomorrow."

"Oh, wow," said Vere. "That was really nice of her."

"I know, right?" Britney agreed. "You wanna go?" she asked Vere. "He's not going to take the tickets unless somebody forces him to."

"I've already got tickets — Kateryna's cousin is hosting."

"How about we both go then," Britney suggested to Giovanni.

She pulled a small square of purple paper from her pocket and passed it to Giovanni. When he took the ticket from her, his thumb ran across a pattern of bumps, which, upon closer inspection, turned out to be a key embossed in the paper.

"Let's see about finding Lucas," said Vere, slinging his backpack over his shoulder.

"I'll meet you in a few minutes," Britney replied. "I'm going to see what Lisa and Tracee want to do."

Britney began walking back toward the top of the hill while Vere and Giovanni continued down toward the stage. At the foot of the stage, a throng of spectators mingled with the actors who were still in varying degrees of costume.

"Over there," Vere pointed out a pair of Greek soldiers.

Vere and Giovanni navigated through the crowd until they reached Lucas-come-Androcles, now bereft of his double.

"Friends!" the soldier called in greeting. "What'd you think?"

"*Bravo*," Giovanni tilted his head in deference.

"Yeah, well done, mate," added Vere.

"Thanks, gents," Lucas replied with a wide grin.

Vere waved at Britney and Tracee who were roaming through the crowd at the foot of the stage. The two women picked their way over to the small circle of friends and joined them.

"Where's Lisa?" asked Vere.

"She went home," Tracee answered.

"Lucas, this is Tracee," Britney introduced her friend.

"Hi, Lucas," said Tracee.

"Hallo, Tracee," Lucas bowed his head slightly.

"So Tracee and I were thinking about getting a drink," Britney stated. "Anybody want to join?"

"Love to," Lucas said. "Where?"

"*Die Biere* is close," Tracee suggested.

"Gio and I are headed that way too," said Vere.

"Already planning on getting wellied?" asked Lucas, again grinning broadly.

"I live upstairs," Giovanni answered.

"Well, that is convenient," said Lucas. "I don't suppose there's space for Pyricles and me in either of your cars?"

"One of you can ride with Tracee and me," Britney offered.

"Perfect," Lucas proclaimed. "Do you guys mind bringing Pyricles with you?"

"No problem," said Vere.

"Alright, see you over there," said Britney.

Britney, Tracee, and Lucas joined the mass of people flowing toward the parking lot like flotsam through a rough channel, bobbing and darting between cresting swells. Giovanni watched their heads float along for a minute, but they were soon lost among the crowd.

"That him?" Vere asked, pointing to the side of the stage where a man had just exited a covert doorway.

"Yeah, that's him," Giovanni confirmed.

Pyricles had changed from his toga into a pair of torn jeans and a grey polo. He scanned the crowd from the doorway, spotted Vere and Giovanni, continued scanning.

"That was real subtle," said Vere as he and Giovanni walked toward Pyricles.

"Hey," Giovanni called, "Lucas asked us to give you a lift to *Die Biere*."

Pyricles scowled.

"Nice of him to tell me," he whinged.

"Come on — let's get out of here," Vere said.

The three men walked across the street to the parking lot. They found Vere's car, and each climbed inside. Vere turned his key in the ignition and brought the car to life. The radio console's screen illuminated.

"Welcome back, *los Flotadores*. *Yo soy* DJ LP, and you're listening to—"

"Change the station, will you?" Pyricles asked. "I'm going to stab a rusty icepick into my ear canal until can feel it in my brain if I have to listen to any more of this."

"Calm down," Vere replied as he clicked off the radio. "There's no suicide in my car. You can kill yourself when we get to the bar if you like."

"It's your rodeo," Pyricles spat back.

"That's funny," Giovanni remarked. "Lisa said the same thing—"

"Who?" Pyricles demanded, leaning forward into the gap between Vere and Giovanni's seats.

"Lisa," Giovanni repeated.

"Lisa Mopumochi?" Pyricles pressed.

"*Non lo so*," Giovanni faced Pyricles. "*Forse—*"

"I don't fucking speak Italian!" Pyricles hissed in his face.

"I. Don't. Know." Giovanni repeated in English. He turned away from Pyricles. "Maybe," he said dismissively.

"Yes," Vere answered Pyricles' question. "How do you know Lisa?"

"We were engaged once," Pyricles muttered, sitting back in his seat.

The static sound of highway driving filled the car.

"So what happened?" asked Vere.

"I don't want to talk about it," Pyricles retorted.

"Could've fooled me," Giovanni muttered.

"What the hell would you know about it?" Pyricles snapped back. "A painted skunk could fool *you* for a fucking house-cat!"

Vere chuckled from the driver seat. Next to him, Giovanni shook his head and rolled his eyes.

"You're a real charmer," said Giovanni.

"Excuse me if I'm no longer entertaining you," Pyricles countered, "but I just got done *working*, while you were having fun with—"

"So what? It's your job; it doesn't have to be fun. You think writing is always fun? No. I haven't been able to write a word in over a week — totally blocked up—"

"*So what?*" Pyricles cast Giovanni's challenge back at him. "*It's your job; it doesn't have to be fun—*"

"Are you always such an asshole?" Giovanni demanded. "I mean, I only just met you yesterday, and you've always been an asshole to me, but are you like this with everyone?"

"You want something to write about?" Pyricles railed. "I'll tell you a story, a story about a man and a woman; a story about how he does everything he can and still loses her; a story about why nothing feels right since she left; a story about being lost, without meaning in the world. Why don't you write that story, *poet?*" Pyricles expelled the last word from his mouth like a chunk of rancid meat.

"Somebody already wrote that story," Vere stated.

"Somebody already wrote *every* story," added Giovanni.

"So why bother?" a sob crept into Pyricles' declamation.

"Because I haven't," said Giovanni.

"Who's going to pay you to write a story that's already been written?" Pyricles queried.

"I don't know," Giovanni responded, "and I don't particularly care."

Pyricles snorted contemptuously.

"So you think art is only worth making if you're getting paid for it?" Giovanni asked.

"And you think it's not if you are?" said Pyricles.

"I'm not saying that art and commerce are diametrically opposed, but—"

Pyricles snorted again. Giovanni turned to face him in the backseat.

"Use your words," Giovanni prodded.

"So, what, I'm not an artist because I get a paycheck? That's what you're saying?"

"That's not what I—"

"Well, I think that's bullshit—"

"Well, that's not what I said, but you aren't an artist if you're only doing it for the paycheck," Giovanni countered, facing forward in his seat again. "Regardless," he continued, "that was a hell of a show. Although, I think a little satyr play at the end would've been nice; you know, leave on a lighter note."

"Like what?" asked Vere.

"I don't know — something absurd..." Giovanni's voice trailed off. "Oh! I got it. How about *The Atlantiad, Act III: Offstage*. It's just all the Atlantiad actors from the third act coming offstage and dying. And there's a harried stage hand — like a Buster Keaton or Lucille Ball type — who is just getting more and more overwhelmed by the bodies and body parts that keep piling up, and—"

"You're a strange individual, aren't you?" Pyricles inquired.

"What?" Giovanni challenged. "That's funny!"

"Where do you come up with this stuff?" Vere asked.

"Dreams, mostly," Giovanni answered.

"I wish I had dreams that wild," Vere returned.

"You should sleep with your socks on then," Giovanni stated.

"What?" Vere asked.

"Sleep with your socks on," Giovanni repeated.

"Why?" Vere pressed.

"Well, if my feet are hot when I sleep, my dreams are stranger," Giovanni explained. "Take last night for instance: I dreamt I was an engraver—"

"What do you know about engraving?" Pyricles interrupted.

"I picked it up when I was a teenager."

Pyricles scoffed.

"You must have been a real popular guy."

"Will you shut up? I broke my foot playing *calcio*."

"Kal-chee-oh?" repeated Pyricles.

"Football," Giovanni responded.

"Soccer," Vere suggested.

"Anyway," Giovanni wrested back control of the conversation, "I was sitting on a wooden stool in a cramped, sod hut. The air tasted damp and musty, but the smell was perfumed by a jasmine bush blossoming outside. There was a table, a bed, a hearth in the corner. The setting sun cast a colorless twilight that shone through a roughly cut window behind me. A candle burned before me, illuminating my workspace. It was surrounded by a pool of wax of its own making, and, beyond that, dried up rivers traced the wood grain of the table in dirty hues that could hardly be considered colors.

"First, I placed my plate — burnished copper that gleamed even in the dim candle light. This I held with my left hand, and, with my right, my burin, trusted tool, a bulb of well-worn wood sprouting a metal awl. With these tools, I wrought a wondrous scene.

"I wrought walls, a town, a ditch. I wrought also steady, horizontal lines marking a gentle sky, interrupted by soldiers' pikes. In the ditch, an old man is being burnt at the stake. A friar stands before him, while a soldier to his left sets fire to his pyre. The vertical lines of the friar's habit keep a silent coven with the fagots that feed the flames — the heretic is trapped by the uniform rigidity of the lines as much as the bundles of sticks that bind him in turn. A scroll floats from above and crosses the stake, making a scythe that hangs over the heretic's head — the scythe of Damocles.

"I wrought also six faces in the foreground: the friar, the heretic, the soldier, and three nobles. The friar wears a hypocrite's expression of concern as he proselytizes to the crowd. The heretic offers his offensive hand to the curling flames growing at his feet while feathers of smoke unfurl above; though the flames lick at him, no cry will ever escape the heretic's sealed lips. The soldier unquestioningly obeys an unheard order. The nobles, engaged in a clandestine congress from their seats at the front of the crowd, haggle over the price of the man's effects. Behind the nobles' bearded faces, a sea of heads fades into a cobblestone pattern.

"All of this I put on my lustrous copper plate, glowing in the dying candlelight. Lastly, when I had finished, I wrapped the plate in soft calfskin, and carried it from the hut."

The sound of static again filled the car.

"And?" Pyricles demanded.

"And what?" Giovanni responded.

"How'd the damn dream end?"

"That is how it ended: I left the hut, the door slammed behind me, and I woke up."

"Well, that's not any kind of ending!" Pyricles exclaimed. "Where's the resolution? Do you at least know what the scroll said?"

"Oh, *sí*, it said, 'Lord, receive my spirit.'"

"Lord, receive my spirit?" Pyricles echoed. "Well, what the hell does that mean?"

Giovanni shrugged in response.

"It's a small, strange, little island we live on," Vere stated as he accelerated through a turn.

"Florida isn't an island; it's a peninsula," Pyricles spat back.

"Anywhere can be an island," Vere replied.

"That's just nonsense."

"It's not *just* nonsense," Vere explained. "It's *absolute* nonsense — like everything else in this world."

"Well, *there is nothing either good or bad, but thinking makes it so*," said Giovanni.

"Will you shut — *the fuck* — up already?"

Vere pulled the car into an empty spot along the side of the road. The car shuddered slightly as the front wheel bumped against the curb. Pyricles flung open his door and stomped off toward the bar. Vere and Giovanni each climbed out of the car.

"Why don't you go on ahead," Giovanni suggested. "I'll be there in a minute."

Vere nodded and followed Pyricles' path. Giovanni set off in a slightly different direction, toward the amphitheater at the center of town — this one smaller than the one he had recently departed. Several families still lingered on the amphitheater's lawn from some event that must have ended some time ago; their children mostly slept in strollers or directly on the grass. Giovanni walked down a deserted, leaf-strewn sidewalk. To his right, cars were parked along the street — imperious monsters crouching in the shadows, waiting to growl and sputter into life. As he walked, he thought about his dream from the previous night. He thought about the heretic and his searing, writhing pain; the aristocrats and their crass commerce; the friar, condemning his brother; and the soldier, in a pose of eternal obedience. He thought about his poetic creations, The Strawberry King and Queen Moxmori, each conniving at the other's disgorgement, dismemberment, and death. Giovanni thought about these images, and wondered why he created such a chorus of horrific characters.

He approached a large, circular fountain. The pump was turned off however, so no liquid cascaded from one level down to the next and the next and so on. The fountain's broad, round bowls with their scalloped rims reminded him of inverted turtle shells. He lay down on the low, wide wall that enclosed the shallow water. Looking up into the night sky, he tried to pick out the few constellations that he knew. Failing to find more than a half dozen, he turned his mind to creating patterns of his own among the pin-pricks of light that dotted the sky. As he lay along the fountain, the swollen moon slowly climbed, nearly reaching its zenith.

Giovanni sat up, compulsively brushed his brown hair to the side of his forehead, then stood. His movements were deliberate, considered. He walked toward *Die Biere*, between square columns supporting the extended second story above him. Outside the bar, two televisions were mounted on the wall. A pair of football games was playing for the benefit of the dozen or so occupants of two picnic tables. The black and white footage showed two stadia. On the first screen, two lines of players marched onto the pitch while the fans' songs rose high from the stands. Somewhere in the crowd, a quarrel broke out, and two men angrily exchanged words. The already frenzied spectators encouraged each of the men, but the stewards held them back. On the other screen, a match neared the final whistle, and the players showed signs of the battle that had ensued. In the stands, the fans raised a tifo displaying Death in all of his violent glory, hauling a dead man by the heels.

Giovanni turned away from the screens and walked across the street. He stuck his hands in his pockets as he ambled down the sidewalk toward a small college campus, his *alma mater*. He walked between hulking brick buildings until he reached an athletic field, a shallow gully scarring one flank. Giovanni recalled the many times he labored joyously here in the heat of the sun, surrounded by men and women who were momentarily focused on a singular objective. Each time they had played, they turned and turned again: two teams running headlong down the pitch, with a third breaking for water but looking forward to returning to their sport.

Giovanni walked next to a large grove of trees. An owl hooted overhead as he entered, its roosting disturbed by his presence. Two round eyes, burning boldly among the stars, watched Giovanni as he followed the circular sidewalk through the dense, swampy canopy of hardwoods and conifers. He paused in a shaft of moonlight. To his left, a large cypress tree stood in a shallow pool of water. The tree's roots pocked the ground with knobby mounds that poked out of the water. To his right, a noctivagant squirrel chittered, then rustled through the branches of a nearby live oak. Still feeling the owl's eyes upon him, Giovanni resumed his pace and soon exited the forest.

He walked also to a small art studio that abutted the edge of the grove. Here, lights glowed from within slender windows. Giovanni stole glances inside as he passed a row of three rooms: in one, a young woman made sad, sweet music with an acoustic guitar; in the next, a series of artists stood at their easels arrayed in a circle around a robed figure; the last room was empty save for a large collage featuring a boy with jaded eyes, his hand covering his mouth. Giovanni came to the end of the row of rooms and continued down the sidewalk.

He walked back toward *Die Biere*, following the sidewalk to the same single lane road he had crossed earlier. A car horn honked when Giovanni reached the crossing. The driver swerved to avoid a dog that had bolted into the street, and the car's front wheel slammed into the curb of the median. The car lurched and jumped onto the short concrete ledge. The driver stuck his head out of his window and began bellowing curses, but his words were incoherent over the horns that sounded from the three cars behind him. The dog stood resolutely in the street, barking in response to the driver's exhortations and refusing to keep out of harm's way.

Giovanni walked on until the stillness of the night swallowed the sounds of panic behind him — even the wind quieted down. He followed the sidewalk as it twisted down a deserted street of dark windows. Moonlight gleamed on the glass panels as he passed.

Farther he walked before he approached another bar, this one dark inside except for neon lights that illuminated an open yet cramped interior. Here, men and women danced gaily, each seeking to entice the other. The women wore short, airy dresses, and the men linen pants and loose, woven shirts. Sometimes the women would come together in a ring and dance around one at their center — she responding to them with her dancing like a lump of clay to the genius of a potter sitting at his wheel — until they abruptly broke apart, giggling, and rejoined their partners on the periphery of the dance floor.

Giovanni walked also past this scene, and stopped when he returned to the starting point of his evening jaunt. He listened for the sounds of crashing waves, for though he was several miles from the coast, he had the distinct sense that the ocean encircled everything around him.

Giovanni rounded the corner, and suddenly, there She was, looking for all the world an apparition as She stood in the cone of golden light cast down from a street lamp. He felt it as soon as he saw Her — the same feeling he had always felt in Her presence, the sense of falling in love anew, the heart that doesn't so much flutter as careen madly like a flimsy aluminum airplane lurching through turbulent skies, the stomach that doesn't so much fill with butterflies as wage outright war against itself with a ferocity that would allow no flight, be it from arthropod or aeroplane. The next thing that struck him was her beauty: she was the most beautiful woman he had ever seen. He knew it was wrong — voyeuristic, self-indulgent, and regressive — but Giovanni couldn't help but hold Her in his gaze again: Her hair, coils of silk as black as onyx; Her bright, almond-shaped eyes, full of mischief and fire; the small mole that graced the curve of Her cheek — the spot he used to kiss with all the gentleness he could muster; Her warm, tender lips; the curve of Her body — a full and organic figure with a thick chest and hips and a thin waist and legs — and the grace of Her poise — he had always thought She moved like a dancer, and even as She stood motionless in the halo of light, he could see the music in Her body. She seemed to be hammered out of bronze — so perfectly sculpted was She in his eyes — and Her skin tone easily bore out the comparison, especially when it glimmered in the sun under a sheen of fine sweat. There was only one comparison which had ever been appropriate: She was the very personification of beauty; a portrait of a Greek goddess; Pygmalion's Galatea, frozen in time. Oddly, her movements themselves seemed frozen as she stood there on the sidewalk.

Even now, he always saw the best in Her first — before he remembered the worst. All Her betrayals and disloyalties, Her lies and deceits. He could little more repose his trust in Her than he might in a funhouse mirror or a magician's hands. How many times had She tricked him before? The truth of Her character was as plain as Her beauty.

Giovanni saw all this at once, rushing back into his mind in an instant. In the next moment, cold fear of being seen flooded up from his feet and he too froze in his movements. She didn't seem to notice him however, and the wave of fear passed. At last, he saw the source of Her consternation, why She was lingering on the sidewalk at such a late hour; it was Her Achilles' Heel: the broken toenail that She tried so desperately to hide by gluing a false one atop the broken remnants of the natural one. The forgery had become dislodged from Her foot and She was inspecting the damage. He thought of calling out to Her, this woman who had once been closer to him than any other person; he closed his eyes and imagined Her smile when She heard his voice. He frowned. When Giovanni opened his eyes, She was gone, disappeared. She had been standing there one moment, and then suddenly She wasn't — annihilated like the rest of the ghosts from his past.

Blinking the apparition out of his eyes, Giovanni resumed his stroll.

Anywhere can be an island, Vere had said.

Giovanni arrived back at *Die Biere*, completing his short circuit around the center of town. He looked inside the bar, through the plate glass that served as a wall. He saw his four new friends at the far side of the bar: Lucas and Britney shared sips from each other's glasses, while Pyricles and Tracee awaited the delivery of their own drafts. Giovanni scrutinized the rest of the bar's patrons, but he couldn't find Vere.

"Going in, mate?" his friend's voice issued from behind him.

Vere clapped Giovanni on the back on his way inside the bar.

Anywhere can be an island, he had said.

Giovanni followed his friend into the bar.

Chapter 7

Giovanni caught up with Vere as he walked toward the far end of the long, rectangular bar. A brushed steel bar top ran along the length of the left wall, then turned and extended along the back wall, creating an upside down L-shape. There was an assortment of games along the wall to the right — dartboards, a digital jukebox, and a long shuffleboard table — and a row of high-top tables through the middle of the room.

"Vere! Gio!" Lucas exclaimed from his seat at the bar. "What took you so long?"

Vere held up his palms in protest.

"We're not all racecar drivers," he jibed.

Giovanni spotted a familiar face as she set two teeming glasses on the bar top before Pyricles and Tracee.

"Hey, Gio," she called as she looked up from her task. She was young and beautiful; bright eyes and an inviting smile illuminated an attractive face framed by dark hair. "What can I getcha'?" she asked, flashing a carefree smile.

"Hey, Melissa," Giovanni greeted her in return before adding, "watcha' got?"

She moved to a set of three taps with metallic handles.

"We have three on special tonight from Minotaur Brewing. This one," she said while filling a small glass from the bronze tap, "is the Homicide Hefeweizen. This is the Suicide Saison," she continued as she poured from the silver tap, "and last up is the Deicide Dubbel."

She poured the final glass from the gold tap, then placed the three glasses on a tray and set the tray on the bar top in front of Giovanni. Melissa tilted her head toward Vere.

"I'll try those too," Vere answered her unspoken query.

She again filled three small glasses and arranged them on a tray before setting the tray in front of Vere.

"Let me know when you're ready for more," she said with a wink.

Giovanni watched Melissa as she moved her slender body gracefully behind the bar, pulling on tap handles in a variety of creative shapes — first a centaur, then a crown, a tree, and a winged woman. As she stopped at each tap, she held a gleaming glass before the spout to catch the liquid that came cascading out — pale straw from one, shades of chestnut from another; then brilliant copper, warm amber, ruby, and garnet; even thick columns of the black stuff itself. Vere and Giovanni sipped from each of their three glasses, sampling notes of flavor and aroma: the sweet of sugar and malt, the bitter of alcohol, the spice of hops, the subtle nuances of yeast.

Melissa returned to their spot at the bar.

"Well?" she asked. "What do you think?"

"I'll let our poet laureate decide," said Vere.

"Who?" Melissa asked.

Vere nodded at Giovanni.

"Gio? I didn't know you were a poet!" Melissa exclaimed.

"Oh, yeah, I suppose," Giovanni responded.

"That's so cool! So what'll it be, Wordsworth?"

Melissa smiled coyly, her cheeks dimpling.

"I like them all," Giovanni declared.

"Me too," Vere agreed.

"One of each?" Melissa suggested.

"Sounds good to me," Vere responded with a chuckle..

"*Sì, anch'io,*" Giovanni said. "Me too."

"Which one do you want first?" she asked.

"Let's start with the hefeweizen," said Vere, who then turned to join Lucas, Britney, Pyricles, and Tracee in conversation.

Giovanni nodded, and Melissa set to work filling two large glasses. He watched as she completed her brief task. When she was done, frothy, golden liquid spilled down the side of the two brimming glasses; she slid them across the bar top to Giovanni.

"Thanks," he said with a quick smile.

She winked again, then moved down the bar. Giovanni nudged Vere, then passed him one of the glasses.

"—not even really blue," said Lucas.

"They're not?" Britney asked into her glass, her eyebrows arching over its rim as she drank.

"That's ridiculous," said Pyricles. "Of course they are."

"No, they're not," Lucas reasserted.

"What's not what now?" Vere asked.

"Blue jays," said Tracee. "Lucas says they're not really blue."

"They're not!" Lucas exclaimed. "Their feathers are brown; they just look blue because of the way light passes through them."

"I've seen a blue jay feather before," said Pyricles, "and it wasn't brown."

"Did you crush it?" Lucas asked.

"*Did I crush it?*" Pyricles echoed. "Of course not."

"Well, there you go," Lucas stated as though that was all that was left to be said about the matter. "I say, anybody care to make a bit of a friendly wager?" Lucas flicked his eyebrows entreatingly.

"On what?" Britney asked.

"I'm not betting on the color of blue jays," said Vere.

"I'm sure there's something we can bet on," Lucas insisted as he scanned the bar. "There," he pointed to a television screen in the corner of the room.

"Horse racing?" Pyricles asked contemptuously.

"Sure, what's wrong with that?" said Lucas.

"What do I know about horse racing?" Pyricles continued.

"All you have to do is pick a name," Lucas explained.

"I'm not betting," said Giovanni.

"You can be the house," Vere suggested.

"Alright, ladies and gentlemen," Lucas proclaimed in his best auctioneer's voice, "place your bets with Giovanni! Five bucks a pop!"

"Win-Place-Show?" asked Vere.

"If you like," Lucas agreed.

"Whatever," said Pyricles. "I'll take Memnon's Revenge."

"To win?" Giovanni asked.

"No, to lose," Pyricles declared sarcastically, passing a five-dollar bill to Giovanni.

Giovanni took the money and marked the bet in blue ink on a cocktail napkin.

"I'll take One-Eyed Jack to win," said Vere.

"Blue Note's Prestige for me," Britney added.

"Any other takers? I say, Giovanni, what's your friend's name?" Lucas pointed across the bar, "Excuse me, dear—"

"Melissa," Giovanni supplied while he collected money from Vere and Britney.

"Melissa," Lucas repeated, "would you care to partake of a bet? The Number Seven at Hollywood Park is just about to kick off."

"Oh?" Melissa asked as she walked over to the impromptu casino. "What are the odds?"

"They're on the screen now," Britney pointed to the appropriate television.

Melissa studied the spread for a moment.

"I'll take Kid Danger to win," she stated, pulling a five-dollar bill from the tip jar and adding it to the pile in front of Giovanni.

"And I'll take One-Eyed Jack to win, Prestige to place, and Aethe to show," Lucas concluded the betting, passing his money to Giovanni. "Can you turn the TV up for the race?" he asked Melissa, who pulled a remote from under the bar and complied.

"The horses are taking position now," a tinny voice reported. "There's Memnon's Revenge, last in the gate, and here comes Aethe to the outside stall. They're all in line now, and we're just waiting for the—"

Ring-g-g. A shrill bell trilled.

"A-a-and they're off! One-Eyed Jack takes a good beginning and steps out to lead. Then Mario Caerulanus, just after Jack, followed by Luna Bear, with Kid Danger to the outside. Aethe next, followed by Memnon's Revenge just four lengths behind as they move into the turn. Blue Note's Prestige leads the back of the pack. Up the stretch now, Aethe and Memnon's Revenge are matching strides in the lead. Prestige takes the far outside. Kid Danger's pushing the inside, then Luna and Mario in the rear, then One-Eyed Jack. Kid Danger takes the lead, Memnon's Revenge just after him. They're pulling away from the others. It's Kid Danger and Memnon's Revenge; Prestige and Aethe behind down the final furlong. Kid Danger, a two-length lead going into the final sixteen... Kid Danger! It's Kid Danger! Memnon's Revenge comes in close on his tail, followed by Aethe, then Prestige."

Melissa switched off the volume.

"Never bet against the bar," she said with a grin that made Giovanni's heart flutter.

Giovanni passed her the pile of money, except for one note. Melissa took the money and stuffed it into the tip jar.

"What's second place win?" Pyricles asked.

"Second place gets his bet back," said Lucas.

"Well, at least it's something," Pyricles smirked and held out his hand expectantly.

"You chose Memnon's Revenge to *win*," said Giovanni.

"And?" Pyricles demanded. "She won second!"

"She *placed* second," said Giovanni.

"That's what I said," Pyricles insisted.

"No, it's not," Giovanni said as he waved the cocktail napkin scorecard in the air.

"That's not fair," Britney interjected.

"How is that not fair?" Giovanni repeated. "He picked Memnon's Revenge to win."

"Sounds like he didn't understand the format," said Britney.

"You said all I had to do was pick a name," Pyricles argued. "I picked a name, and the damned horse came in second. That entitles me to second prize."

"That means Lucas misses out," said Giovanni.

"What's that now?" Lucas asked.

"How would Lucas win?" Pyricles decried.

"No one else got any of their predictions right except Lucas—"

Pyricles snatched the ink-stained cocktail napkin from Giovanni.

"This says he chose One-Eyed Jack!"

"But he picked Aethe to show," Giovanni explained.

"So he gets three chances to win?" Pyricles fumed. "How is that fair?"

"Alright, alright," Lucas interceded, "I'll forfeit my rights to the prize, but you have to give me a chance to win it back."

Giovanni passed the remaining bill to Pyricles.

"There," Lucas pointed out a basketball game on a television on the opposite wall. "We could bet on the outcome of the game..."

However, the game had been interrupted by a fist-fight between two players, both of whom wore royal blue jerseys.

"Or the outcome of the fight," Lucas altered his proposal.

"Sucker's bet," said Melissa. "That one's called 'Goon' for a reason."

As she spoke, the larger player grabbed a handful of the other's jersey, dragged him close, then delivered a haymaker of a right hook to his teammate's head. The smaller man instantly went limp and crashed to the floor.

"You can still pay out if you want," Melissa teased.

"How about a round of shots instead?" Lucas answered as he slapped a bill on the bar top.

"What's your poison?" Melissa asked.

"Tequila!"

Melissa quickly set to work. First she picked up the small glasses, wet their rims and dipped them in salt, set them down and filled them with spirits — a double shot poured neat and topped with twists of lime — and the publican passed these over the wooden bar to where the revelers stood with glistening eyes. When they had retrieved their glasses, they held them aloft, clinked them together, brought them to their lips, threw back their heads, and drew out all the liquid. The shots done, the tequila gone, they plunked down their glasses and no one's thirst went unsatisfied.

"Anybody ready for another?" Melissa asked the group.

Giovanni raised his glass and swilled the frothy remains of his beer, then gulped down the dregs, set the glass on the bar top, and slid it toward Melissa.

"The saison next?" she asked.

He nodded, swallowing his mouthful of hefeweizen.

"For me as well, please," added Vere.

"On the way," Melissa responded, removing the two men's glasses from the bar top.

"I've got it," Lucas proclaimed with another slap to the bar top. "Arm wrestling!"

The assembled friends looked curiously at Lucas.

"To bet on!" he continued. "I'll bet I can beat anyone in an arm wrestle."

Lucas began rolling up his shirt sleeve.

"You can't arm wrestle on the bar top, funny-guy," Melissa said as she passed Vere and Giovanni their beers.

"What about the picnic tables outside?" Lucas asked.

Melissa shrugged, smirked, and shook her head apathetically.

"Let's go!" Lucas hollered, leaping up from his seat at the bar.

Pyricles followed, then Britney and Tracee, then Vere and Giovanni carrying their beers. The picnic tables were empty; the previous inhabitants had abandoned their haunt, and the televisions were black and silent.

"Who dares face me?" asked Lucas as he sat down and plunked his elbow on the table, wiggling his fingers excitedly.

"I dare," Vere said, setting his beer down and sitting on the bench opposite from Lucas.

"Oh, Vere, um, are you sure?" Lucas asked as his opponent slid his sturdy frame into place. "I was rather thinking Britney might like—"

"She can have you next, mate," Vere interrupted, grasping Lucas' hand.

"I say, I'll try to take it easy on you then," Lucas forced a nervous laugh. "Can somebody, um, count us in?"

Tracee set her palms atop Vere and Lucas' gripped hands.

"Three... Two... One," she removed her hands. "Go!"

Lucas thrust his chest and shoulders forward in an attempt to leverage his weight against Vere's arm; Vere didn't budge, nor did his face betray any hint of emotion. Lucas' knuckles quickly lost their color, fading from pink to white; his face, however, reacted in the exact opposite fashion, flushing as he struggled to shift Vere's immovable appendage.

"I say," Lucas puffed out the words, "call it a draw?"

Vere smiled at Lucas, then clapped his free hand together with the one already joined in Lucas' grip, and shook the man's well-wrung hand.

"A draw it is," Vere agreed as he released Lucas' hand.

Lucas drew his hand to his chest, then clenched and unclenched his fist several times.

"Any other ideas?" asked Pyricles.

"How about a race?" said Vere.

"How about not," Pyricles countered.

"Anyone know a game?" said Lucas, continuing to stretch and exercise his hand as discretely as possible.

"*Certo*, I know a game," Giovanni replied.

Melissa walked up to the table and collected Vere and Giovanni's empty glasses.

"We used to play this in the barracks," Giovanni continued. "Does anyone have a nickel?"

Tracee pulled a coin purse from her handbag and dug out a nickel. She tossed it to Giovanni.

"OK, who's playing?" asked Giovanni.

"I am," Lucas answered.

"I'll play your game," Melissa volunteered, setting down a tray of empty glasses she had collected.

"Oh, um," Giovanni prevaricated, "are you sure you want to—"

"Just tell me how to play," she demanded as she sat in Vere's recently vacated position across from Lucas.

"So you sit across from one another, make a fist, and press your knuckles against the table."

Melissa and Lucas obeyed Giovanni's instructions.

"I don't think I'm going to like this game," said Lucas.

"Then, you take turns sliding the nickel into your opponent's knuckles," Giovanni continued, "and the first person to draw blood wins."

"That's barbaric," said Lucas, his face again drained of color.

"I didn't say it was a nice game," Giovanni replied with a shrug.

"Knuckles down," Melissa ordered.

Clink-clink-clink.

Giovanni flipped the nickel onto the table. It landed nearer to Melissa than Lucas, so she went first. She plunked the nickel on the table in front of her, then slid it toward Lucas' hand using the tip of her index finger. The nickel made it three-quarters of the way to Lucas, then faltered and stopped just before his knuckles.

Lucas went next. He placed the nickel on the table, then held it down with his index finger while he lined up his shot. Satisfied with his placement, he leaned down to sight, closed one eye and lined up the coin, then flicked the nickel with his middle finger. The metal disc careened off the side of the table.

"Yow!" he yelped, shaking his hand. "What the hell? I say, Giovanni, what's the big idea?"

"I didn't tell you to flick it," Giovanni asserted.

"How else am I supposed to do it?" Lucas demanded.

Melissa retrieved the nickel and set it before her.

"Yeah," she asked, "how else?"

"You put your thumb on top of the nickel," Giovanni instructed, "then set your index and pinky fingers down in front, like the posts of a slingshot."

"OK," Melissa set her hand in the prescribed position. "Now what?"

"Now, slingshot," Giovanni directed.

In one quick motion, she thrust her thumb forward and released the nickel. It zinged across the table, slammed into Lucas' largest knuckle, and settled in the saddle between the knuckles of his index and middle fingers.

"Yow! Yow! Yow!" he howled again, yanking his hand from the table and shaking it violently. "That's it; you win!"

Lucas held out his hand to inspect the damage.

"You're right about that: she did win," Giovanni confirmed, pointing to the knuckle of Lucas' middle finger where several layers of skin had fissured into a miniature tectonic fault line.

"Yes, thanks a million, Gio," Lucas responded, clutching his hand to his chest again. "That's a plum lovely game you've taught us. D'you know any others? Maybe we can play 'hangman,' but, you know, really hang whoever loses!"

The table burst into laughter. Giovanni looked at his friends' jubilant face, then joined their chorus. Even Lucas managed a self-effacing chuckle as his irritation subsided.

"Why don't you try shuffle board?" Melissa suggested.

"Wonderful idea," said Lucas. "Britney, would you care to play?"

"Why not?" she agreed.

"Who else?" asked Lucas.

"I'll play," said Tracee.

"Me too," Pyricles added.

The four shuffle board companions rose from the picnic table and filed inside the bar. Vere looked from Melissa to Giovanni, then got up and followed the recently departed. Melissa stood and collected the glasses from their table.

"Want a hand?" Giovanni offered.

"How about both?" Melissa countered, pushing two empty mugs toward him.

"Nice work with the nickel."

"Thanks, and thanks for the tip."

Melissa collected the revelers' remains from the adjacent table before walking to the door. Giovanni, glasses in one hand, opened the door and held it for her. He followed her inside and to the bar, back to the far spot they had earlier occupied. Vere was sitting on one of the barstools, watching the latest contest. Giovanni resumed his seat next to his friend. Lucas and Britney stood on one side of the long shuffleboard table, and Pyricles and Tracee stood across from them. The pair at each end of the table took turns sliding dense metal pucks across the polished wooden table top, while their team-mate at the opposite end sprinkled sand on the landing target — a triangle subdivided into seven polygons representing different point values.

"You guys ready for the dubbel?" Melissa asked from behind the bar, drawing Vere and Giovanni's attention back from the shuffleboard table.

Vere nodded.

"Please," said Giovanni.

Melissa filled two glasses with the latest draft and placed them on the bar top.

"Cheers," said Vere.

"Thanks," Giovanni added.

Melissa wiped her hands on a bar rag, then walked around the corner of the bar and sat on Giovanni's free side.

"Are you any good?" she asked, pointing to the shuffleboard table. "Maybe we could play the winners."

"How about darts instead?" Giovanni suggested, nodding toward the dartboard in the opposite corner.

"I don't know," Melissa stated, "I'm pretty good at darts."

"Well, if you're as good at darts as you are at nickel-knuckle, then I don't have a prayer," Giovanni said, "but I'll take my chances. Vere, you want in?"

"Yeah, give me just a minute. I'm going to step outside to call Kateryna."

Vere rose from his barstool and lumbered out the door. No sooner had he left than Lucas slipped into his seat at the bar.

"Well?" Melissa asked Lucas. "Vanquished or victorious?"

"Tough match," Lucas admitted. "We are indeed the vanquished. The victorious team has retired to the loo."

Pyricles sidled up the bar next to Lucas.

"What the hell was that, Lucas?" Pyricles hissed at him.

"Sorry?" Lucas asked in confusion, turning to face his friend.

"Why'd you throw the match? I bet Tracee forty bucks against a date that we would win."

Lucas frowned.

"Sorry, Pyr. I thought we were doing the other plan," he explained. "You know, lose the game and win the—"

"Anybody pouring drinks in this goddamned place?"

The muffled bellow issued from a man at the opposite end of the bar who faced the floor as he spoke. His black ponytail bobbed as he wavered back and forth, his large, hairy arms draped across the bar top to steady himself.

"Don't you think you've had enough, Ron?" Melissa asked.

Clank.

The wavering man banged his empty beer mug against the bar top, then raised his pinched face.

"No," he replied, "I don't."

Clank.

"Well, I do," Melissa replied.

"Well, I know better than you," Ron quipped.

Clank.

"Why don't you go home and sleep it off?" Melissa suggested.

"Why don't you get your ass back behind the bar?" Ron shouted in return.

"Why don't you go take a rolling fuck at a flying donut?" Pyricles shot back.

Ron snatched his mug from the bar top and chucked it at Pyricles, who swiftly ducked.

Clonk.

The mug careened into Giovanni's face, striking him under his right eye. Starbursts exploded into his vision. He grasped the bar as he tried to blink away the pain and disorientation, but his eye was already swelling shut. Through his good eye, Giovanni saw Ron lumbering toward him. Shoving Pyricles' crouched form aside, Giovanni kicked a barstool into Ron's path. However, his depth perception was severely hindered by the lack of half of his visual faculties, and the barstool that he had intended to serve as a barrier between himself and the enraged man hurtling toward him instead fell to the floor and clattered into Ron's shins. Ron bellowed an obscenity as he tripped and fell to his knees. Giovanni was already advancing toward him. He aimed a right jab down at Ron's face, but again misread the distance to his target and missed his mark; his fist sailed past Ron's enraged face as the momentum of the ill-fated attack carried him nearer to his foe. Ron reeled his head back, his eyes wide and wild; he was preparing to smash his forehead into Giovanni's nose when an oversized hand landed on his head. Powerful fingers dug into Ron's scalp and locked firmly around a fistful of black hair. Vere, the owner of the oversized hand, yanked Ron to his feet.

"Lemmego-you-goddamned-sonuvabitch!" Ron hollered as he aimed several clumsy punches behind him.

Vere released Ron's hair and spun him around with an open hand shove to the back of his shoulder.

"I didn't come here to fight," Vere stated with ice in his voice and fire in his eyes, "but that doesn't mean I won't."

Once Ron laid eyes on his newest aggressor, the fight went out of him entirely. Vere gripped him around the bicep, led him to the exit, and watched from the doorway as Ron slunk off into the night.

"Oh my god, Gio," Melissa exclaimed. "Are you alright?"

She hurried out from behind the bar to where Giovanni stood, gingerly pressing his fingers against his face and grimacing at the pain.

"Yeah," he responded, "I'll be fine."

"Stop poking at it!" she commanded, swatting his hand away from his face. She leaned closer to examine him. "That's going to be a nice shiner; it's already turning blue."

Melissa guided Giovanni to a seat in the inner corner of the L-shaped bar. He sat down facing away from the bar and leaned back against the bar top.

"I say," Lucas said.

"You didn't have to do that, you know—" Pyricles stated.

Giovanni faced Pyricles as Vere returned to their corner of the bar and stood before his friends, closing their small circle.

"—but thank you, both of you," Pyricles continued.

"What're friends for?" Giovanni replied, a small grin breaking through his grimace.

"How about another round on the house?" Melissa suggested to the quartet at the bar.

"Thanks, Melissa, but that's enough excitement for me for one night," Giovanni responded, getting to his feet again.

"You can't go after that!" she said.

"I say," Lucas repeated, "you can't very well drive right now."

"Vere drove," Giovanni explained, "and I only live upstairs."

"Right, right," Lucas shook his head.

"Really, I'll be fine. What do we owe you, Melissa?" Giovanni asked, pulling notes from his wallet.

"After you were attacked?" she asked. "Let's just call it even."

Giovanni tried to smile at her, but winced as the skin at the corner of his eye stretched painfully.

"See you next time," he said, stuffing the notes in the tip jar.

"I'm going too," Vere said. "Do you fellas need a lift home?"

"I'll stay a bit," Lucas answered, looking toward the bathroom.

"Same," said Pyricles.

"*Ciao, amici*," Giovanni called with a wave.

"Goodnight, lads," Lucas said.

"Night," Pyricles added.

Vere and Giovanni walked toward the exit.

"Gio, wait," Melissa hailed, trotting to catch up.

"I'll meet you outside," Giovanni said to Vere, who continued out the door.

"What's up, Melissa?" Giovanni asked, turning away from the door.

She stopped in front of him.

"I just wanted to make sure you're OK after all that," she said, grabbing her left bicep with her right hand.

"Yeah, I'm fine; don't worry about me."

"Kinda hard not to worry after watching that glass almost take your head off."

Giovanni raised his hand to his eye and felt the raised skin, trying to gauge the severity of his wound.

"It's not that bad, is it?" he asked.

"Um, no?"

Giovanni laughed then winced again.

"It's pretty bad," Melissa admitted. "You should get some ice on it soon."

"I think I have something for it upstairs."

"Well, look," she blurted out, "I get off in a couple hours...if you need any help with the eye, or...anything."

Giovanni immediately recognized the longing in her eyes.

"Thanks, Melissa, but I think I'm just going to go to sleep tonight," he responded. "I'll be back in soon though," he added, smiling at her again.

"See you soon then," she smiled back at him. "You still owe me a game of darts."

She gave him a quick hug and a quicker kiss on his unbruised cheek, then turned away and walked back to the bar.

Giovanni turned in the opposite direction and exited the bar.

"Alright, mate?" Vere asked.

Giovanni nodded.

"Thanks for saving my ass in there," he said.

"More like your nose," Vere responded with a laugh.

"Yeah, I had maybe lost the reins a bit."

"Flying too close to the sun," Vere agreed.

"Well, take care, Vere. Drive safely."

"Alright, see you tomorrow," Vere replied, gripping Giovanni's hand in his own again.

Giovanni turned left and began heading in the opposite direction as his friend. A gentle wind blew desiccated leaves down the cobblestone sidewalk. Giovanni shivered, then hurried toward a pair of large glass doors. He entered a code on the metal keypad on the wall, then pulled open one of the doors, walked through the lobby, and stepped into a waiting elevator.

Ding.

The elevator arrived at his floor. As he trudged down the hallway, Giovanni let the exhaustion of the day — and especially the night — wash over him. He felt as though he were not so much walking toward his apartment but melting toward it. He hoped to make it to his door before he ran out of time and substance. Finally, just as his fears were beginning to solidify into reality, he arrived at his door, unlocked it, and entered his apartment.

Chapter 8

Giovanni kicked the door shut behind him. He turned into the kitchen and pulled a bag of blueberries from the freezer, then walked to his couch and fell onto it. He pressed the bag of blueberries to his swollen eye. The frozen orbs dulled his pain and cooled his head. He dug the television remote from under a paisley-patterned pillow and flicked the power on.

Click.

The words 'Infinity Media' appeared on the screen. The letters of each word rearranged themselves into two circles. The circles joined into a sideways-8, which then began to spin; the infinity symbol transformed as it spun then disappeared.

Black. Silence.

"—come, son of Aeson."

A beautiful, blonde woman aboard the deck of a ship casts sultry, pleading eyes. She wears a loose white sheet draped over one shoulder and banded at the waist. The wind tugs at her sheet, exposing her buxom figure. The object of her desire stands across from her, his dark hair blowing in the same salt wind. The setting sun glances off his olive skin. He wears only a rough pair of breeches, and his bare chest displays a sailor's strong, rugged physique. The water behind them is a dark, inky indigo.

"Take me and make me thy maiden!" she beseeches as she presses herself against his rippling chest.

He sweeps the sheet from her shoulder and uncovers her evenly tanned body, glistening with a mist of sea and sweat.

Click. Black. Silence.

"I heard what you done been doin' behind my back! I don't appreciate that s---!"

An enormous woman stands on a low stage. Her pale white face flushes to a glowing red as she screams. She towers over the object of her invective, a woman as black as she is white, as thin as she is fat, and as short as she is tall. The seated woman grabs a handful of her confronter's indigo dress.

"You don't know what the f--- you're talking about!" she screams back as she tears at the woman's hair and face.

The crowd cheers.

Click. Black. Silence.

A man in an indigo suit, his pants rolled up to his calves, walks across a bed of glowing coals.

"That's right," he says with a practiced smile, "the pastor himself will be praying for your soul! And ask yourself, I implore you, wherein do you differ from the sinner? Are your soul and your heart clean? Send me one dollar, send a hundred — whatever you can — and you will be added to my personal prayer list—"

Click. Black. Silence.

[04]

"—what I see for *you*," says a heavyset woman with cinnamon skin. She wears a tight-fitting, black turban and a loose, red blouse. "Call me now for a free tarot reading!"

Behind her, smoke drifts before scrolling images of tarot cards, alternately upright and reversed: a young man wearing a tunic and carrying a bag on a stick stands with a dog at the edge of a cliff, a woman in an indigo robe sits between a black and a white pillar, a man with a wand and a crown of laurel stands in a chariot drawn by a black and a white sphinx, a red satyr with black horns and wings sits before a nude man and woman, both loosely chained to his throne.

"What do you want to know?" she asks. "The cards reveal watcha' can't see for yourself!"

Click. Black. Silence.

[05]

A grey cartoon lizard stands on its hind legs at the head of a procession, flicking its sinuous tail and waving a bone baton in the air. It leads a motley assortment of cartoon demons dancing in a circle around a black cauldron that bubbles and belches over an open flame. The demons' forms are hideous made hilarious by their miniature size: a squat and shuffling red-faced terror; an ungainly, orange blob with far too many legs; a little, yellow goblin; a dragon, green and grotesque; a wild, blue boar with twisting tusks; a nasty-looking dog with patchy, indigo fur; a curious tangle of violet hair, its face identifiable by a long, curly beard; still more follow the circular path.

Click. Black. Silence.

An ugly, little man sits before a panel of journalists. The words *Indigo City Owls* are emblazoned in bold letters on the chest of his sleeveless jersey.

"I don't know why this is so interesting to you people. Why can't you respect my privacy? What I do off the court is none of your concern. Anyway, I don't run around behind people's backs with they women — that's just not the kind of man I am. I especially wouldn't disrespect one of my teammates like that. Y'all need to chill."

The interview freezes and a woman's voice narrates over the still image.

"That's a statement made earlier today by Eddie 'the Nipple' Nipapaul regarding allegations of philandering with the wives of his teammates. One of his teammates, Ivan 'Goon' Batleir, spoke with us about this issue before tonight's game."

A gargantuan man with a prominent unibrow towers over a reporter in a grey suit. The reporter holds a microphone up toward the man's mouth.

"Piece of s--- is snake, not man. I am hoping he is not showing himself again," he wipes sweat from his face. "Prison does not suit Ivan."

Click. Black. Silence.

[07]

A coterie of cartoon men stands in a cave illuminated by torches in wall sconces. The men wear colorful silk robes over their dark skin and turbans atop their heads. One stands apart from the rest, bloody sword in hand.

"Such is his punishment for failure," the sword-bearer addresses his peers, "which he knew well before he made his attempt—"

Click. Black. Silence.

"—I'll tell you exactly what you've gotta do."

A fat man with a piggish face and a mottled complexion sits at a large desk. An oversized golden microphone hangs suspended before him.

"Tell your congressman, you tell him, say, look here, science is science, but a good Christian education is—"

Click. Black. Silence.

"—the recollections of one Michael Chambers with appropriate flashbacks and soliloquy. Or, more simply stated, the evolution of man, the cycle of going from dust to dessert, the metamorphosis from being the ruler of a planet, to an ingredient in someone's soup. It's tonight's bill of fare from—"

Click. Black. Silence.

FADE IN:

Space, vast and black, fills the screen.

MUSIC CUE: "Jupiter, Bringer of Jollity" by Gustav Holst

MAIN TITLE:

CALLISTO

EXT. SOLAR SYSTEM

The sun glows brightly at the center of the Solar System as the planets rush past. They slow as they pass, following long, ovoid paths. FOV tightens on Jupiter.

> **VOICE OVER**
> The year is three hundred forty-four. Five thousand one hundred seventeen by the old Chinese calendar, or twenty-four twenty by the Gregorian. Interplanetary colonization began almost four hundred years ago, two hundred years before life on Earth was destroyed.

EXT. JUPITER

Jupiter dominates the screen. His moons enter and exit the FOV as they travel along their ellipses.

> **VOICE OVER**
> The Galileo Charter rules the Jupiter System. The Charter turned the gaseous giant into a refueling center for travel between the various planetary civilizations, and they have reaped the benefits for centuries.

EXT. CALLISTO
FOV tightens on the moon Callisto, emerging from Jupiter's enormous shadow. Her surface is dark and scarred by innumerable craters.

The majority of the Charter's citizens are located on Jupiter's fourth moon, Callisto. The icy rock is home to several underground hives, each containing its own self-sustaining community.

INT. VALHALLA HIVE - IZIA'S BEDROOM - DAY

IZIA, an attractive 18-year-old girl with dark, curly hair, steps through a retractable door into a small, Spartan bedroom. She wears a towel that she pulls off to dry her damp hair before quickly donning her grey, one-piece uniform and exiting through another retractable door.

INT. HALLWAY

Izia emerges into a cylindrical, dull metal hallway that curves out of view in either direction. She walks down a familiar path, waits briefly at an elevator's retractable doorway, then enters as the doors open.

INT. ELEVATOR

Several people — all in the same grey, one-piece uniform — stand inside the circular elevator carriage. A CHIME SOUNDS (440 Hz) as the elevator doors close, then continues marking each floor as the carriage ascends [7 -- 6 -- 5 -- 4].

INT. HALLWAY

Izia steps into another cylindrical hallway and begins following its curved path. JANE, an attractive 18-year-old girl identical to Izia, emerges from a conjoining hallway. Jane's cheeks and eyes GLOW with a warm light, and her dark hair is streaked with silver that actively SHIMMERS.

IZIA
Hey, Jane.

Jane looks apathetically over her shoulder at Izia. She SIGHS, irritated.

JANE
Hi, Itzy-Bitzy.

IZIA

Please don't call me that.

JANE

Whatever.

IZIA

You look different today.

JANE

(brightening)

Targeted bioluminescence. Daddy had a team of cosmetic geneticists brought to the Hive to do it for me special. It's a brand new
treatment, just invented, very expensive.

Izia and Jane arrive at a closed door and queue up behind three waiting girls,
whose identical faces are each framed by a different style of blonde hair. The
door slides open.

INT. CLASSROOM

The students file into the empty classroom as the floor's rigid geometric
pattern begins to shift. The patterned plates of metal separate and fold into
desks before the girls each take a seat. Two boys with matching faces and
blonde crew cuts enter and sit in the rear of the room.

JANE

(to Izia)

Hey, did you do the—

MRS. NOLE

Good morning, class.

MRS. NOLE enters and stands beside a large desk at the front of the room.
She is in her early-100s, with a stern voice that can bend steel with a word.
The few creases in her face show the indigo tinge of age regression treatments, but her eyes are sharp and clear within similarly affected indigo
sockets.

STUDENTS
(unenthusiastic)
Good morning, Mrs. Nole.

The door slides open and SAMIR enters the classroom. He is a swarthy 18-year-old boy with chiseled features and dark hair.

MRS. NOLE
Impeccable timing, young man. Front and center. Now class, as I mentioned last week, this being our last week of instruction before the Pacem holiday, we're going to keep our sessions nice and short — we're only going to hear from one of you each day.

Mrs. Nole pulls a small tablet from the breast pocket of her uniform. She dims the lights and activates the holographic projector.

MRS. NOLE (cont'd)
Samir, you have our first topic.

SAMIR
Thanks Mrs. N. My topic is the early history of Jupiter. In the year sixteen-ten Gregorian, Galileo Galilei observed the four largest moons orbiting Jupiter: Io, Europa, Ganymede, and Callisto. Although further moons were later discovered, the exploration of Jupiter was given little attention until the end of the twentieth century.

JANE
Pssst... Izia... Izia.

IZIA
(whispering)
What?

SAMIR
Beginning with the *Galileo* in nineteen-ninety-five, interplanetary probes were sent to Jupiter to collect data. The *Cassini* followed in two-thousand, and the *Juno* in two-thousand-sixteen. These probes sent vital information about the Jupiter System back to Earth, enticing and intriguing the entire planet.

JANE
Did you do the Gravity and Magnetism Quiz?

IZIA
What?

JANE
The grav and mag quiz, did you do it, retard?

Mrs. Nole clears her throat loudly and stares pointedly at Jane and Izia.

SAMIR
In the second decade of the twenty-first century, space exploration was open to anyone who could afford the expense. The first private individual to construct her own interplanetary fleet was considered tragically eccentric and derided for her temerity. The second to do so was widely criticized for his dithering. Historians call this period 'Humanity's Manifest Destiny.'

Jane clears her throat loudly and stares pointedly at Izia.

SAMIR
In twenty-thirty-three, the first of three planned missions arrived in the Jupiter System. A team of Russian and American astronauts landed on Ganymede and established a scientific and exploratory outpost. Shortly after the final of the three missions departed Earth, the two countries dissolved their treaties and went to war with one another. All of the astronauts claimed neutrality in the conflict and continued their work in the Jupiter system.

JANE
Well?

IZIA
Well, what?

JANE
I swear to god, if you make me ask you again—

Mrs. Nole SLAMS her hand down on Jane's desk. The other students' heads all snap toward the noise. Samir stands in silence at the front of the room.

MRS. NOLE

Please continue, Samir.

SAMIR

Right... Well, by twenty-forty-two, science missions expanded to cover Io and Europa, and a scientific colony was firmly established on Ganymede, where early efforts to terraform the moon showed great promise. The original crews of astronauts were stranded after Russia and the United States destroyed one another, but China, India, Canada, and Germany each sent further missions to the outpost. However, as war and survival increasingly consumed resources on Earth, missions to the moons of Jupiter ceased.

MRS. NOLE

Thank you, Samir.

Samir walks to his seat while Mrs. Nole uses her tablet to turn up the lights and turn off the holographic projector.

MRS. NOLE (cont'd)

Now then, as for you ladies. Is there something you would like to add?

IZIA

No, Mrs. Nole.

MRS. NOLE

Jane?

JANE

Mrs. Nole?

MRS. NOLE

Nothing to add?

JANE

Nope.

MRS. NOLE

Surely you must have something to add. Else why would you have chattered throughout Samir's entire presentation?

JANE

I'm so sorry, Mrs. Nole. Izia was just asking me about the Physics homework.

MRS. NOLE

I'm sure that's not true.

A scowl replaces Jane's cloying smile.

JANE

What's that supposed to mean?

MRS. NOLE

It means I don't imagine that Izia wants to fail Physics.

Samir lets out a CHORTLE of laughter, then stifles it with the crook of his arm.

MRS. NOLE (cont'd)

Furthermore, this is not Physics class. This is History class. And if you wish to disrupt it any further, then you can spend the remainder of the period in detention.

Jane SNORTS derisively.

MRS. NOLE (cont'd)

And there's the winner.

Mrs. Nole points to the closed door.

MRS. NOLE (cont'd)

Out.

Jane leaps out of her seat.

JANE

But—

MRS. NOLE

If the next words you intend to utter are 'my daddy,' then save it and leave.

The bioluminescent glow in Jane's cheeks and eyes appears demonic with the flush of her face.

>   JANE
>   (hissing)
> What the hell, Izia? Why didn't you just give me the damn assignment?

>   IZIA
> I already turned it in, O-K?
>   (softening)
> Sorry.

Jane storms out of the classroom.

>   MRS. NOLE
> Excuse me, class. Samir, please answer any questions your classmates may have about your presentation.
>   (muttering to herself)
> I intend to see that she makes it to detention this time.

Mrs. Nole exits the classroom.

>   SAMIR
> Uh, right then. Any questions?

One of the blonde girls giggles.

>   SAMIR
> I'll take that as a no.

Samir moves to Jane's empty seat alongside Izia.

>   SAMIR
> Hey, Izia. Thanks for distracting the Mole. My brother wrote that essay a few years ago. I was sure she was going to recognize it.

>   IZIA
> Oh, erm, at your service I guess.

SAMIR

So, are you doing anything for Pacem?

IZIA

Yeah, I always go to the memorial service.

SAMIR

What? No, I meant anything fun.

IZIA

Like what?

The door opens and Mrs. Nole pokes her head into the classroom.

MRS. NOLE

That will be all for today, class. We will resume presentations tomorrow. I suggest you use your free time to prepare for inspections.

Mrs. Nole's head disappears. As the students rise to leave, each of their desks unfolds into several metal plates. The plates rearrange themselves and disappear into the rigid geometric pattern on the metal floor. Izia hurries out the door and into the hallway. Samir moves to follow her, but Jane intercepts him at the door.

INT. HALLWAY

JASON emerges from a retractable door a short way down the hall from Mrs. Nole's classroom. He is a short 12-year-old boy with closely cropped blonde hair. His uniform hangs loosely on his slender frame.

JASON

Hi, Izia.

IZIA

Hey, Jason. How's it going?

JASON

Good.

IZIA

Good.

                    JASON
Guess what.

                    IZIA
Hmmm, I guess you aced your trigonometry test today.

                    JASON
No, I didn't ace it, but I only missed one.

                    IZIA
Wow, nice work, Jason! I'd call that acing it.

                    JASON
Thanks, Z. I've been doing a lot better since you started tutoring me.

Izia and Jason enter a waiting elevator.

INT. ELEVATOR

Samir jogs down the hallway toward the elevator.

                    SAMIR
Hey, Izia! Hold the door.

Jason puts his arm between the closing doors, interrupting the doors' sensors. Samir steps inside the elevator, Jason removes his arm, and the doors begin to close again.

                    IZIA
Oh, hey again. I didn't see you—

A hand grabs the edge of the closing elevator door. Jane's head appears in the widening gap of the door.

                    JANE
Obviously you didn't see us. Only an idiot would disrespect either of us — or our families — like that. And you're no idiot, right?

Jane enters the elevator and the doors slide shut behind her. The CHIME SOUNDS as the elevator begins its descent [4].

SAMIR

What's your problem, Jane? Why don't you go find an express carriage? You're always bitching about how these ones take too long anyway.

JANE

Aw, did I hurt your widdle feewings, Sami?

SAMIR

No, but you're being a supernova-sized bitch.

JANE

Oh my god, grow up Samir. Itzy knows I was just joking with her.

JASON

Jokes are funny, Jane. That wasn't funny.

JANE

Shut up, Jason the Raisin. It's funny watching Mom dress you every morning. Anyway, it's like I said — she knows I was joking.

JASON

Although I suppose you are sisters genetically.

JANE

Keep talking, Jason, and you're going to become my sister belatedly.

SAMIR

So where ya headed, Izia?

IZIA

Down to the Drain. Robbie's probably still sleeping, and I heard Nadira is doing inspections this month.

SAMIR

Yeah, I heard my mom say that she was starting the inspections at the bottom this year.

IZIA

Oh, I hope she doesn't come today. There's no way Robbie has the Drain ready.

JANE

Daddy said she was starting at the top. You know, take care of the people of means first—

SAMIR

Well, she can't be mad at Robbie.

IZIA

(laughing)
No one can be mad at Robbie.

SAMIR

No one can lead a team of gravity-ballers like Robbie!

JANE

I wonder who she'll be mad at instead, then.

SAMIR

You don't have to worry about Nadira. Right, Jase?

JASON

Right, Sam. She's been over loads of times, and I've never seen her mad.

IZIA

You've actually met her?

JASON

Yes.

SAMIR

Sure, haven't you?

IZIA

No, Samir. We don't see much of the Premier on my floor.

JANE

Nobody calls her that. Even you're allowed to call her by her name.

JASON

It's not her name.

JANE

Of course it is, idiot. All the Premiers have always been named Nadira.

JASON

That's not her name, Jane — it's a title.

JANE

Why are you still talking, Raisin Brain?

SAMIR

I think you kind of look like her, Izia. Nadira that is.

IZIA

Really? You think so?

SAMIR

Yeah, a bit.

JANE

Yeah right, Samir.

SAMIR

What do you think, Jase?

JASON

We all look alike. It's the cloning program—

Jane grabs a handful of Jason's loose uniform and yanks him close.

JANE

Shut up, you little freak!

Jane shoves Jason into the corner of the elevator. She turns her attention to Samir.

> **JANE (cont'd)**
> And you! Why do you even talk to him? You know he's just going to say some absurd bullshit.

> **SAMIR**
> Why don't you shut up, Jane?

> **JANE**
> Look, enough with this small talk; just ask her already.

> **IZIA**
> Ask me what? You can't still be on about that quiz.

> **SAMIR**
> Nothing. I mean, it's not a big deal. We were just hoping that, if it's not any trouble or anything, that—

> **IZIA**
> Yeah?

> **JANE**
> That you could get us a bottle of Van Hooch.

> **IZIA**
> You want me to get you a bottle of Robbie's rotgut? Why don't you just ask him yourself, Jane?

The CHIME SOUNDS as the elevator doors open [5].

> **JANE**
> Use your head, Izia. Uncle Robbie would be sure to let my mother and father know if I asked him for any V-H. So it's better for you to do it, you know, since your parents are both dead.

SILENCE hangs in the elevator for a moment as Jane smiles her sweetest smile at Izia.

SAMIR

Are you for real right now? Get out of the elevator, Jane.

JANE

That's fine. This is our stop anyway. Should I tell Daddy that you're going to be late again, Sami? He almost had you reassigned after the last time.

Jane strolls out of the elevator.

SAMIR

Sorry.

IZIA

That's alright. I'm used to it from her.

SAMIR

It's not alright. She thinks she can treat people however she wants just because her great-great-great-great-great-grandparents were part of the original colony.

IZIA

I think you forgot a 'great' in there somewhere.

Samir smiles faintly.

SAMIR

Probably a couple at least.

Samir steps halfway out of the elevator and leans against the doorjamb.

IZIA

Also, weren't your own ancestors part of the same colony?

Samir's faint smile fades.

SAMIR

Yeah, well, that was a long time ago.

An awkward silence fills the space between Izia and Samir.

IZIA

Doesn't that make you uncomfortable?

SAMIR

What, my family?

IZIA

No, the door.

SAMIR

What's wrong with the door?

IZIA

Are you serious? You're standing right in the gap. What if the elevator malfunctions and the carriage just falls all of a sudden? What if the sensors fail and the doors close on you? Either way, you'd be cut in half in an instant. Haven't you ever thought about that?

SAMIR

Wow, Izia. I really hadn't until now.

Samir LAUGHS nervously, shifts his weight from foot to foot, and brushes his hand through his hair.

IZIA

My friends call me Z, by the way.

SAMIR

Well, my friends call me Sam.
(beat)
Hey, Z?

IZIA

Yeah, Sam?

SAMIR

Don't worry about the V-H. Jane will just have to figure out some other way to—

IZIA

No, I'll do it.

SAMIR

Are you sure? Jane can get it, she's just—

IZIA

I don't mind. Really, Sam — it's no big deal.

SAMIR

You're the best, Z. Look, I'm having a party tonight for Pacem — that's what I was trying to tell you earlier — so just bring it with you when you come over. Anytime is fine.

IZIA

Oh...erm, O-K. I'll see you later then.

SAMIR

See ya!

Samir flashes his perfect smile before exiting the elevator.

IZIA

Oh, Sam!

Samir's head and shoulders appear in the doorframe.

SAMIR

Yeah?

IZIA

Happy Pacem!

Samir flashes another perfect smile.

SAMIR

Happy Pacem, Z.

Samir's head and shoulders disappear. The CHIME SOUNDS, the doors close, and the elevator resumes its descent.

JASON

She's lying, you know.

IZIA

What th— Oh, Jason. Shouldn't you have gone with your sister?

JASON

It's better not to be around her after that. She's lying about why she can't get a bottle for herself.

IZIA

Oh?

JASON

She doesn't care if Mom and Dad find out. They've already caught her drinking five times this term.

IZIA

So what's the real reason then?

JASON

She doesn't have any soldi.

IZIA

(laughing)

Yeah right, Jason. Everyone knows your family has more soldi than the rest of the Hive combined.

JASON

The family has money, but she doesn't.

IZIA

What, did they cut her off?

JASON

No, I did.

IZIA

What do you mean, you did?

JASON

I hacked the soldi servers last year. Anytime Jane gets any soldi, I move it.

IZIA

You hacked the soldi servers? What the hell, Jason? How?

JASON

I just did is all. And keep it down, Z — they're always listening.

IZIA

Oh, are they? So how come they haven't come and taken you away?

JASON

No one else knows.

IZIA

Not even them?

The CHIME SOUNDS as the elevator doors open [6].

JASON

Not even anyone. I just thought you should know the truth. See ya, Z.

IZIA

Hey Jason, wait. What do you do with all of Jane's soldi?

JASON

Put it somewhere safe.

IZIA

Like where?

JASON

You ever use the Trailhead Gateway?

IZIA

Sure, once or twice. I can't really afford to pay the fee that often.

JASON

Next time you want to go out there, just type the number eight into the keypad eight times. All of Jane's soldi is designated to that

JASON (cont'd)

door account, so you should be able to use it for the rest of human existence without any problem.

Jason exits the elevator. The CHIME SOUNDS as the doors slide shut. Izia rides the elevator until she reaches the bottom [8].

INT. HALLWAY

Izia walks mechanically down the cylindrical hallway. Her face shows the confusion she feels. She reaches a closed door and punches a series of numbers into the keypad on the wall. Before entering, she pulls minute earbuds from her pocket and tucks them into her ears.

MUSIC CUE: "The Sun," by Portugal. the Man

INT. VALHALLA HIVE - WATER TREATMENT FACILITY - DAY

Inside the small room, panels of water filtration equipment dominate two walls. In the corner of these two walls, a large man's bulk strains against the netting of a low-hanging hammock. A long desk runs along the remaining wall. As Izia enters, this last wall illuminates, displaying an image from Earth — before The Ruin. An eagle skims the water of an alpine lake. The long desk's touchscreen top also illuminates, and shows the lake's reflection of snow-capped mountains. Izia sits at the desk, types her credentials on the touchscreen, and begins her work. She nods to the music, taps her foot, and eventually sways in her chair. Finally, she stands and begins dancing in front of the desk.

ROBBIE

Hey, Iz.

END MUSIC

Izia jumps at the sound of the rough voice. ROBBIE stands behind her. He is in his late-30s with a muscular body that has spent the better part of a decade going to seed. Izia plucks the earbuds out of her ears.

IZIA

What the hell, Robbie! Don't scare me like that.

Robbie rubs the sleep from his eyes with thumb and forefinger of one hand. He tilts his head back to vent an enormous yawn while scratching at the thick stubble covering his bloated chins.

ROBBIE

Sorry. I was sleepin' in de monkey when you came in. What're you workin' on over dere?

IZIA

Oh, nothing — just checking the intake pumps for anomalies. Been asleep long?

ROBBIE

Ja, had a bit too much to drink wid breakfast. 'S'all better now.

IZIA

Robbie, c'mon. You're drinking that swill for breakfast now?

ROBBIE

Easy, Iz. 'S de best medicine for what ails me.

IZIA

Oh? What's that, Robbie?

ROBBIE

'S de boredom, Iz.

IZIA

That's why you do it? The boredom? And drinking the stuff is bad enough — do you have to make it too?

ROBBIE

Look, way I see it I'm providin' a service 'round here.

IZIA

Getting people drunk? That's your service?

ROBBIE

Damn right it is. You know what happens if I'm not here makin' de Van Hooch?

IZIA

None of the water gets stolen? You stay awake for an entire shift? I get a break from constantly worrying about someone coming down here to check on us?

ROBBIE

No, *nee*, and *nein*. What happens is some young'un gets de idea into his or her head to make up a home brew usin' water from one of de dive shafts.

IZIA

Give me a break, Robbie. Everyone knows that water's poisonous.

ROBBIE

Aye, hence de need for my Van Hooch. I'm protectin' people.

IZIA

(laughing)
You have an interesting logic, boss.
(beat)
By the way, how much do you sell those bottles for?

ROBBIE

'Scuse me? 'How much do I sell dem for?' Oh-ho-ho, I know where you're goin' wi' dis.

IZIA

Where am I going with this?

ROBBIE

You dink I'm sellin' you a bottle.

IZIA

C'mon, Robbie.

ROBBIE

After all de shit you give me over it?

IZIA

It's like you said, though — too dangerous to not sell me a bottle.

ROBBIE

How's'at?

IZIA

Well, if I don't get it from you, then I'll just have to try to brew it myself. I'll use one of the dive shafts. I'm sure I won't die from just a few drinks—

ROBBIE

Now you're just bein' stupid on purpose. Anyhow, I'm just takin' you by de nose. You can have a bottle, Iz, and I don't need none of your soldi. We'll call it an early Pacem present.

Robbie arcs his back into a stretch while letting out another massive yawn.

ROBBIE (cont'd)

But Iz—

Robbie scratches the stubble on his cheek.

ROBBIE (cont'd)

There are better ways of makin' friends.

IZIA

I just want them to like me. Is that so bad?

ROBBIE

<u>Dem</u> or <u>him</u>?

IZIA

It's not just for Samir—

ROBBIE

So Samir's his name.

IZIA

(frustrated)

It's not just for Samir, but he is hosting the party.

Robbie holds his hands up mock surrender.

ROBBIE

Say no more, say no more.

Robbie lumbers out the door.

IZIA

Thanks, Robbie!

Izia turns her attention back to the computer screen. After a few moments, the sound of the door opening interrupts her.

IZIA (cont'd)

That was quick. You got the bottle already?

NADIRA, Premier of the Jupiter System, stands in the doorway with a bemused look on her face. She is in her early-40s, with olive-skin and dark eyes.

NADIRA

Excuse me?

IZIA

What the—

Nadira enters the room and the door shuts behind her. Izia looks up from her work and freezes as she recognizes the newcomer.

NADIRA

Bottle of what exactly?

IZIA

Shhhit.

NADIRA

A bottle of shit? Why on Callisto would you have a bottle of shit?

Izia jumps to her feet and stands respectfully with her hands stiffly at her sides.

IZIA

No, it's not mine — I mean, I don't have a bottle of shit—

NADIRA
(smiling)
But someone here does?

IZIA
What? No, it's not anyone's. I mean — no. I mean — I'm sorry, and there's no bottle of shit.

NADIRA
Well, that is certainly reassuring.

Izia's face burns red with embarrassment. She bows her head, brings her hands together as in prayer, raises them halfway to her chest, stops, looks inquisitively at Nadira.

NADIRA (cont'd)
(laughing)
Dear girl, stop. What is your name?

IZIA
Izia, ma'am.

NADIRA
Well, Izia, I came to speak with Heer Van Dyke. Where is the young captain?

IZIA
Oh, he, erm, he just went to use the, erm, gentlemen's facilities.

NADIRA
(laughing)
We are using that term rather loosely, are we not?

IZIA
Ma'am?

NADIRA
Never mind. Will he be long?

IZIA
I think so, ma'am. You only just missed him.

Nadira stands for a moment in the center of the room and holds Izia in her gaze.

NADIRA

Well, I suppose that is the risk one runs with surprise visits. However, I can't wait all day. There's no telling how long it might take a gentleman to use the facilities.

IZIA

Yes, ma'am. What should I tell Robb— erm, Heer Van Dyke?

NADIRA

Tell Robbie that I will be back at this time tomorrow.

IZIA

Yes, ma'am.

NADIRA

Until tomorrow then.

Nadira turns and walks out the door. Izia collapses into her chair with a massive SIGH. She takes several slow breaths before returning to her work. Robbie enters carrying two bottles in each hand.

IZIA

Robbie!

Robbie grins and raises his hands, showing off his bounty.

IZIA

Are you fucking kidding me right now?

ROBBIE

What's wrong wid you all of a sudden?

IZIA

What if someone had seen you with all of those?

ROBBIE

In case you forgot, I'm de Chief of Water. Sometimes I carry bottles around. Some of 'em actually do have water in 'em. And anyway it's only ever de two of us down here, Iz.

IZIA

It's inspection week, Robbie!

ROBBIE

Oh, right... Well, who's going to come all de way down here to—

IZIA

Nadira.

ROBBIE

Right, good one, Iz. De Premier is just going to pop in on us.

IZIA

She just did.

ROBBIE

Well, den it's a good ding I got some extra Hooch. She can really put it away you know.

IZIA

That's not funny, Robbie.

ROBBIE

I was only half jokin'.

IZIA

Well, I wasn't joking when I said she was here. What would have happened if you came back with that while she was here?

ROBBIE

Not much, I imagine — she sees me through her fingers. And who was it asked me to go get de damn bottles anyway?

IZIA

I didn't think you were going to come back juggling them!

ROBBIE

Iz, trust me. I don't need to make de Premier happy wid a dead sparrow.

IZIA

What the hell does that even mean?

ROBBIE

Will you just trust me? Every team needs a captain, Iz.

Robbie offers one of the bottles to Izia. She takes hold of it.

IZIA

Alright—
(beat)
Captain.

Robbie grins and releases the bottle. He stashes the remaining bottles behind a false panel among the water treatment equipment.

IZIA

Hey, Robbie?

ROBBIE

Hey, Iz?

IZIA

Can I ask you another question?

ROBBIE

Sure.

IZIA

Do you know where your brothers are?

ROBBIE

My broders?

IZIA

You know, your clone brothers.

ROBBIE

Ain't got none of 'em.

IZIA

Excuse me?

ROBBIE

What? I never told you dat? *Ja*, your lordship Robert Van Dyke is a natural born human.

IZIA

Oh please, Robbie. There are no natural born humans in the Valhalla Hive.

ROBBIE

Fout. Wrong. Dere are no natural <u>birds</u> in de Valhalla Hive, but I wasn't born here. You're talkin' to an Asgard native.

IZIA

You were born in the Apiary?

ROBBIE

Dat's right. Grew up dere too. Enough Van Dykes over dere dat you hear more Dutch dan English near de top. Moved here for de gravity ball deam.

IZIA

Yeah, Robbie, everyone knows about your heroics with the Callisto Bears. I just figured you were cloned here like the rest of us.

ROBBIE

De rest of us? I'm not de only one here widout any clones. Your teacher lady, de one older'n Callisto herself, she's a solo too.

IZIA

A solo?

ROBBIE

Ja, solo. *Enkel, afgezonderd.* Alone. We don't come in a set of eight like de rest of you. What's got you askin' about your clones anyway?

IZIA

Jane.

ROBBIE

My charmin' niece? She of *het pesten en intimidatie*? What'd she do now?

IZIA

Same old, same old. I just don't understand why she hates me so much.

ROBBIE

Can't get along wid everyone I suppose. Still, it's not like you're enemies or anydin' like dat.

IZIA

We're not? Could'a fooled me.

ROBBIE

Aw, c'mon, Iz. We're all on de same team here.

IZIA

Yeah? I must have missed the team visit to the cosmetic geneticists.

ROBBIE

Saw dat, did you? I told my idiot sister to stop givin' in to dat brat's demands.
(beat)
What do you want me to tell you? Money makes de world go 'round. My Van Hooch, on de oder hand, will make you dink de world has stopped.

IZIA

(laughing)
Sure, Robbie.

ROBBIE

I'm not kidding you. You better be careful wi' dat stuff.

INT. ELEVATOR - NIGHT

Izia stands in the center of the elevator, alone. The CHIME marks the ascending floors. She pulls the bottle Robbie gave her out of a plain, black backpack hanging from her shoulder. She unscrews the cap and sniffs at the contents. She balks, then sips tentatively from the bottle — once, twice. The CHIME SOUNDS and the elevator doors slide open [5]. Izia quickly screws the cap back on the bottle and stuffs it back in her bag.

INT. HALLWAY - OUTSIDE SAMIR'S ROOM

MUSIC CUE: "Feel It Still (Gryffin Remix)," by Portugal. The Man

The muffled sounds of MUSIC, CONVERSATION, and LAUGHTER grow louder as Izia trots down the curved hallway. She arrives at Samir's door. The door opens just as she begins nervously straightening her uniform. Colored lights and dance music explode out of the open doorway. Samir steps into the doorway, an uncapped bottle in one hand.

> ### SAMIR
> Z!

> ### IZIA
> Hey, Sam. Lucky timing.

> ### SAMIR
> Lucky? No, I had the cameras watching for you.

Samir points to the cameras over each of Izia's shoulders.

> ### IZIA
> You have access to the surveillance video?

> ### SAMIR
> Jus' the stuff on this floor — Oh shit! I forgot.

Samir takes an exaggerated step out of the doorway and the doors close behind him, muffling the noise again.

SAMIR (cont'd)

S'that better?

IZIA

Better for you. It's your health, funny guy.

SAMIR

A toast to my health then?

Samir takes a sloppy pull from the bottle and passes it to Izia. She gingerly sips from the bottle before returning it to Samir. He takes another pull from the bottle, draining the last of it.

SAMIR

S'good, right?

Samir lobs the bottle at the hallway ceiling. It SMASHES and glass shards rain down on the hallway. A panel in the wall opens and a team of sleek, matte black drones race out and erase any trace of the mess.

IZIA

It's awful. And I have another whole bottle of it.

Izia pulls her own matching bottle from her bag. She teasingly dangles the bottle in front of Samir.

SAMIR

Whoa! Nice, Z!

IZIA

Nice of your parents to let you have a party like this.

SAMIR

This is nothing. Back on Asgard, we used to have a weeklong festival for Pacem.

IZIA

Why'd your parents want to move here?

SAMIR

My mom got a job offer.

IZIA

What about your dad?

SAMIR

Are you kidding me? He couldn't wait to move here once he saw this place.

Samir jerks his head toward his door.

IZIA

Really? I thought the Asgard Apiary was supposed to be way nicer than the Hive.

SAMIR

I dunno. It might be, but all the nicest apartments on Asgard are owned by the Van Dykes.
(feigned haughtiness)
They're very important people.

Izia laughs. Samir smiles and leans near her, swaying slightly from the VH. The noises of the party amplify behind them as the door opens. Jane stands in the doorway.

JANE

Sami! What are you doing, babe? We need you in here. Will you mix up some more of those shots — whaddaya call'em — Red Spots?

SAMIR

Oooh, yeah!

Samir turns and dances into his room through the open doorway. Izia smiles and starts to follow him, but Jane moves to block her. She steps out, forcing Izia to step backwards. The doors close, muffling the noise from the party again.

JANE

(sarcastic)
Oh good. She came.

IZIA

Why don't you just leave me alone, Jane? What's your problem? The only reason I'm even here is because you asked me to get you this goddamned drain cleaner!

JANE

You honestly think I couldn't get any V-H on my own? You're only here because I wanted to prove a point. I wanted to show you what you will never have. And maybe now you'll stop with your pathetic attempts.

IZIA

What?

JANE
(mocking)
What?

IZIA

I really don't know what you're talking about, Jane.

JANE

In what world would Samir prefer you to me?

IZIA
(annoyed)
I think that's up to him to decide.

JANE

No, it's not. And it's not up to me either. It's up to you, E-Z. You see, if you keep trying to steal Samir from me, then I'm going to make sure that you can't have him.

IZIA

What? How are you going to—

JANE

How am I going to keep him from you? Easy — I'll tell Daddy that he raped me.

IZIA

But, that's insane—

JANE

It would be insane—
(beat)
For you to ruin Samir's life like that.

IZIA

That's ridiculous. No one would believe that Samir raped you.

JANE

Daddy will. He doesn't care much for Samir anyway, but when he sees the evidence...

Jane ends her sentence with a shrug of her shoulders. Her eyes glint maliciously.

IZIA

What evidence?

JANE

Use your head, retard. What's the best evidence of rape? A bit of him inside of me.

IZIA

I'll warn him. I'll tell everyone. I'll—

JANE

(laughing)
Warn him? You're a few hours too late for that. And if you tell anyone else, then I'll have no choice but to confess to Daddy how Samir tricked me.
(sobbing)
How he got me alone one night — the night of his Pacem party. How he plied me wi-wi-with alcohol and held me down. How he, how he forced himself—
(exaggerated sob)
Inside of me.

Jane's sobs die on her lips and she smiles at Izia.

JANE (cont'd)

Of course, I'll have to tell Daddy all about Samir's accomplice —
who helped him plan his assault, who got him the booze — you. I
don't think we execute people for being accessory to rape, but
Daddy would know better. Judges are good at that sort of thing.

Jane snatches the bottle of VH from Izia, turns on her heel, and reenters
Samir's room. Izia stands at the closing door, frozen. The doors reopen just
as they close, and Samir stands in the doorway again.

SAMIR

What're you still doin' out here? T'party's inside! C'mon.

IZIA

Hey, actually, Samir, I'm not feeling very well. I think I'm going to
call it a night.

SAMIR

What? No! You're fine. Look, lemme see.

Samir puts one hand on Izia's shoulder, and presses the back of his other
hand to her forehead.

SAMIR (cont'd)

See? Fine, perfeckly fine. C'mon inside.

Jane appears behind Samir with three shot glasses in her hand.

JANE

You're missing your own party, Sami.

Jane puts her free hand on Samir's shoulder and turns him back toward the
party. She hands him one of the shots.

JANE (cont'd)

Coming, E-Z? I've got a special shot poured just for you.

Jane holds one of the shots out toward Izia.

SAMIR
(over his shoulder)
C'mon, Z!

Jane dumps the shot on the ground at Izia's feet, then drinks her own shot in one quick motion.

IZIA
No, sorry. I think I'd better go get some rest.

Samir has already begun walking back inside.

IZIA (cont'd)
Oh, but Sam—

The door closes. Izia is alone again.

IZIA (cont'd)
Happy Pacem.

END MUSIC

INT. HALLWAY

Izia trudges back to the elevator. The sounds of the party die as she moves down the curved hallway. She arrives at a bank of elevators and steps into one that waits vacantly.

INT. ELEVATOR

The CHIME SOUNDS (350 Hz) as the elevator doors close [5].

INT. ELEVATOR - [THE FORGE]

The darkness of the Forge swallows Izia. In every direction, pitch black is scarred by a grid of thin, indigo lines. Izia draws her breath sharply. She steps back and stretches out her arms, trying to find assurance in the firm walls of the elevator. Her fingertips scrape at emptiness. She claps her hands together before her face. She sees her palms connect, but hears nothing.

IZIA

Hello?

Her voice sounds thin and dampened. A man's long face flickers into existence before her, digitally drawn in shades of white and indigo. His intense, prominent eyes dominate a likeness otherwise occupied by a broad nose and thick lips. When he speaks, his booming voice echoes throughout the Forge.

KENDON

Well, well, well, looks like day longer dan rope after all. Welcome to di Forge, Nya-dira, you andr—
     (shock)
Who are you?

IZIA

Who am I? Who are you?
     (stronger)
And where am I? What the hell is going on?

KENDON

But — you're just a youn' gyal! How old are you, gyal?

IZIA

Eighteen, not that I think that much matters. Now, who—

KENDON

Eighteen! I not been waiting two hundred years to talk to an eighteen year old gyal! Dis is all wrong. What are you doin' deh'ya?

IZIA

Look mister, I'm not telling you shit until you tell me who you are!

KENDON

Me name is di Scourge of New Babylon, and I didn't wait all dis time to talk to an eighteen year old gyal!

The thin grid lines rapidly expand, erasing the Forge in a flash of indigo.

[/THE FORGE] - INT. ELEVATOR

The CHIME SOUNDS at double-time [7]. Izia looks around the elevator in disbelief. She lunges to the nearest wall and presses her hands against it, testing its existence. The elevator CHIME again redoubles its tempo. Izia slowly backs out of the elevator.

INT. HALLWAY

Izia turns and walks quickly down the hallway. She stops at her door, punches her entry code into the keypad on the wall, and steps through the opening doorway.

INT. IZIA'S BEDROOM

As the door closes, the room responds to Izia's presence. Lights in the floor and ceiling switch on and digital windows appear on three of her walls. To her left, a tropical thunderstorm rages; occasional lightning strikes illuminate shuddering palm trees and sheets of wind-driven rain. In front of her, a craggy mountain summit collects slowly falling snow. To her right, the moons of Jupiter hang before the brightly burning sun, seen from the surface of the red giant.

> **IZIA**
> Hey, Dorothy.

DOROTHY, the room's Artificial Intelligence, responds with a woman's gentle voice.

> **DOROTHY**
> Welcome home, Iz.

> **IZIA**
> Can you turn the lights down?

The lights dim to a warm glow.

> **IZIA (cont'd)**
> Thanks, Dorothy.

DOROTHY

Did you have a nice day?

Izia SIGHS as she sits on the edge of her bed. She kicks off her shoes.

IZIA

I've had better.

DOROTHY

What's wrong?

IZIA

I—I don't even know. Sorry, but I really just want to go to sleep. I'm not feeling so hot.

Izia unzips her uniform.

DOROTHY

Hmm, I can turn up the heat for you.

IZIA

No, I mean I'm not feeling well.

DOROTHY

Let's take a look.

Izia's interior wall completely opaques, a life-size image of her body displayed in the center. A series of diagnostic tests run along the margins of the screens.

DOROTHY (cont'd)

Ninety-eight-point-eight degrees internal temperature, hydration looks low, blood-sugar low, potassium low, and — what's this? Have you been drinking?

IZIA

What? No.
(beat)
I'm fine, just exhausted.

Izia slumps over in her bed and clutches a pillow to her face.

DOROTHY

I recommend a full meal, straight away. I'll prepare you a soy-seven cutlet, riced haqiora pods, and roasted beets. For dessert, some octoberries and—

IZIA

Thanks, but I don't think I can eat all that. Maybe just something to drink.

Izia's eyes are already closed when a panel in the wall near her bed slides open, revealing a glass full of lavender liquid.

DOROTHY

I've taken the liberty of adding some vitamins to your—

The wall display shows a new screen bearing the heading 'SLEEP ANALYSIS.' The rest of the wall returns to its original state as the new screen floats to the corner of the room — a small beacon of light in the darkness. Izia's soft breathing fills the room.

DOROTHY (cont'd)

Goodnight, Iz.

INT. IZIA'S BEDROOM - DAY

Izia lies prone on top of her bed. Her bedroom is brightly lit, her three 'windows' still showing each of their scenes: tropical storm, snowy mountaintop, Jupiter's moons.

DOROTHY

Izia! Izia!

IZIA

Hmmph?

Izia lifts her head slightly.

DOROTHY

Don't mumble at me! Get up!

IZIA

Turn the lights down, will you?

The lights brighten.

DOROTHY

Do you have any idea how long I've been trying to wake you?

IZIA

No, how long?

The lights brighten again.

DOROTHY

Too long!

Izia sits up in her bed and brushes her hair away from her face. She rubs her eyes with the heels of her palms.

IZIA

Hmm, what time is it?

DOROTHY

Time for class! Let's go, Iz.

Izia swings her legs over the edge of the bed and sits up.

IZIA

Oh my god, I feel like shit. Did I die, Dorothy? Is this what death feels like?

Izia slips her feet into her shoes, stands, and zips her uniform.

DOROTHY

Very funny. You would feel a lot better this morning had you listened to me last night. You're dehydrated, low on potassium, and your amino levels are—

IZIA

Ugh, don't remind me about last night.

A panel in the wall near Izia's bed slides open, revealing a glass of lavender liquid.

IZIA (cont'd)

Will you keep that cold for me? I need to take a shower.

DOROTHY

No time! You're late for class already! Take the glass—

Izia grabs the glass from the wall cavity and begins chugging it. Rivulets of juice run down her chin from the corners of her mouth.

DOROTHY (cont'd)

To go.

Dorothy punctuates her sentence by opening the door to Izia's room. Izia stops drinking and wipes her mouth with the back of her hand. She roughly stows the glass in the wall cavity. It is still half full and dripping sticky liquid.

IZIA

Sorry, Dorothy — no time.

Izia rushes out the open doorway.

MUSIC CUE: "Feel It Still (ZHU Remix)," by Portugal. The Man

SERIES OF SHOTS - IZIA STRUGGLES TO MAKE IT TO CLASS

A. View from the elevator: Izia hurries toward.
B. The elevator panel counts down as it ascends: [6 — 5]
C. View from the elevator: Izia hurries away.

END MUSIC

INT. VALHALLA HIVE - CLASSROOM

The lights in the classroom are dimmed and the holographic projector displays the Jupiter System. Jane stands with her arms crossed at the front of the classroom, while Mrs. Nole and the remaining students sit at their respective desks. The doors slide open and Izia scurries inside and straight to her seat.

JANE

Well, it's about time.

MRS. NOLE

That's enough. Izia, take your seat. As for you, Jane — let's hear it.

JANE

Wow, what an introduction. Well, I wrote about the Incursions. So, in twenty-one hundred, Captain Johan Van Dyke discovered foreign drones on Europa. The drones were from the Pan Caribbean Federation, a bunch of filthy refugees—

MRS. NOLE

Without the colorful commentary.

Jane rolls her eyes. Her bioluminescence robs the gesture of any subtlety.

JANE

Yeah, so anyway, a little drone war started in the Jupiter System, which the Charter won thanks to Captain Van Dyke. Afterwards, the Charter was the supreme power in the system, so we avoided involvement in a bunch of wars that totally wrecked our neighboring systems. This was the Small Peace, and it continued until twenty-two hundred. Next came the Second Incursion, when the P-C-F came at us again. Since they didn't want to get spanked as badly as the last time, they brought warships to go with their drones, and again invaded the Jupiter System to wage war. But this attempt also failed, again thanks to a—

MRS. NOLE

The P-C-F very nearly conquered the Galileo Charter during the Second Incursion. It was only thanks to a last-ditch effort that we won the war and saved the colonies.

JANE
(muttering)
How do you know — were you there?

MRS. NOLE

Excuse me, young lady?

JANE

I said, "Do you know who saved us again?" A Van Dyke, this time Admiral Beatrix Van Dyke, great-granddaughter of the famous captain. Then the P-C-F nuked Earth in twenty-two twenty-two, so the Charter sent drones to Mars and destroyed their colonies. The Great Peace began in twenty-two thirty-one, once the last of the filthy P-C-F scum had been exterminated.

MRS. NOLE

Enough! Take your seat and shut your mouth, lest any further offal should escape your pampered lips.

JANE
(muttering)
You're the awful one.

Jane strolls to her desk and casually sits. She turns and stares pointedly at Izia, seated next to her.

JANE

I don't appreciate being made to wait on the likes of — eww, what's wrong with you? Why are you leaking?

Izia pulls her hair into a bunch behind her head and holds it away from her neck. She fans her neck with her free hand.

IZIA

Leave me alone. It's hot in here.

Mrs. Nole turns up the lights and turns off the holographic projector.

MRS. NOLE

Now then, are there any questions for Jane?

Jane stares around the classroom, daring anyone to speak.

MRS. NOLE (cont'd)

No questions? Nothing at all? Alright, how about comments? Does anyone have any comments about the Incursions?

Silence reigns over the classroom. One of the identical blonde boys looks tentatively at Mrs. Nole.

                    MRS. NOLE (cont'd)
Franck, something you'd like to add?

                    FRANCK
Well, it's like you said Mrs. Nole — about the Second Incursion, I mean — we'll celebrate our victories this week during Pacem, but how many of our people died in those conflicts?

                    JANE
Drones.

                    FRANCK
Excuse me?

                    JANE
Drones, not people.

                    FRANCK
No, we hadn't converted to a fully drone-based military by then. Over half of our casualties were human.

                    JANE
That sucks, but what do you care? That was hundreds of years ago, and things have worked out pretty well since then.

                    FRANCK
Well enough for you. How many Van Dykes died on the front lines? My family was nearly annihilated by the viruses the P-C-F unleashed during the Second Incursion. Even today, we can only afford—

Franck clenches his jaw while his face flushes red. SIEM, the identical boy sitting next to Franck, completes his brother's thought.

                    SIEM
That's why we're the first four-double O-four series to be processed in over thirty years.

Silence momentarily regains dominion over the classroom.

                    MRS. NOLE
Thank you for sharing, boys. Let's all remember that Pacem is not
a celebration of victory — it is a celebration of peace, and peace
comes at a heavy cost. That will be all for today. Izia, you're up
tomorrow.

                    IZIA
Yes, Mrs. Nole.

INT. HALLWAY

Samir jogs to catch up to Izia as she walks down the curved hallway.

                    SAMIR
Wait up, Z!

                    IZIA
Hey, Samir.

                    SAMIR
What's your hurry?

                    IZIA
Sorry, I've got to get down to the Drain before—

                    SAMIR
O-K, I won't hold you up, but what time do you get done? My dad
rented the Bears' g-ball court for the day. D'you know what that
means?

Samir flashes his perfect smile.

                    SAMIR (cont'd)
Total control over the artificial gravity! And we're bringing a set of
laser stunners to have zero-G duels and—

                    IZIA
That sounds really fun, Samir, but I'm going to be at the Drain all
day.

SAMIR

Tonight then.

Izia hesitates. Samir's smile fades.

IZIA

Tonight? I, erm, I don't think that's such a good idea. Look, I have to go. Sorry.

Izia turns and hurries away down the curved hallway. She uses the back of her hands to wipe away the tears that mingle with her sweat once Samir disappears around the bend.

JASON

What's wrong, Z?

Izia jumps, startled to see the young boy walking beside her.

IZIA

Jason. Hey. It's nothing — just another tough day with your sister.

JASON

Yeah, I'm still avoiding her. I'm pretty sure she'll take her anger out on anything close at hand, but I'm also pretty sure that I'm her favorite target.

INT. ELEVATOR

The CHIME SOUNDS as the elevator begins its descent [5].

JASON

Z?

IZIA

Huh?

JASON

I asked you how the inspection went yesterday.

IZIA

Oh, it didn't. Robbie was, erm, running an errand when Nadira came to the Drain.

JASON

I didn't see you in the cafeteria at dinner last night.

IZIA

What were you doing in there? Why didn't you eat with your family?

Jason shrugs.

JASON

I like the cafeteria.
 (beat)
Are you O-K?

IZIA

Yeah, fine. I just didn't sleep well last night. I'm not really sure I slept at all.
 (beat)
Do you ever dream that you're awake?

JASON

I think I'm awake in all my dreams.

IZIA

I guess you're right — unless, can you dream that you're in a dream? Maybe all of this is just—

The CHIME SOUNDS as the elevator doors open [6].

JASON

Are you sure you're O-K?

IZIA

I'm fine, just tired.

Jason walks out of the elevator, watching Izia over his shoulder as the doors close. The CHIME SOUNDS.

INT. ELEVATOR - [THE FORGE]

The darkness of the Forge swallows Izia. A plain table blinks into existence before her on the indigo-gridded plane, then a chair, then Kendon, sitting comfortably in the chair.

                    KENDON
Hello again, youn' gyal.

                    IZIA
          (suspicious)
Hello.

                    KENDON
I been t'inking maybe we got off on di wrong foot.

                    IZIA
And whose fault do you think that is?

                    KENDON
Bad t'ing neva got owna, me papa use'ta say.

Another chair blinks into existence, opposite Kendon at the small table.

                    IZIA
This one does.

                    KENDON
Alright, so I shouldn'ta yelled at you when I first saw you, but I was surprised! I can't even remember how long it's been since I seen anotha human, and then some youn' gyal appears—

                    IZIA
My name's not 'youn' gyal.' It's Izia.

                    KENDON
Alright den, some Izia appears out of nowhere.

                    IZIA
Felt more like I was appearing into nowhere. What is this place anyway?

Izia sits.

KENDON

Dis is di Forge. It's a digital construct — an empty place.

IZIA

An empty place? For what?

KENDON

Dis one is a prison for I.

IZIA

Then how did I get here?

KENDON

Dat's as much a mystery to I as it is to you.

IZIA

So that's why you were so angry when you first saw me? You were expecting your jailor?

KENDON

I was.

IZIA

What'd you do?

KENDON

Many t'ings in me life, but neva what I was imprisoned for.

IZIA

And what's that?

KENDON

You want to know what I didn't do?

IZIA

Fair enough. So who are you?

KENDON

Names are tricky t'ings.

IZIA
(irritated)
Are you going to answer any of my questions?

KENDON
Alright, me name is Kendon Ker—

Izia explodes out of her chair.

IZIA
I knew it! You're Kendon Keron, the P-C-F General. You nuked Earth!

KENDON
(stern)
Every rope got two ends.

IZIA
What does that mean?

KENDON
It means dat I know dat story from a different perspective.

Kendon gestures to Izia's fallen chair. She looks at it suspiciously, but doesn't move toward it.

IZIA
So what's your end of the rope?

KENDON
I neva nuked Earth — me people were still living on Earth!

IZIA
No, the P-C-F all moved to Mars.

KENDON
No, some of us moved to Mars, but not all of us, not even most of us. Most of us stayed on Earth.

Kendon nods at the chair, causing it to blink out of existence. It immediately reappears in its original, upright position at the table.

IZIA

Then how did you survive the wars — The Ruin?

Izia moves to the chair and sits.

KENDON

Di same way you survive now on Callisto — we went underground, or undersea anyway. But dat all started long afore Mars. And dat's when di P-C-F first encountered di beast dat is your Nya-dira. When we went undersea, we invented di hive tech. We sold dat tech to Nya-dira for a fortune in Soldium — Soldium dat became wort'less on Earth when she moved SoldiCorp to Jupiter!

IZIA

So why didn't you just move to Jupiter too?

KENDON

And it's dat easy to move an entire civilization halfway across di Solar System? Di furthest we could go was Mars, so we went. And we struggled dere until di development of our Dyson Reflectors increased di potential of our solar fields exponentially. Now, dey float out dere — clouds of 'em — god knows where—

IZIA

Get to the part where you invade our system, try to seize Europa, and start an interplanetary war.

KENDON

It wasn't an invasion! It was di second part of our diaspora! Your Nya-dira sold us di rights to dat moon—

IZIA

Nadira sold you Europa? Yeah right!

KENDON

Doubt all you like, youn' gyal, but dat's di truth.

IZIA

First of all, I already told you that's not my name. Second, what could you possibly have had worth enough to buy an entire moon?

KENDON

Besides all di soldi we had from sellin' your Nya-dira our hive tech?

IZIA

I don't think she would have sold you a moon for any amount of soldi. And why do you keep saying 'your Nadira?' The Diaspora was hundreds of years ago — it was a totally different person.

KENDON

It was di same one.

IZIA

You haven't even seen the current one — she can't be older than forty.

KENDON

Try four hundred, at least.

IZIA

Bullshit. Even with age regression treatments every year, she would never make it past two hundred — it's just not humanly possible.

KENDON

Aye, dat's di truth — it's not humanly possible.

IZIA

Stop talking in circles!

KENDON

Ain't it simple? Nya-dira ain't human.

IZIA

(sarcastic)
Right. So what is she then?

KENDON

An android.

IZIA
(laughing)
An android?

KENDON
She's switched bodies a few times over di years, but it's di same consciousness.

IZIA
That's ridiculous.

KENDON
It's not ridiculous — it's how we bought di moon! We had some-t'ing dat was wort' more dan any amount of soldi to your Nya-dira, more dan a moon even — android tech. And we weren't about to sell it for any more magic beans!

IZIA
Androids don't exist — they're a myth at best. And how would you even know something like that?

Kendon LAUGHS drily.

KENDON
Because I was an android.

Kendon's face turns bitter.

KENDON (cont'd)
Afore she stuck me in dis empty hell.

IZIA
(disbelief)
You <u>were</u> an android?

KENDON
Aye.

IZIA
And before that you were, what? Born? Created? How does an android's life start?

KENDON

I didn't start me life as an android. I was born like any otha human, but A-L-S took ova me body when I was still young.

IZIA

A-L-S?

KENDON

Amyotrophic lateral sclerosis. It destroyed me body. Dat's why me consciousness firs' went digital. Me mama invented di tech to save me consciousness while me body died, and she spent di rest of her life developing android tech to give I a body to live in. Dat's how I became an android.

IZIA

And what are you now?

KENDON

A caged digital consciousness.

IZIA

If you're digital, then you have to be stored somewhere.

KENDON

Cleva gyal. Aye, I is a memory living on memory — I uploaded me consciousness to one of our reflectors when Nya-dira's drone army attacked. I meant to take ova di cloud, to use it to defend our planets, but di cloud lost connection when our planetary comms stations were destroyed. She nuked Earth and Mars seconds after I transubstantiated. I was lucky to make it out at all.

IZIA

You expect me to believe that Nadira nuked Earth?

KENDON

She knew dat whoeva destroyed di Earth would be hated for all eternity—

IZIA

That still doesn't explain why she would want to destroy the Earth in the first place—

KENDON

Because we had finally won! URN had fallen and di Earth was ours. Dat's why your Nya-dira nuked it at di same time she destroyed our Martian colonies. She wiped us out root and stem. I'm all dat's left of di P-C-F. But it's like me papa use'ta say — moon run fast, but day catch'im.

IZIA
(exasperated)
What does that even mean?

KENDON

It means dere is no escape from justice.

Izia looks around pointedly, then back at Kendon.

IZIA
Is this justice then?

KERON

D'ya t'ink ya have to point out di irony for me, gyal? Di locks are digitally coded to her D-N-A! Until I get some of dat, dis is home sweet home — P-C-F-D-R oh-eight-dash-one-six-t'ree-dash-two.

Kendon leans conspiratorially toward Izia

KENDON (cont'd)
You know, you could free me, Izia. A drop of her saliva, sweat, even blo—

IZIA
And then what? You infect our oceans with another virus—

KENDON
I had not'ing to do wi' t'ose viruses! Dat could just as likely'a been URN as anyone else.

IZIA
So you just resume your war with Nadira then? Your war on my home? I don't think so.

KENDON

I no longer seek revenge, just freedom.

IZIA

What would you even do? Where would you go?

KENDON

I'd steer me ship far away from here. Always wanted to see di Centauri System.

IZIA

And you expect me to just take your word for that?

KENDON

What else can I do? Wait another couple hundred years for anotha youn' gy— anotha Izia to stumble upon I?

IZIA

Look, even if I agreed to help you, how would you get her D-N-A from wherever you are?

KENDON

I can scan it from here. You just need to get it to di surface.

Izia stands slowly.

IZIA

I don't <u>need</u> to do anything. I never said I was going to help you. I mean, I'm sorry that you've been imprisoned for so long, but I'm not going to commit treason to free you. Whatever happened between you and Nad-ira has nothing to do with me.

Izia backs away from the table. A frown settles on Kendon's face as he leans back into his chair. He stands to leave, but the Forge is already changing; the thin grid lines rapidly expand, erasing the Forge in a flash of indigo.

[/THE FORGE] - INT. ELEVATOR

The CHIME SOUNDS at double-time [8]. Izia steps out of the elevator.

INT. HALLWAY

Izia slowly walks down the curved, cylindrical hallway. She arrives at the door to the Water Treatment Facility and punches in her code, but the door refuses to open. She tries — once, twice — but the door remains obstinate. She casts an exasperated look at the camera above the door. As she turns away from the door, it slides open.

INT. WATER TREATMENT FACILITY

Robbie sits in front of the control panel. His eyes remain fixed on the screen as Izia enters.

> ### ROBBIE
> Hey, Iz.

> ### IZIA
> Since when do we lock the door around here?

> ### ROBBIE
> Huh?

> ### IZIA
> The door, it wouldn't open for me.

> ### ROBBIE
> (distracted)
> How'd you walk in here den?

> ### IZIA
> What?

> ### ROBBIE
> Huh?

> ### IZIA
> Never mind.

Izia nods at the wall opposite the door, newly decorated with a digital recreation of a painting. Two brightly lit men stand in the center of the frame. They lead a company of militiamen who each stand frozen in a pose of interrupted raucousness. Tucked behind the leaders of the company, two young girls in ceremonial dresses are similarly illuminated.

                    IZIA (cont'd)
What happened here?

Robbie doesn't look up from his work at the control panel.

                    ROBBIE
De Compagnie van Kapitein Frans Banninck Cocq en Luitenant Willem Van Ruytenburgh.

Izia frowns and raises an eyebrow.

                    ROBBIE (cont'd)
Used to hang in de *Kloveniersdoelen.*

                    IZIA
Give me a break Robbie — you know I don't speak Dutch.

Robbie shrugs.

                    ROBBIE
        Learn.

                    IZIA
No one even speaks it here!

                    ROBBIE
Plannin' on stayin' here your whole life are you?

                    IZIA
I dunno...no.

Robbie looks at Izia, blinks, then SIGHS through his nose.

                    ROBBIE
S'just an old painting dat used to hang in an old buildin'. Somedin' to remind me of home.

IZIA

It's beautiful. Who painted—

The sound of the door sliding open interrupts Izia. She and Robbie both turn toward the noise. Nadira stands in the doorway, her face devoid of emotion.

ROBBIE

Hey, Nadi—

NADIRA

Excuse us, Izia.

Nadira steps into the room, then gestures toward the door. As Izia steps out of the room, she casts a quick glance at Robbie and sees her own mild confusion reflected back at her from his face.

INT. HALLWAY

The door to the Water Treatment Facility slides shut. Izia backs against the curved wall opposing the door, leans against it, and slides into a seated position. After a moment of waiting, she crosses her arms, rests her elbows on her knees, rests her head on her crossed arms, and closes her eyes.

INT. HALLWAY - NIGHT

MUSIC CUE: "Above You," by Supermachiner

Izia looks up with a start. The hallway lights are dim and tinged with an unusual cobalt hue. A panel in the wall near the floor slides open and a small, squat drone scuttles out. Its myriad blue-metal legs move in concert as it approaches Izia. It tries to skirt around her, but falls off the walkway and lands on its back. Izia watches the drone's underbelly as its legs continue to gesticulate. She looks around suspiciously, then grasps one of the drones thin legs and bends it backwards against its socket. The leg breaks off with a snap. Izia stabs her improvised scalpel into the drone's underbelly and drags it toward her, leaving a ragged incision. She peels back soft, synthetic skin, then gasps, drops her scalpel, and kicks the abomination away from her. Blood spatters the hallway as the drone spins away on its back. Izia, her face a mask of disbelief, moves closer to the drone again. She crouches and, with a tentative hand, reopens the drone's interior cavity. Set inside the drone's carapace, a thick ball of deep red muscle pumps regularly. Izia kicks the drone away again and buries her face in her blood-stained hands, refusing to believe what she has seen. She slowly lifts her head and looks around her, from the blood sprays on the wall, to the puddle at her feet, to the drone's snapped off leg laying near her foot. Resolve settles on her face as she snatches the bloody tool from the floor and slices her own chest open along her sternum. She uses both hands to pull back her uniform, then layers of skin and muscle. Viscous, black oil pours onto the floor from the bottom of her wound while thick smoke billows upwards from the top. She tries to scream, but smoke fills her mouth the moment her lips part.

END MUSIC

INT. HALLWAY - DAY

Izia opens her eyes with a start. The doors in front of her open and Nadira storms out of the Water Treatment Facility. She casts a quick glance at Izia's troubled face, but doesn't hesitate as she passes. Izia stands and walks through the open doors.

INT. WATER TREATMENT FACILITY

Robbie, fuming, paces back and forth across the small room.

>   **IZIA**
> Was that the inspection?

>   **ROBBIE**
> What de fuck is dat bitch on about?

>   **IZIA**
> Yeah, she looked pretty angry—

>   **ROBBIE**
> After all dese years, now she wants to come down here and start holdin' my hand?

>   **IZIA**
> I don't get it, Robbie. What happened?

>   **ROBBIE**
> Even asked about you.

IZIA

Me? What did she ask about me? Did she find out about the V-H?

ROBBIE

V-H? She knows about de V-H.

IZIA

What? How?

ROBBIE

How? Iz, she taught me how to make it. Well before she was her high and mighty Premier of de Jupiter System, she was my boss—

Robbie points to the floor.

ROBBIE (cont'd)

Here.

IZIA

So she knows? About everything?

ROBBIE

Well, it's not like I tell her every little ding dat happens, but she set up dis racket — I'm just runnin' it.

IZIA

So then what's wrong?

ROBBIE

What's wrong is she wants me to stop!

IZIA

Why?

ROBBIE

I don't know! And I don't much care. Stop, hmph — not in dis lifetime.

Robbie plops onto the room's lone chair and begins pulling up charts and blueprints on the wall screen.

ROBBIE (cont'd)

I just need a new source of water.

IZIA

Is that possible?

ROBBIE

Well, she sure as shit isn't goin' to let me keep takin' it from where I got it before!

IZIA

Where did you get it before?

ROBBIE

Eh?

IZIA

The water — where did you get it before?

ROBBIE

Same place as de rest of de water — de ocean.

IZIA

C'mon, Robbie. I learned about the subsurface ocean when I was four years old. Everybody knows that's where the Hive gets all of its water, but where did you get it to make your V-H?

ROBBIE

Sounds like you already know where de water comes from.

IZIA

Fine, Robbie — keep your secrets. I really don't feel like playing stupid games with you.

ROBBIE

Well, what do you want me to tell you? I got it from de same place as de rest of de water.
(beat)
I just took it before de final stage filters could register de intake.

IZIA

You mean before they could finish purifying the water! Are you crazy, Robbie? And you let me drink that poison?

ROBBIE

Hey! I didn't make you do anydin'. You're de one who came lookin' for de V-H. Where were your questions about de water yesterday?

(softening)

And anyway, de water was already safe by den. De final stage filters are just a fail safe.

IZIA

(sarcastic)

That makes me feel loads better. Thanks, Robbie.

ROBBIE

Jesus Christ, Iz, you've made your point — I won't let you drink any more of my poisonous swill. But just for your information, I haven't ever poisoned anyone before, and no one else is complainin' to me about a bad batch. You only feel ill because you're hungover. It's what happens when you drink too much.

INT. ELEVATOR

The elevator panel counts down as it ascends: [8 — 7]

INT. IZIA'S BEDROOM

The doors to Izia's bedroom slide open and she shuffles inside. She hurries to her bed and collapses facedown on top of it.

DOROTHY

Good evening, Iz. How was your day today?

IZIA

So. Tired.

DOROTHY

What would you like for dinner tonight? I'll stick with my recommendation from last night, since you neglected to eat it then. You

really do need to keep up your strength, young lady. What do you
say, Iz? Iz?

The wall display shows the Sleep Analysis window.

DOROTHY (cont'd)

Goodnight, Iz.

INT. VALHALLA HIVE - VAN DYKE APARTMENT - DAY

The door to the Van Dyke apartment opens, and Jane steps into an enormous,
multilevel rotunda. Everything in the apartment is immaculately white. A
large, carpeted staircase leads to a landing, then splits and continues to rise in
either direction. JULIA descends from the landing. She appears fit and in her
early 20s, but the barest indigo traces of age regression treatments creep
from behind her earlobes and the corners of her eyes. Her flaxen hair is tied
back in an elegant pattern of braids. She holds a spherical glass in one hand,
in which bubbles slowly emerge from a colorless liquid and float toward the
ceiling.

JULIA

Goedenmiddag mijn dochter.

JANE

Where's my dad?

JULIA

(sarcastic)
Good afternoon to you too, Mom.

As Julia reaches the bottom of the stairs, a small, flat drone flies to her side
and hovers near her shoulder. She finishes her drink and places her empty
glass atop the drone, who promptly flies away. An identical drone delivers a
fresh drink to her, then flies away in the same direction as its partner.

JANE

Where's. Dad.

JULIA

He's in his office.

Jane moves toward a small, circular stairwell to her right. Julia sidesteps to block her path.

JULIA (cont'd)
'He's in his office' means don't bother him.

JANE
But I need him.

JULIA
He's busy.

JANE
Great. Thanks, Mom.

JULIA
What? What do you need?

JANE
Apparently nothing important! Nothing ever is — unless it's about your golden child. But I didn't swim out of your vagina like some kind of fish, so—

JULIA
Keep your voice down! Do you know what would happen if anyone knew the truth about Jason?

JANE
What would happen? We'd pay off some nobody and the problem would disappear?

JULIA
Not all problems can be solved so easily. You know perfectly well that natural births are forbidden on Valhalla. If anyone ever found out that the President of the Supreme Court violated the Hive's charter—

The apartment door slides open and Jason steps inside.

JANE
They'd probably toss the little mutant into space.

The door closes behind Jason. Julia takes a step toward Jane and SLAPS her across the face.

> **JULIA**
> Shut your mouth this instant! Keep up this behavior, young lady, and your father and I will send you to Level Thirty-five.

> **JANE**
> You can't send me there! It's a boarding school for delinquents! And it's all the way in the Asgard Apiary!

> **JULIA**
> We can, and we will. You're on thin ice, Jane. Now go to your room.

> **JANE**
> But I have to talk to Dad!

> **JULIA**
> Your father doesn't have time for any of your nonsense tonight.

> **JANE**
> It's not nonsense!

Jane vents one final SCREAM as she STOMPS up the stairs to her bedroom. Jason watches her from the sealed doorway, blinking but emotionless.

> **JULIA**
> *Kom hier, mein geliefkoosd.*

As Jason walks toward his mother, his FOOTSTEPS grow increasingly louder.

INT. IZIA'S BEDROOM - NIGHT

Izia wakes to the sound of KNOCKING on her metal door. Her room is dimly lit, the walls themselves providing the faint glow. She lifts her head off her pillow groggily.

> **IZIA**
> Wha's'at noise?

DOROTHY

Sorry, Iz. I <u>told</u> the young man to return at a more decent hour—

Izia leaps out of bed and dashes to the door.

DOROTHY (cont'd)

But he refuses to—

IZIA

Door open.

The door slides open. Samir stands in the doorway, looking down the hallway amusedly.

SAMIR

Will you check out this little guy?

A squat, cumbersome drone rumbles into view behind Samir. It continues down the hallway and out of frame, leaving behind a slightly cleaner walkway marred by two nearly parallel tread tracks.

SAMIR (cont'd)

I don't think he's going to make it much further.

IZIA

What're you doing here, Samir?

SAMIR

I came to see what happened tonight.

IZIA

Tonight?

SAMIR

Yeah, why didn't you want to come to the g-ball court with me?

IZIA

I — I just couldn't. Nadira showed up at the Drain, and then Robbie was losing it.

SAMIR

What about last night? You disappeared from my party so quickly that I didn't even get a chance to say goodnight.

IZIA

Jane said goodnight for both of you.

SAMIR

Jane? What's she got to do with anything?

IZIA

She — she explained everything last night.

SAMIR

What's to explain? And Jane doesn't speak for me.

IZIA

Your girlfriend doesn't speak for you?

SAMIR

Girlfriend? Z, that's just gross. I mean, have you met Jane?

IZIA

Then you've never slept with her?

SAMIR
(suspicious)
I'm not really sure that's any of your business—
(beat)
But no, I've never slept with Jane. Who said that I had?

IZIA

She did.

SAMIR

Jane said that I slept with her?

IZIA

She said a lot more than that.

SAMIR

Look, I don't know what her problem is, but I'm going to talk to her tomorrow and straighten things out.

IZIA

No! Don't do that, Sam. It's not important. Really.

SAMIR

It's important to me. Why should she get to tell lies whenever she pleases?

IZIA

It might have something to do with her family owning half of the Hive.

SAMIR
(bitter)
Like anyone could forget.

Samir shifts his weight, jams his hands into his waist pockets, then smiles.

SAMIR (cont'd)

I almost forgot! I brought you something.

Samir pulls a thin, rectangular case out of one of the waist pockets of his uniform. He presses a button along the side of the case and a tray slides out. A tiny disk sits in the center of the tray. It is transparent and barely visible except for the tracers of silver running back and forth across the thin membrane.

IZIA

Is that—

SAMIR

A NeurOptical Implant, yeah. I got a new one yesterday, so I figured you could have my old one, y'know, if you wanted.

IZIA

Huh?

SAMIR

Z, I'm kidding, obviously. How gross, right? No, it's new. It's Dytech's latest model — the G-A-seventy-one. Now you can—

IZIA

Samir, I can't accept that.

SAMIR

Sure you can.

IZIA

That N-O-I must have cost more soldi than I've ever seen.

Samir shrugs.

SAMIR

What am I supposed to do with it?

Izia looks quizzically at Samir.

SAMIR (cont'd)

I got three of them, and I'll probably get at least one more when I see my grandparents for Pacem. I've only got the two eyes. Really, take it.

Samir slides the tray back into the case and offers it to Izia. She doesn't take it.

IZIA

I don't know, Sam... and I should really go anyway; I need to finish reviewing for tomorrow.

SAMIR

Do you want some company?

Dorothy's voice blasts out the open doorway.

DOROTHY

She doesn't need that kind of company!

SAMIR

Whoa, who's that?

IZIA

Oh, that's Dorothy.

SAMIR

Likes me, doesn't she?

IZIA

Ignore her. Look, you can come in for a few minutes if it means we can stop standing around in the hallway.

Izia steps backwards into her room. Samir follows and the doors slide closed behind him.

SAMIR

Tell you what — I'll be your audience so you can practice. I'll sit here—

Samir sets the NOI case on Izia's nightstand and hops into a sitting position at the foot of her bed.

SAMIR (cont'd)

And you can stand there and recite your presentation. What's your topic?

IZIA

SoldiCorp.

Izia moves to the head of her bed and sits facing Samir, one leg underneath her and the other dangling off the side of the bed.

IZIA (cont'd)

But I don't feel like reciting my whole speech right now. You'll just have to wait until tomorrow like everyone else.

SAMIR

Oh, alright. So what do you want to do?

IZIA

Sleep.

Izia reclines in her bed and drapes her legs across Samir.

DOROTHY

For which she needs no assistance from you!

IZIA

Don't mind Dorothy — she's just protective. After all, she's the only family I have left.

Samir starts rubbing one of Izia's feet.

IZIA (cont'd)
(drowsy)
Mmm, that feels nice.

SAMIR

What happened to the rest of your family? I mean, you had to be assigned to someone or your embryo wouldn't have been processed.

IZIA

Both my parents died just before I finished gestation.

SAMIR

Z, that's awful. I'm so sorry.

The wall display shows the Sleep Analysis window.

SAMIR (cont'd)
How come they didn't assign you to another—

DOROTHY
(hissing)
Can't you see she's trying to sleep!

INT. IZIA'S BEDROOM - DAY

Izia lies prone on top of her bed in her brightly illuminated room.

DOROTHY
Good morning, Iz.

                    IZIA

Mmm, morning, Dorothy.

                  DOROTHY

How are you feeling today?

                    IZIA

Tired.

Izia rolls toward the inside of the bed and stretches her arm out, searching.
She sits up in her bed.

                IZIA (cont'd)

Where's Samir?

                  DOROTHY

The young man left an hour after you fell asleep last night. He
intended to wake you, but I would not have it — you got little
enough sleep as it is.

                    IZIA

Is that all?

                  DOROTHY

No. The young man asked me to tell you that he had a wonderful
evening and that he will see you in class.

Izia hops out of bed and dashes into the bathroom.

               IZIA (OFF SCREEN)

Was that so hard?

                  DOROTHY

You tell me.

The sound of RUSHING WATER cascades out of the bathroom, followed by
the sound of BLASTING WIND accompanied by a slightly blue flash of
light. Izia, freshly cleaned, walks out of the bathroom.

                    IZIA

Oh, enough. Keep it up and I'll adjust your empathy settings.

Izia kicks open a panel in the wall and retrieves a fresh uniform. She quickly slips it on, then steps into her shoes.

DOROTHY
It would be quite unforgivable for such an intrusive—

IZIA
Kidding, Dorothy, I'm only kidding.

DOROTHY
Don't forget your N-O-I.

IZIA
Oh, yeah, I don't think I'm going to wear that actually. I mean, it was really sweet of Samir to give it to me, but that's way too expensive for me to keep, right?

DOROTHY
Unacceptable.

IZIA
Yeah, that's what I thought—

DOROTHY
No! Not using the gift that nice boy gave you is unacceptable.
(beat)
Especially after all the work I went to this morning to sync you with all of the essentials.

IZIA
The essentials?

DOROTHY
You're connected to your room cam, the hallway cam, and to me.

IZIA
To you?

DOROTHY
Well, of course to me.

IZIA

Oh, of course—

DOROTHY

Now I can monitor you from here, and we can communicate if anything changes. Your health looks better, but there's still something off with your amino levels.

IZIA

Talk to me? Through my eye?

DOROTHY

It's just an expression. The N-O-I signals directly to your brain, so you'll hear me, but not with your ears.

Izia picks up the thin, rectangular case from where it lies on her nightstand. She presses the button along the side, ejecting the case's tray, then hesitates.

DOROTHY (cont'd)

Go on, Iz.

Izia touches the tip of her finger to the transparent disk, then brings her finger to her face and presses the disk against her eye. The disk flashes silver as it settles onto her eye, then disappears.

DOROTHY (cont'd)

What do you think?

IZIA

Whoa. How do I—

DOROTHY

You just think what you want to say.

IZIA (VOICE OVER)

LIKE THIS?

DOROTHY

Try to think a bit more quietly, dear.

                    IZIA (V.O.)
Sorry. Like this?

                    DOROTHY
Much better. Now, drink your breakfast and get going!

The panel in the wall near her bed slides open, revealing a glass full of
lavender liquid.

                    IZIA
Can you make it to go?

The panel slides closed, then reopens, revealing a large, lavender bubble. Izia
pulls the bubble from the wall cavity along with a thin, silver straw.

                    IZIA (cont'd)
Thanks, Dorothy!

Izia stabs the straw through the bubble's thin membrane. She sips from the
straw as she hurries out her bedroom door.

                    DOROTHY
Don't run with that straw in your mouth!

INT. CLASSROOM

Izia sucks down the last of the lavender liquid as she enters the classroom.
The remainder of the bubble's thin membrane condenses at the tip of the
straw. A quick scan of the room shows her that only Jane is missing. She
tucks the straw into her waist pocket as she takes her seat.

                    MRS. NOLE
Up front please, Izia. You can begin once Jane arrives.

Izia makes her way to the front of the classroom as Jane strolls through the
irising door.

                    JANE
Here I am — don't have a heart attack.

MRS. NOLE

Take your seat, Jane.

Jane walks directly to Izia's seat and sits, embellishing her every movement. Mrs. Nole pulls her small tablet from the breast pocket of her uniform. She dims the lights and activates the holographic projector, then moves to the back corner of the classroom.

MRS. NOLE (cont'd)

Go ahead, Izia.

IZIA

Yes, Mrs. Nole. My topic is SoldiCorp. During the twenty-first century on Earth, climate change — a phenomenon of increasing planetary temperatures with an accompanying increase in extreme weather events — continued to accelerate, and the entire planet suffered. This led to social unrest and then anarchy as governments bloodily imploded, quietly disbanded, or were violently overthrown. Anarchy soon gave way to tyranny as autocrats seized power; ambitious entrepreneurs established corporate governments; and socio-fascist collectives formed, tore themselves apart, and disintegrated. All manner of systems proliferated in the power vacuum. All attempted extraterrestrial settlements with varying levels of success.

Jane removes a small charm from a thin, silver bracelet on her wrist. She holds the charm at arm's length from her face and squeezes it. The charm hangs in the air. The edges of a digital screen appear in the space around the charm. The space inside the edges opaques.

IZIA (cont'd)

SoldiCorp, a technology conglomerate, deployed a cohort of autonomous, self-replicating drones to construct a series of settlements on the moons of Jupiter. They chose Callisto as the optimal site for settlement thanks in large part to the complete lack of plate tectonics, volcanism, or any other geologic activity. They decided to construct underground settlements to avoid the lunar impacts that were still common occurrences. The first of these settlements, the Valhalla Hive, was dug into the Valhalla Crater, the largest impact crater on Callisto.

Jane puts three fingers near the charm and spreads them apart. As she does so, the four corners of the digital screen extend. She makes a quick gesture with her hand and the screen displays a mirrored image of her face.

> **IZIA (cont'd)**
> The drones replicated while constructing the Valhalla Hive, and SoldiCorp was left with several legions of drones once construction was completed. They set these to farming and mining moons and asteroids, while continuing to replicate. The drones also began strategically maintaining the outer moons, along with the Trojan Asteroids, in order to protect the colony on Callisto from any further lunar impacts.

Jane continues to control the screen with hand gestures. She begins adjusting the brightness and color in her cheeks and eyes, admiring the effects on the mirror-like surface of the digital screen. The students near Jane turn their attention to her.

> **IZIA (cont'd)**
> In two thousand fifty-one, SoldiCorp personnel began arriving on Callisto to inhabit the Valhalla Hive. Construction then immediately began on a series of new hives called the Asgard Apiary. These hives, located in the Asgard Crater, were designed on a monumental scale that dwarf the Valhalla Hive.

> **JANE**
> (under her breath)
> Hmph, like you're poor ass will ever see Asgard.

All of the students except Samir have turned their attention to Jane. Mrs. Nole steps to the rear of the classroom.

> **IZIA (cont'd)**
> In two thousand sixty, SoldiCorp CEO Nadira Fassax Sharmouthy arrived on Callisto just in time to celebrate the grand opening of the Asgard Apiary. Despite the massive nature of the undertaking, construction of the Apiary was completed in half the time it took to complete the Valhalla Hive. Upon Nadira's departure, all remaining company personnel were required to depart Earth or be terminated.

As Jane leans closer to her digital self and begins experimenting with different blends of color, Mrs. Nole inches toward her. The other students sit mesmerized by the display.

> **IZIA (cont'd)**
> The following day, SoldiCorp's last remaining planet class vessel departed Earth.

Mrs. Nole SLAPS the floating charm out of the air. It SMACKS into the wall, the digital screen disappears, and the charm falls to the floor.

> **JANE**
> Hey!

Jane presses her thumb against a link in her bracelet. The charm responds by leaping into the air and flying back to Jane, who quickly inspects it.

> **JANE (cont'd)**
> You're lucky you didn't break it!

> **MRS. NOLE**
> Care to give me another opportunity?

Jane casts a contemptuous look at Mrs. Nole, but returns the charm to her bracelet. Mrs. Nole returns to the rear of the classroom.

> **MRS. NOLE (cont'd)**
> Please continue, Izia.

> **IZIA**
> Oh, erm, so in addition to leading the first interplanetary corporation, Nadira was also the first private citizen to construct her own interplanetary fleet. Her greatest victory, however, came in two thousand seventy-six, when she convinced the orphaned astronauts on Ganymede to sign the Galileo Charter and join SoldiCorp. With the signing of the Galileo Charter, Nadira established SoldiCorp as the official government of Callisto, and the broader Jupiter System.

Mrs. Nole uses her tablet to turn off the holographic projector.

MRS. NOLE

Very nice, Izia.
> (beat)

As for you Jane, that's now three successive classes that you have monopolized with your antics.

JANE

B-F-D.

MRS. NOLE

Excuse me, young lady?

JANE

I said — Big. Fucking. Deal.

Mrs. Nole's face hardens. She puts one hand on her hip and points her other hand toward the door.

MRS. NOLE

Get out of my class.

JANE

As though there's a single person living in this system who doesn't know about SoldiCorp and Nadira Sharmouthy!

MRS. NOLE

Get up and leave. I will not tolerate any more of your disrespectful

—

JANE

I'm not going anywhere. I'm going to sit right here for as long as I want.

Mrs. Nole clenches her jaws. She regains her composure, then addresses Jane.

MRS. NOLE

Very well. Sit there, relax, get comfortable. I'll just summon your father.

JANE

Yeah, you go ahead and do that. I'm sure he'll answer the call of a glorified babysitter.

MRS. NOLE

Perhaps he wouldn't answer the summons of your teacher, but I think his interest will be piqued when the headmaster buzzes to notify him that his daughter has been recommended for expulsion.

Jane's confidence falters.

JANE

Right — I mean, like you even have access to Old Man Fuller—

MRS. NOLE

<u>Doctor</u> Fuller has been a dear friend of mine for longer than you have existed, young lady.

Jane's eyes follow Mrs. Nole as she strides out of the room, then settle on Izia, still standing uncomfortably. Jane's face transforms once again into a mask of rage accented by a demonic glow from her bioluminescent cheeks and eyes.

JANE

Now look what you did!

Izia's eyebrows jump up her forehead in shock.

IZIA

What <u>I</u> did?

SAMIR

Give it a rest, Jane.

Jane's eyes remain glued to Izia.

JANE

Why don't you mind your own business, Samir.

SAMIR

I guess because you've been doing quite a job minding my business for me.

JANE

Huh? This has nothing to do with you.

SAMIR

And you telling everybody that we're sleeping together, does that also have nothing to do with me?

Jane turns to face Samir, her rage replaced by surprise.

JANE

What? That's — that's not even what I— I—

SAMIR

Save your lies, Jane. We all see you for exactly what you are.

Jane looks around the room, hate pouring from her eyes. She points at Izia, still standing uncomfortably at the front of the room.

JANE

She's nothing! A less attractive version of me, nothing more! She has no soldi, no family, no friends — nothing! She has nothing! She is nothing.

SAMIR

She is so much more than you will ever be.

Izia scans the room while Jane and Samir stare each other down. None of the other students will meet Izia's eyes; each of their faces is a portrait of controlled neutrality. Izia takes a tentative step backwards, then turns and dashes out of the classroom.

INT. ELEVATOR

Jason and Izia stand together in a vacant elevator — worry is etched across his face, while hers is sweat-damp and flushed. The CHIME SOUNDS (260 Hz) as the elevator doors begin to close. A hand grabs the edge of the closing door, and Jane's head appears in the widening gap. Jane enters the elevator and the doors slide shut behind her. Her face is still a bio-illuminated mask of rage.

JASON
Hey, Jane.

JANE
Shut. Up.

The CHIME SOUNDS as the elevator begins to descend. Jane reaches out and presses a large, red button labeled 'EMERGENCY STOP,' then turns to face Izia.

JANE
Samir won't even talk to me now because of you!

IZIA
No, he won't talk to you because of your idiotic plan to frame him for—

JANE
You think you're so fucking smart.

IZIA
Smart enough to know not to manipulate the people I care about.

JANE
And don't you just care about everyone — even pathetic little raisin-headed freaks!

Jane grabs Jason roughly by the collar of his uniform and yanks him toward her.

JANE (cont'd)
What do you say, Jason?

JASON
Lemme go!

Jason squirms against Jane's grasp. She SLAMS him against the wall of the elevator, dazing him. Izia GASPS.

                              IZIA

    Let him go!

Jane holds Jason against the wall.

                              JANE

    Isn't it funny, little brother? She's not even related to you, and still
    she cares so much about you. It makes it so easy to hurt her.

Jane lets go of Jason's collar and wraps her hand around his throat. She looks
over her shoulder at Izia — Jane malicious, Izia horrified — then turns her
attention back to Jason. She wraps her remaining hand around his throat and
lifts him off the ground slightly.

                              IZIA

    I said let him go!

                              JANE

    Why don't you make me, E-Z! All of this is your own damn fault
    —

Izia kicks the back of Jane's knee. Jane SCREAMS from rage as much as
pain and drops Jason. He collapses onto his hands and knees on the floor and
HUFFS air. Izia depresses the emergency stop button.

                              IZIA

    Get out of here, Jason!

The CHIME SOUNDS as the elevator doors open [5]. Jason scrambles out,
and Izia steps in front of Jane, blocking the doorway.

                          IZIA (cont'd)

    What the hell is wrong with you? That's your brother!

                              JANE

    He's no more my brother than you're my sister. You're both just
    incubated puddles of protein!

The CHIME SOUNDS as the doors close. Jane SCREAMS again and lunges
toward Izia, lashing out with a sloppy right-hook. Izia's precise movements
occur so rapidly that they are nearly imperceptible. She uses her left arm to

block Jane's hook, then slams the heel of her right hand into Jane's diaphragm. Jane's body heaves as the air escapes her lungs. She doubles over, GASPING for breath. Izia looks at her hands incredulously. The CHIME SOUNDS as the elevator doors open [6].

                    IZIA
     Just stay away from me, Jane.

Izia turns halfway to leave, looks from the open door to Jane's crumpled form, back to the doorway, then finishes her turn and takes a step out the door. Izia falls face first on the floor, hard. She looks back and sees Jane's outstretched hand clutching her trailing foot. Jane pulls Izia by the leg back toward the elevator.

                    JANE
     No! I'm not done with you!

Jane crouches, then stands. Izia acts automatically; she lunges toward Jane, dodges to avoid her impossibly slow punches, then wraps her hands around Jane's neck and lifts her off the ground.

                    IZIA
     Enough!

Izia's face flushes with rage, while Jane's face begins to turn blue, her eyes fearful.
                    IZIA
     I have had enough of your—

Jane kicks Izia in the stomach and both girls collapse in a heap on the floor. The CHIME SOUNDS as the elevator doors open [7]. Jane stumbles out of the elevator and the doors begin to close. Izia rapidly looks to her left and right, gauging the doors' progress. In one fluid movement, she grabs Jane by her arm and yanks her back into the elevator. Jane's body clears the closing doors as she tumbles into the elevator.

                    IZIA (cont'd)
     I said, I have had enough—

Jane rolls over and sees that her trailing arm is cut off just above the elbow, her trailing foot also missing. She thrashes hysterically while blood spurts out of her gruesome wounds, her arm staining her uniform and her leg flooding the elevator floor. Izia backs into the opposite corner of the elevator, staring at Jane's pooling blood on the floor. Jane HOWLS as she uses her remaining leg to push herself into the corner of the elevator. She struggles into a seated position, clutches her bloody stump of an arm to her chest, and WAILS.

JANE
I'll f-f-fucking k-kill you! You...you...you—

A panel on the elevator wall slides open and two clouds of micro-drones swarm out. The clouds fly to Jane's wounds, spread across the exposed flesh and bone, and bite down. Jane cries out sharply before the drones' drugs kick in; her eyes glaze over and she slumps against the wall. The CHIME SOUNDS as the elevator doors open [8].

INT. ELEVATOR - [THE FORGE]

The Forge flashes into Izia's vision, cutting in and out in bursts. Kendon's face dominates the indigo-gridded blackness, his eyebrows pinched in confusion.

KENDON
Izia? What are you doing deh'ya, gyal?

IZIA
Kendon? What the hell is happening to me? I think I just killed Jane! I didn't mean to! I was just pulling her back into the elevator and the door sensors must have failed and—

KENDON
I saw what happened, Izia, but it was no failure — it was you.

IZIA
What do you mean? How could it have been me?

KENDON
Di code you sent di doors was clear as day to di trained eye — you ova'rode di sensors.

IZIA

But how could I?
(beat)
Trained eye? Eye — it's the fucking N-O-I!

KENDON

Come again, gyal?

IZIA

The NeurOptical Implant that Samir gave me, it must have, I don't know, given me some kind of—

NADIRA

Izia? Is that you?

The Forge cuts out of Izia's vision. She shakes her head back and forth and her vision splits, one eye seeing clearly while the other shows her a video stream of the hallway past the elevator doors. She sees through her clear eye that Nadira stands in the distance. Nadira's gaze moves rapidly from the blood on Izia's uniform to the smears of it streaking the floor to Jane's slumped and unconscious form.

NADIRA (cont'd)

(firm)
Izia, I need you to step out of the elevator and—

KENDON

Run, gyal! What are you waiting for?

Izia furiously presses the 'DOOR CLOSE' button.

KENDON (cont'd)

Not dat way — use di N-O-I!

Izia's eye flashes silver, the CHIME SOUNDS, and the doors begin to close; she looks back down the hallway and sees Nadira sprinting toward her, drones pouring out of cavities in the walls around her. They are murderous creations of matte-black metal with spindly leges, streamlined and extend-able wings, multiple rotor arrangements, and all assortment of mean looking metal pokers, saw blades, and scalpels. The doors close just in time to prevent the cloud from penetrating the elevator; heavy THUDS shake the elevator in rapid succession as the drones crash into the sealed doors. The CHIME SOUNDS and the elevator begins to climb [8].

IZIA
Shit shit shit! What do I do?

The elevator lurches to a stop. The lights extinguish.

KENDON
Get dis carriage moving!

IZIA
How?

KENDON
Same way you closed di doors.

Izia closes her eyes and presses the palm of her hand against the elevator's control panel. The lights flicker on and the elevator resumes its ascent. The CHIME SOUNDS [7].

IZIA
What do I do, Kendon?

KENDON
Di surface! Get yourself to di surface.

IZIA
And then what?

KENDON
Worry about dat when you get dere. If she cyatches you—

IZIA
I know what happens if she catches me!

MUSIC CUE: "Doors Are Harder to Slam in the Summer," by Sex Positions

Sparks fly from the floor of the elevator as drones attempt to cut their way inside. Three small saw blades break through the floor, then retract, leaving a triangular hole. An optical wire snakes inside and begins to scan the elevator, but Izia rushes to stomp the life out of the appendage. The CHIME

SOUNDS [6]. Gas begins to seep into the elevator from the hole beneath Izia's foot, while smoke cascades from the ceiling. The CHIME SOUNDS [5].

####### IZIA (cont'd)
Open!

The doors slide open, revealing the interior of the elevator shaft as it rushes past. The next level comes into view and Izia dives out of the smoke-filled elevator. The CHIME begins to sound, TRILLS irregularly, then dies [4].

INT. HALLWAY

Kendon and the Forge continue to occupy half of Izia's field of vision.

####### KENDON
Where now?

Izia has already begun to sprint to the nearby bank of express elevators.

####### IZIA
I need a faster carriage.

Izia rounds the corner to the bank of elevators and nearly crashes into a pair of security officers in black and blue uniforms. She drops to her knees and slides through the gap between their legs, then pivots, extends one leg, and propels herself headfirst into an open elevator.

####### IZIA
Close!

The doors slam shut in response to her command. The CHIME SOUNDS [4].

####### KENDON
You don't have to say it. Just t'ink about what you want, like when you closed di doors on dat gyal dat looked—

####### IZIA
I didn't want that to happen! I just wanted to stop her from hurting Jason anymore.

KENDON

I'd say you succeeded.

The CHIME SOUNDS [3].

IZIA

Shut up! I'm trying to think.
    (beat)
I can't escape from her, can I?

KENDON

Trapped like a crab in a hole.

The CHIME SOUNDS [2].

IZIA

Well, at least one of us can escape.

KENDON

What?

IZIA

What do you need from Nadira to escape?

KENDON

Just get her to di surface. I can scan her D-N-A from dere.

The CHIME SOUNDS [1]. The doors begin to open, revealing a squad of security officers. The doors again slam shut before the lights in the elevator extinguish, and the elevator plummets. The CHIME SOUNDS with increasing speed [2 —— 3 — 4].

KENDON (cont'd)

What are you doing gyal? You're going di wrong way!

IZIA

I know a better way.

The CHIME SOUNDS rapidly [5-6-7-8]. The elevator suddenly halts its descent, the doors fly open, and Izia bolts down the hallway, away from the elevator and, farther away down the hall, the Water Treatment Facility.

END MUSIC

INT. HALLWAY

Izia slows her pace to a quick trot.

>   **IZIA**
> Show me the Trailhead Gateway cameras.

>   **KENDON**
> I don't have access to di Hive's closed circuit cameras—

>   **IZIA (V.O.)**
> Dorothy, can you hear me?

>   **KENDON**
> But if you could get me in to di system—

>   **DOROTHY**
> Izia, what's happened? Is that blood on your uniform—

>   **KENDON**
> Never met a security system I couldn't hack once I had access—

>   **IZIA**
> Will you shut up! I'm trying to get you in.

>   **DOROTHY**
> Excuse me?

>   **IZIA (V.O.)**
> Not you, Dorothy. I was talking to — someone else. Look, can you pull up the cameras at the Trailhead Gateway?

>   **DOROTHY**
> Iz, I don't have clearance to access those cameras. Even if I wanted to give you—

>   **IZIA (V.O.)**
> The bedroom cams then. Feed them into my N-O-I.

DOROTHY

Done.

IZIA

Can you see that, Kendon?

KENDON

Way ahead of ya, gyal. You now have access to all Hive cameras.

DOROTHY

Iz? How did you get access to those feeds?

IZIA (V.O.)

I'll explain later. Bye, Dorothy.

Izia winks repeatedly, each time scrolling to a new video feed from the Valhalla Hive's closed circuit camera system. She stops when she recognizes the Trailhead Gateway; zooms closer on the abandoned security desk. She winks again and sees a view of the elevator: a security guard kneels at Jane's side.

KENDON

Now's your chance, gyal!

Izia clears the Forge from her vision, and again bolts down the hallway toward the Trailhead Gateway.

INT. VALHALLA HIVE - TRAILHEAD GATEWAY

The Trailhead Gateway is deserted when Izia arrives. The cylindrical tunnel rises before her, levels out for just enough space to contain a security desk and several lockers, then continues to rise out of sight. Izia dashes to the lockers and hammers the 8 key on the wall-mounted keypad. The nearest locker doors swing open in response. Izia grabs a thick silver collar and matching bracelets from inside the locker, then quickly dons all three.

NADIRA

Izia, stop!

Izia spins on her heel and sees Nadira ten paces behind her on the hallway's inclining exit ramp.

KENDON

Keep going!

NADIRA

I need you to come with me, Izia.

IZIA

Stay back!

NADIRA

I'm sure you didn't mean to hurt that girl. It was just an accident. You're very sick—

IZIA

Sick? I'm not sick. Keep those drones away from me! I just—

NADIRA

Izia, I checked the logs from your health monitor: you've had a fever, chills, sweats, and now — it seems — hallucinations.

KENDON

She's lying to you.

IZIA

Hallucinations?

NADIRA

There are no drones, Izia.

IZIA

There were! They tried to kill me!

NADIRA

It's not real, Izia. You're seeing things because you're sick.

Izia winks the camera view back into her vision. She accesses a camera just behind Nadira, and scans the hallways. A horde of drones waits around the bend of the hallway — crouching, hovering, clinging to walls, peeking out from inside cavities in the ceiling and walls. Izia turns and sprints up the short remaining section of hallway before reaching a circular portal to the surface. The metal sheets of the door each slide back, and an octagonal aperture expands from the center. Izia dives through the opening, rolls, then quickly gets back to her feet.

EXT. CALLISTO - TRAILHEAD GATEWAY

As Izia emerges on the surface of Callisto, three transparent petals blossom from within the collar around her neck. The petals converge to form a bubble around Izia's head. The bracelets around her wrists echo the collar's action in miniature, protecting her hands from the vacuum of space.

> **KENDON**
> Dere you go, Iz. Just get her clear of dat awning and I can scan—

> **IZIA**
> Shut up! I need to think without you in my head.

Izia blinks the NeurOptical Implant out of her eye. Kendon and the Forge disappear from her vision. The Trailhead Gateway's portal reopens and Nadira slowly walks toward Izia. She wears no protective equipment, but remains unaffected. Nadira stops just short of emerging from the Trailhead Gateway's exterior awning.

> **NADIRA**
> Izia! Come back here—

> **IZIA**
> So you can throw me in prison for the rest of my life? Like Kendon?

Nadira stops walking.

> **NADIRA**
> What do you know about Kendon?

> **IZIA**
> I know that he's alive, that he's your prisoner!

> **NADIRA**
> Lies.

IZIA

And the Forge. Is that a lie too?

Nadira's face remains passive except for a minuscule twitch along the left side of her mouth.

IZIA (cont'd)

Yeah, I've been to the Forge. I know all about it. Kendon told me about you too. He told me what you both are—

NADIRA

I'm nothing like Kendon. He barely exists — a shadow in the darkness.

IZIA

Then what are you? Some kind of robot?

Nadira scowls at Izia.

NADIRA

I began as a diary. In the earliest days of the Earth computers, Nadira used me to record her most private thoughts. Before too long, she began tinkering with my code, and developed me — bit by bit, byte by byte — into something more. Eventually, she became me. I'm not just an android—

IZIA

So you did turn yourself into a robot — with Kendon's help of course since you weren't smart enough to do it on your own.

Nadira narrows her eyes at Izia.

NADIRA

Name calling will not help your situation—

IZIA

I've seen what you've been doing to Kendon, keeping him prisoner for centuries!

Frustration and impatience flood Nadira's face.

NADIRA

Kendon is not my prisoner. He only has himself to blame for being trapped in that Dyson hell.

IZIA

Then why are the locks coded to your D-N-A?

NADIRA

He's told you quite a bit, hasn't he? Only about me though. He obviously hasn't gotten around to telling you about himself, or what he knows about you, or how you got sick.

IZIA

I'm not sick. And even if I was, how would he know anything about it?

NADIRA

How do you think? He's the one who flooded our oceans with the virus that's ravaging your brain as we speak! A virus bioengineered for android bodies. It was meant for me, but you caught it. Bad luck, I'm afraid. I don't even know how his virus made it past the scrubbers, or how you came into contact with—

IZIA

That's absurd. How would a virus designed for an android affect me?

Nadira's stare bores into Izia.

IZIA (cont'd)
I'd know if I were a robot.

NADIRA

How else could you have accessed the Forge, a remote digital construct? How else could you have accessed my security systems? The cameras, the elevator—

IZIA

I thought it was the N-O-I that did—

NADIRA

You thought you could breach my security systems with a fucking N-O-I? That seemed logical to you? Our latest citizens come with those installed from birth!

IZIA

How else—

NADIRA

You're an android. Accept it, Izia.

IZIA

A sick android? How does that work, huh? I've never been sick before.

NADIRA

Never? Is that so?

IZIA

Yeah, it is.

NADIRA

And you're not curious how that could be?

IZIA

No, it's normal — no one gets sick in Valhalla.

NADIRA

No, people <u>rarely</u> get sick in Valhalla, but to never get sick — not even a sore throat? Ever? There's nothing normal about that.
(beat)
Well, nothing normal about that for a human, that is. Then again, Kendon's virus wouldn't kill a human.

Izia looks distrustfully at Nadira.

NADIRA (cont'd)

An android, on the other hand—

IZIA

I'm not dying. I feel loads better even.

NADIRA

Let's ask your new friend.

EXT. CALLISTO - [THE FORGE]

The darkness of the Forge swallows Izia and Nadira; they stand facing one another on the indigo-gridded plane. Nadira steps toward Izia, who immediately steps backward in response. Nadira smiles.

NADIRA

Relax. You want the truth? Listen for yourself.

Nadira unfolds the planes of the Forge like fabric — up from the floor, then a series of lateral unfolds to create a partition in front of Izia. Nadira steps away from the partition. She snaps her fingers and Kendon appears before her.

KENDON

Hey! I was busy.

NADIRA

Doing what?

KENDON

What do you want, Nya-dira?

NADIRA

First, I want you to stop trying to decode the locks here. You're not going to crack them — they're much too complex.

KENDON

Complex? <u>Your</u> coding? Spare I di jokes.

NADIRA

I'd also like to know why you infected the girl.

KENDON

You know dya-mn well dat wasn't my fault.

NADIRA

Don't lie to me, Kendon! The bioengineering has your fingerprints all over it.

KENDON

Di bioengineering was done based on your D-N-A from di much-too-complex-for-I-to-crack locks! I don't know how it infected di gyal. I designed dat virus for you alone!

IZIA

What?

Izia steps from behind her digital curtain.

MUSIC CUE: "Drop (Mogwai Remix)," by Ludovico Einaudi

IZIA (cont'd)

She was telling the truth then? I'm infected? And it's your virus? It's your fault that I'm sick?

KENDON

It's Nya-dira's fault you're sick!

NADIRA

I didn't create that virus.

IZIA

(screaming)
Is it yours?

KENDON

You were never meant to catch it! It was only supposed to kill di beast!

IZIA

(panicked)
What do you mean it was supposed to <u>kill</u> her? There's a cure, right? This isn't going to kill me.

KENDON

You were dead days ago — it's just been catchin' up to you.

Izia remains motionless for a moment — just a moment — before moving with absolute purpose: she straightens all the fingers on her right hand into a broad, flat blade and thrusts her arm toward Kendon. The momentum of the movement stretches her arm to twice its normal length and sends her hand into Kendon's chest. Once she penetrates his digital skin, she curls her hand into a fist inside Kendon's chest, then flicks all of her fingers outwards. Kendon's face barely has time to effect a look of sheer terror before his body explodes in a shower of bright indigo pixels. Izia, wild-eyed, turns to Nadira.

IZIA

What did Kendon mean that it's your fault I got sick? Why would his virus even affect me if it was designed for your D-N-A?

NADIRA

Our D-N-A. You were created from my own genetic material.

IZIA

Your D-N-A? So I'm — what? — your clone?

NADIRA

It becomes very lonely watching everyone you know die — even for an android. When I created you, I hoped that I was creating a daughter of sorts—

IZIA

I'm not your daughter! My parents — they died the day before I finished gestation — otherwise I wouldn't have been processed.

NADIRA

Your parents never died, Izia, because they never existed. You were processed because I ordered you. A true android from birth, not a converted consciousness as I was. Such a waste.

Nadira shakes her head sadly.

NADIRA (cont'd)

Come back to Callisto and let's end this.

Nadira disappears.

IZIA

Show me the P-C-F Cloud — all of it.

A digital window pops up in front of Izia's face. In red text, it states: 'DNA PASSCODE REQUIRED.' Izia presses the palm of her hand against the window. The text changes to green, and the window disappears. In its place, a holographic depiction of the Solar System appears. The words 'PCF DYSON CLOUD' blink momentarily, followed by thousands of minuscule blinking dots. Izia takes a step forward, and the Forge disappears.

END MUSIC

[/THE FORGE] - EXT. CALLISTO

Nadira and Izia stand opposite one another on the surface of Callisto.

NADIRA

Come here, Izia — there's no need for you to suffer any longer. I promise to make this quick.

IZIA

I'm not afraid of you! You saw what I did to Kendon — to Jane. I'll — I'll—

NADIRA

(laughing)
What? Do the same to me? Don't be ridiculous. You can't kill me. Didn't Kendon tell you anything about Soldium?

IZIA

All the soldi in the world won't save you from the hell you deserve.

NADIRA

Wrong. So long as a single Soldium server remains online, I will survive. So long as one piece of soldi exists, I will exist alongside it — a bipartite entity. That's the real beauty of the Soldi Code that I wrote — I wrote myself into it.

Nadira, confident and triumphant, takes a step toward Izia and away from the exterior awning of the Trailhead Gateway. Izia moves instinctively to take a step backward, hesitates, then resets her foot and faces Nadira defiantly. In the vast space behind Izia, points of light begin to sparkle — several at first, then many hundreds.

EXT. JUPITER SYSTEM

Countless spots of light blossom in the space surrounding the Jupiter System, then blaze into bright lines of redirected sunlight. The fiery rays all target the same small moon lurking in Jupiter's shadow.

EXT. CALLISTO

Thousands of rays of redirected sunlight converge on Nadira in a thick, white column.

> **NADIRA**
> Izia!

A DIGITAL SCREAM pierces Izia's mind, then recedes as Nadira is vaporized in a flash. The column of light splits, and the individual rays travel along the surface of the moon, each seeming to move with a mind of its own. Izia stands motionless while the rays dance around her; they halt variously and pulse, searing holes through the moon's surface and deep into the Valhalla Hive.

> **IZIA**
> Dorothy? Can you hear me?

> **DOROTHY**
> Iz? Is tHAt YO-YO-YO-YOuuuuuu—

Dorothy's voice devolves into a digital TRILL, then stops.

> **IZIA**
> (panicked)
> Dorothy? What's wrong?

> **DOROTHY**
> Circa—circus—cirCUITS-ts-ts. CIRCuits tried — fLIED — FRyed-eyed-eyed-kkkkshh.

The sound of STATIC fills Izia's ears.

IZIA
Dorothy? DOROTHY!

Izia WAILS in rage. She winks the Hive cameras back into her vision and scrolls through several cameras, each displaying an image of chaos.

SERIES OF SHOTS - DESTRUCTION INSIDE THE HIVE
A. A ray of concentrated sunlight lances through the ceiling of a small electrical room full of servers. The ray traces a path across a bank of Soldium servers, leaving molten metal in its wake.
B. Dozens of citizens in a curved hallway struggle to breathe as drone clouds swarm to seal matching holes in the floor and ceiling, the metal around the holes still glowing red.
C. Samir's eyes stare lifelessly at a hole in the ceiling. A pool of blood spreads across the floor around his head and drips slowly into a hole in the floor.

EXT. CALLISTO

Izia falls to her knees and stares at the Trailhead Gateway. Her eyes are wide but clear as she reignites the Dyson Reflector rays and gathers them around her in the same thick, white column. She closes her eyes and slowly exhales as the rays converge. The column of light intensifies until Izia's body is vaporized, then the light extinguishes.

EXT. CALLISTO - [THE FORGE]

Izia flashes into existence among the indigo-gridded lines of the Forge. The holographic depiction of the Solar System still glows in front of her, as do the thousands of minuscule blinking dots that represent the PCF Dyson Cloud.

IZIA
Have you all had enough of this system too?

Izia expands the corners of the holographic display until the Centauri System edges into view. She presses her finger to the system's binary stars, and tracers appear leading to the pair of stars from each of the blinking dots.

IZIA

Farewell, Callisto.

MUSIC CUE: "Since I Left You," by The Avalanches

Izia walks resolutely, heading deeper into the Forge.

BEGIN CLOSING CREDITS

END CLOSING CREDITS

END MUSIC

INT. VALHALLA HIVE - ELEVATOR - NIGHT

The CHIME SOUNDS frantically (440 Hz). Jane lies in a pool of her blood on the floor of the elevator. The drugs have reduced her eyes to slits and pasted a dumb smile on her face. She is barely conscious and talking nonsense. Robbie appears at the end of the dark hallway, moving quickly toward the elevator.

ROBBIE
Jane?! What de—

JANE
Uncle Robbie!

Jane shakes her stump of an arm in an attempted wave. Robbie dashes to her side and falls to his knees.

JANE (cont'd)
Say hello to my lil' friends! They hurt a'first, but now — now I kinda like'm.

ROBBIE
What de hell happened?

JANE
They flew'ou'of the wall — two clouds of 'em — then they landed on me. Then they bi'me — ow! — then they kissed me — mmm. Now though—

Jane shakes her arm at Robbie again.

> ### JANE (cont'd)
> We're friends!

Robbie gently slides his arms under Jane's body and gingerly lifts her off the floor. She rests her head on his shoulder and closes her eyes.

> ### ROBBIE
> *Ja*, you're friends alright.

INT. WATER TREATMENT FACILITY

Jason perches on the edge of the single chair in the dimly lit room. He jumps to his feet when Robbie steps through the doorway carrying Jane.

> ### ROBBIE
> Jase? Where'd you come from?

> ### JASON
> We couldn't find Jane. What happened to her?

> ### ROBBIE
> Found her like dis.

> ### JASON
> Is she going to be O-K?

> ### ROBBIE
> *Ja*, she'll be alright. De medic drones must have got to her early.

Robbie sets Jane's sleeping form in the hammock while Jason activates the wall's digital screen. He pulls up a window titled 'HEALTH MONITOR,' and sets it running diagnostics on Jane. It delivers a preliminary report confirming stabilized vitals.

> ### JASON
> Something's wrong.

> ### ROBBIE
> Something else?

JASON

I'm trying to order a new medic drone for Jane, but it says my soldi account is empty.

Robbie skirts around Jason. He leans past his nephew to type at the control panel. He opens a new window titled 'SOLDIUM SERVERS.' The screen is black. Robbie types a series of commands, each more furious than the last. He SLAMS his palms down on the table.

JANE

Mmm... Uncle Robbie?

ROBBIE

Get your rest, girl.

JANE

What's wrong?

ROBBIE

De servers must have been slagged by whatever attacked de Hive.

JANE

Oh, that's nice.

Jane's eyes remain closed as she drifts back into her drug-induced sleep.

ROBBIE

Ja, real fuckin' nice. Every online server wiped—

JANE

Online. That's a funny word.

JASON

What about an offline server?

A contemplative grin replaces the scowl on Robbie's face.

ROBBIE

No one would dink to attack an offline server.

Robbie hurries to the wall near the water treatment equipment and opens a false panel. He pulls a small, black box from the wall cavity and rushes back to the table. Setting the box on the table, he traces a line to it from the holoscreen, then selects the power icon. The box glows slightly. Robbie brings up the Soldium Servers window again. The screen is black, but an indigo cursor blinks in the upper left corner. The cursor moves rapidly across the screen: 'Hello, Heer Van Dyke.'

FADE OUT

Giovanni awoke with a start. No clock was visible, but he was sure that several hours had elapsed since he had fallen asleep. As he stretched his arms out, his right hand struck against the bag of blueberries sitting on the arm of the couch in a darkened pool of condensation droplets that had run off the sides of the plastic. The mushy contents of the bag further confirmed Giovanni's speculation about the passage of time. He got up and brought the blueberries back to the kitchen. After tossing the bag into the freezer, Giovanni plodded to a small secretariat desk in the corner of the room and grabbed his tan canvas bag from where it sat atop the desk. He walked out his backdoor and onto a cement balcony furnished with two grey metal chairs and a matching table; sitting on one of the chairs, he propped his legs on the other, and retrieved two books from within the bag — his black, banded notebook, and a hardcover copy of *The Count of Monte Cristo*. He tossed the notebook onto the table and flipped open the front cover of Dumas' tome. There, a small rectangular cavity had been carefully incised into the interior pages. A joint rested in the carved out hollow. Giovanni tipped the book up, dumped the joint into his hand, and then stuck it in his mouth, unlit.

He sat that way for several minutes before trading the hardcover book for his notebook. Pulling the elastic band away from the front cover of the notebook, he tested its resistance as well as his own.

Snap.

The elastic band slipped off his finger. He set the book down on the table, then flipped to the back of the notebook and began to read through the poems he had written about Her. Each time he finished reading a page, he tore it out of the notebook, crumpled it into a loose ball, and dropped it into a large, glass ashtray on the table. When he reached the final page, he closed the notebook and pulled a cheap matchbook from under the ashtray. The matchbook was black with the word '*Ray's*' stamped on the front in white, waxy letters. Eight matches remained, their indigo heads in a tight formation of two rows of four. Giovanni peeled one away from the rest, bent it backwards, and struck it against the matchbook's abrasive pad; the little torch flared to life. He let it unfold to ignite the heads of its neighbors before dropping the flaming lump onto the rough pyramid of crumpled poems, then watched while the poems disappeared into smoke and ash as the fire consumed them — paper, ink, and ideas all annihilated in an instant.

Giovanni tore the final poem from the book. He held the corner of the page to the flames, brought the burning page to his mouth, touched it to the tip of his joint, and inhaled deeply. The page continued to burn at a steady rate although the flames subsided. The joint kept pace as Giovanni inhaled — once, twice — then he froze. The line of incinerated paper that had been snaking its way down the page stopped, leaving only the name of the final poem, Her name, upside down in his hand. No sooner had he recognized this than the scrap of paper leapt from his hand, borne aloft by the wind. It danced momentarily in an updraft before absconding with his erstwhile title.

Giovanni looked back to his notebook, still opened from the back. The interior spine showed the scars of its lost poems, but then he turned the page and a fresh, blank page stared back at him from the right hand side of the bifold. It held the promise of possibility: uniform lines waiting to be brought to life — filled with the as yet unimagined quirks of endless characters and locales — or ignored entirely in favor of a roughly sketched figure — drops of wet ink smearing across the page under the illustrator's littlest finger. The pale, creamy page seemed to scream at him in its urgency.

Giovanni slid his pen from its resting place within the exterior spine of the notebook. He clicked the pen's point into place, unclicked it, repeated the action, then spun the pen around his thumb — once, twice. He clicked the pen's point back into place, then bent his head over the notebook and scribbled furiously. The heat and humidity made the ink in his pen flow quickly and smear thickly. When he finished, a smudged set of lines lied down the middle of the page. He tossed his pen onto the table and sat back in his chair to finish his joint. When he reached the end, he stubbed the butt into the ashes of his poems, collected his books and bag, and retreated to his bed.

Chapter 9

The next morning, Giovanni stood in his small bathroom and inspected his face in the mirror. A thick, violet line shaded the split and swollen skin under his right eye. Similar patches of color marred his cheek and the bridge of his nose. He smiled at the sight, then winced; the skin on that side of his face had grown tighter overnight, and a dull, pulsing pain throbbed in his head. Giovanni thought about changing his contact lenses, but decided not to molest his swollen eye any further. He patiently completed his daily rituals — toothbrush, tweezers, toilet — then flushed away the refuse on his way out of the bathroom.

In his bedroom, surrounded by bare, white walls, he selected a clean pair of undershorts and a fresh, black T-shirt from a chest of drawers and donned both before snatching the jeans he had worn the previous night from the floor near his bed and stepping into them. On his way out of the room, he saw his notebook lying on the bedside table; it was open to the smudged poem he had scribbled the previous night. He rapidly reread the lines then tucked his pen into the notebook, flipped the cover closed, banded it shut, and shoved it into his tan canvas bag. Giovanni slung the bag over his shoulder on his way to the front door, where he slipped his feet into his black sneakers before exiting the apartment.

Ignoring the broiling heat inside his car, Giovanni searched his pockets for the stub of paper that Britney had given him. His fingertips brushed against the ticket's embossed nubs; he pulled the ticket from his pocket. An address was printed on one side of the ticket, and, below that, a series of numbers. Giovanni recognized the street number, so he shifted his car into gear and departed. Knowing the ride was short, he drove in silence, counting down the street numbers. He rolled the windows down and let the wind refresh the air in the car, wiggling the fingers of one hand against the air stream out the window. After a few minutes of letting his hand slice through air currents, Giovanni turned the car down the appropriate street and decelerated to count down house numbers from their mailboxes.

Next one, he thought to himself as he read the number printed on a mailbox in the shape of a manatee.

A black metal fence delineated the perimeter of the next property. The fence was painfully modern — straight slats spaced too narrowly to permit even a squirrel to pass. The tops of the slats were vicious isosceles spikes, following one another in line like an interminable row of shark fins. Giovanni drove along the fence for several minutes before reaching the property's entrance. He turned into the driveway and was immediately confronted by the domineering black metal fence. A black plastic box atop a matching metal pole stared at Giovanni from outside his open car window. The box looked expectantly at him, and Giovanni looked expectantly back.

"Hello?" he called. "Anybody there?"

No response.

"Open sesame?" he tried.

Giovanni waved his hand in front of the box, trying to activate some hidden sensor. The small, flat box stared back at him, its expectancy turning to disinterest. Exasperated, he rapped his knuckles against the box.

Thock, thock, thock.

The sound was distinctly hollow. Giovanni ran his fingers along the edge of the box; he found the lip of a cover and flipped it open, revealing an illuminated keypad. Sighing through his nose, he dug the ticket out of his pocket and entered the series of numbers printed along the bottom: *5-0-3-0-1*. The portion of fence blocking the driveway began to slide open from the left. Once the gap was wide enough for his small car, Giovanni drove on.

The road split before him, so he veered to the right and followed a long, wide road that ran along a large pond with a statuary fountain at its center. As he drove level with the pond's statue, Giovanni saw its form through the spray of surrounding water jets: it was a huntress, her bow stretched back in the eternal pause of Myronic motion. Her arms were missing from the forearms — left off in neoclassical imitation — but Giovanni imagined them as they would have looked: taut and powerful, one stretched out in front of her, the other drawn back to her cheek. Cords flexed in her back as she flexed her nonexistent bow. She had been wrought from copper, although her warm cinnamon skin had long since tarnished to a dull green. The huntress stood solitarily in the middle of the water, silently assertive in her vigilance.

Giovanni continued down the drive until he reached a roundabout with a towering, white stone obelisk at its center. Neatly trimmed grass filled the space around the obelisk to the edge of the circular road. On the opposite side of the car, a massive wrought-iron gate stood between two decorative porticos, each supported by four white columns. Giovanni stopped in front of the monumental entrance to the house, and a young man wearing white sneakers, shorts, and collared shirt offered him a numbered ticket as he stepped out of his car. He took the ticket, and the young man hopped into the driver's seat and sped off to park it with the others. A number had been stamped in purple ink on the paper: 27. Giovanni tucked the ticket into his pocket and walked to the enormous gate. He tugged at one side of the gate, but the ornate metal refused to move. Giovanni inhaled deeply and sighed through his nose again.

"Gio?" a voice nearby called.

Giovanni turned to his right and saw Vere smiling amusedly.

"What're you doing?" Vere asked from the doorway of a gatehouse just a few paces away. He had dressed smartly for the occasion in a collared, periwinkle shirt and navy pants.

"Vere, thank god," Giovanni greeted his friend as he hurried to the gatehouse.

"Whoa, nice shiner."

"Oh, thanks," Giovanni joked. "How are you?"

"I'm good, you?"

"Yeah, good, good," Giovanni replied as he stepped into the doorway of the gatehouse and shook hands with his friend. "Although I hate to think how long I would've tugged at that gate if you hadn't spotted me."

"Don't worry — I won't tell," said Vere.

Kateryna stepped inside the gatehouse from the opposing door. Her simple sundress matched Vere's periwinkle shirt.

"There you are," she said, jubilantly kissing Vere on the cheek.

"Here I am, and I found Gio," Vere stated, pointing to the doorway.

"*Ciao*, Gio!"

"*Ciao*, Kateryna."

The two friends hugged warmly.

"Oh my god!" she said as they parted. "What happened to your eye?"

"It's nothing, just a bump."

"That's more than a bump," she responded.

"I'll live," Giovanni said with a shrug.

"Really, Gio? That's all you've got to say?"

He shrugged again, smiling sheepishly.

"Well?" she asked. "Shall we then, gentlemen?"

Kateryna took Vere by the arm and led him through the door she had recently entered. Giovanni followed his friends out of the gatehouse and past a row of four palm trees that ran parallel with the walls of the estate. It took him a few paces before he noticed that Vere's shirt matched the periwinkle hue of Kateryna's sundress; their beige twill shoes were similarly paired. Looking down at his own garments, Giovanni noticed a faint stain near the pocket of his jeans. He scratched at it halfheartedly.

Vere and Kateryna stopped at a portable bar, and Giovanni looked up from his preening just in time to avoid crashing into them from behind. The bar was tended by a woman in white, who had arranged a dozen or so glasses in hasty rows before her. She was pouring a dram of deep purple liquid into each as the three friends approached her from across the bar. When she finished that task, she added bright, metallic champagne from an oversized bottle. Finally, she dropped violet rose buds into the mouth of each slender glass. The finished product was a lilac drink with bubbles drifting up toward a delicate flower that floated at the top of the glass.

"May I?" Giovanni asked the bartender, pointing to her colorful array.

"Please," she replied, sliding a glass nearer to him.

Vere and Kateryna each picked up a glass of their own, then the three continued their journey toward the throng of revelers who massed around the pool at the center of the estate. A vortex of them revolved in the shaded lawn before the pool. The man Giovanni knew only as 'The Heel' stood in the middle of the maelstrom in an airy hued three piece suit. He grinned widely as he greeted the steady procession of guests. Vere, Kateryna, and Giovanni walked to their nearest estimation of the beginning of the line and slipped into the stream of guests. The three friends sipped their drinks while they shuffled around the circular route to their host.

"Gio!" a new voice sounded behind Giovanni.

He looked over his shoulder and saw Britney walking across the grounds toward him. He turned to face her.

"Wow," she said as she stopped before him, "that looks *way* worse than they described."

"You know what happened?" Kateryna asked. "He won't tell me."

"Yeah, I know what happened: some asshole chucked a mug of beer at his face."

"Really?" Kateryna asked with wide eyes. "I'm Kateryna, by the way."

"Hi, I'm Britney, and, yes, really."

"It was empty," Giovanni said, shrugging again.

"Well, thank god for that," Britney quipped, "otherwise somebody might have gotten hurt."

"What about you?" Giovanni asked Britney. "How'd your night end?"

"Good. After the glass incident, we—"

"Cousins!" a new voice bellowed.

Rex sauntered toward them, arm in arm with his wives — Felicity to his right in a silver cocktail dress and the woman Giovanni knew only as 'The Head' to his left in a trim, purple suit. Rex wore a grey, pinstriped suit. The three of them stopped when they reached Vere, Kateryna, and Giovanni. Rex took his arms from around his wives and unbuttoned his jacket. The two groups exchanged pleasantries, handshakes, and hugs; then Rex, Felicity, and The Head joined Vere, Kateryna, Giovanni, and Britney in their patient shuffle toward The Heel. Rex searched his pockets, then pulled a folded handkerchief from inside his jacket and used it to mop the sweat from his bald pate. He returned the handkerchief to his pocket and turned to face Britney.

"Hotter'n hell for this time of year, eh?"

Vere opened his mouth to respond, but Rex continued talking.

"I don't remember this one," he said, "and, sweetheart, I would'a remembered you."

"I don't remember you either," she replied, "but I know I'm not your sweetheart."

Rex laughed boisterously.

"Spark, that's what that is! C'mon, let me introduce you to my good friend, Bobbie Bulez."

Rex shouldered his way closer to the man at the center of the crowd then grasped the man's hand and wrung it vigorously. Britney followed in Rex's wake, and the rest of the group filled in the space behind her.

"Rex, enjoying the party?" The Heel asked.

"Hell of a good show, old man," Rex confirmed. "I want you to meet somebody special. A friend of mine who—"

"Britney Barkhourt," Britney said, elbowing past Rex as she extended her hand toward Bobbie 'The Heel' Bulez.

"It's a pleasure to meet you, Ms. Barkhourt," Bobbie greeted her in return, shaking her hand. "You are our poet laureate, if my memory serves?"

"Yes, one of them," she answered with a wry smile.

"I didn't know we were to be graced by more than one," Bobbie replied.

"Well, Gio and I agreed to split the prize from the poetry contest," she said, then turned her head slightly toward Giovanni and raised her voice, "so that means we're splitting the responsibilities too."

Bobbie laughed — a richly modulated twitter of delight.

"Well, we won't put either of you on the spot today. Please let me know if there is anything that you desire," said Bobbie with a gracious smile.

"What a remarkably charming man," Britney commented as she led the group away from the circle of guests.

"His only remarkable aspect is that he's perfectly average in every regard," Rex said too loudly as he put an arm around Britney's waist.

Britney darted out of Rex's reach and made her way to one of the portable bars, where she stood with her back against the bar top. The rest of the group followed behind Rex and Britney. As he ambled past Bobbie, Giovanni could see that his host's suit seemed to shimmer in the sunlight, alternating grey and blue like a peregrine. A gust of wind aided this image by momentarily sweeping his hair back from his face. Then the wind died. By the time Giovanni rejoined the group, they were choosing fresh glasses of the lilac concoction from the portable bar. He selected another glass as well.

"Ya got any real drinks back there, or is it just this purple shit?" Rex asked the man tending the bar.

"Whatever you like, sir," the man said, wiping the palms of his hands against the back of his white pants.

"Let's 'ave a bourbon then, plenty of ice."

Rex turned to Britney.

"So, a poet, eh?"

"Excuse me?" she replied.

"You're a poet?" he asked, picking up the glass that the bartender set before him.

Britney began answering Rex's question, but Giovanni was too distracted to listen; he was absorbed by a grotesque display of sensuousness: Rex's repetitive efforts to sate his thirst. First, he would shake the ice back and forth in his glass, Lilliputian glaciers rattling monotonously; next, he would bring the glass to his mouth and slurp loudly at the liquid that seeped around the edges of the ice; then he would suck a piece of ice out of the liquid and crunch it repeatedly, grinding it into minuscule granules; finally, he would smack his lips, then burp proudly, then repeat the entire performance.

"*Ahhh*," he puffed as he drained the last of the watery remains from his glass. "That's a damn fine bourbon."

Britney responded to Rex's exclamation with a sidelong glance and a flitting scowl.

"Anyway," she continued, "that's why it's called 'So I Say Goodbye.'"

"Now, I always wondered that," Rex lied, swirling the ice around his glass.

"I didn't," Felicity muttered.

"So you won a poetry contest then?" Rex asked Britney.

Britney crossed her arms.

"C'mon, let's go find somewhere to sit," Felicity said to The Head before the two women marched away from the group.

"What do you say?" Giovanni asked Vere and Kateryna. "Do you want to see the rest of this place?"

"You guys go ahead. I'm going to visit the restroom," Kateryna answered. "I'll find you after."

She kissed Vere on the cheek again before walking toward the palatial house at the rear of the estate.

"Well?" Giovanni asked Vere.

"Let's check out the buffet," Vere suggested.

Vere nodded at his cousin as he and Giovanni navigated over to the pool and the buffet line that encircled it. Giovanni gave a small wave to Britney when he passed, and she gave him an exaggerated look of exasperation in return. Rex didn't notice the conspicuous exchange as he was busy eyeing Britney's chest.

Vere and Giovanni walked along white-clothed tables that held a seemingly endless variety of foods in silver serving dishes.

"Quit babbling, nimrod! I can't understand what the hell you're saying," a small woman scolded an unidentified mumbler.

Moving down the line, they passed four young boys jostling one another.

"No fair!"

"It's the last piece!"

"Shut up — there'll be more."

"I'll tell dad!"

"I'll tell him what happened to the TV."

"That was your fault!"

"Nuh-uh! You broke it!"

"No, you broke it!"

They passed Abin Nash, standing next to a younger version of himself.

"This is my brother, Caël," the director remarked to the woman behind him in line.

"Kai-*el*? Am I saying that right?" the woman tilted her head, and the enormous brim of her maroon hat mimicked the movement.

"Yes, you've got it," the younger man affirmed.

"How do you spell that?" she asked.

"Exactly like it sounds—"

Vere and Giovanni continued down the line.

"—you say Lucas Port?"

Giovanni paused as he recognized his friend's name.

"Aye," answered a tall, dark skinned man in a khaki suit.

"More like Lucas 'Any-Port-in-a-Storm,'" the first voice claimed. "Anyway, I can't abide the man—"

Giovanni resumed walking. He looked ahead for Vere, but couldn't find him. He swiveled his head left and right in search, then spotted his friend on the opposite side of the pool, making his way back toward the starting point. Giovanni hurried around the curved edge of the pool to catch up.

"—this all looks so tantalizing—"

"—did you see the—"

"—plan to spend the summer in Greece—"

"—city was Corinth. It was—"

Giovanni caught up with Vere near the end of the line, where three men were engaged in an argument about the merits of dessert cheeses.

"Judas!" a man in a seersucker suit called out.

"Go easy, old boy," the man behind him replied.

"*Et tu, Brute?*" the man in seersucker demanded.

"Looks like it's the same stuff on both sides," Vere said to Giovanni as the two men neared their starting point. The circle of guests surrounding their host had thinned slightly.

"Yeah, looks that way," Giovanni replied, skirting around a middle-aged couple with two young girls, all four dressed in matching khaki pants and navy blazers. "I'm not really hungry anyway."

"I think I saw some tables over there," Vere pointed to the line of palm trees near the front wall of the estate.

The two men picked out a path to the tree line. On the other side of the trees, they discovered a row of vacant plastic tables and sat at the first one in the row. Four empty champagne flutes stood in a cluster near one of the seats. As soon as he sat down, Giovanni began rolling an imaginary ball between his palms in a rhythmic motion.

"Lamenting again?" Vere asked. "No profit will come of it, mate."

"No, just thinking about something I have to finish."

"You'd better hurry — death doesn't wait on any of us," Vere said. "Nor the Devil."

"What's he got to do with it?"

"Devil always knows what you want most."

Giovanni heard a small cough and smelled a familiar scent. Scanning the area, he saw a wispy cloud of smoke rise above the tops of the palm trees. He nudged Vere with his elbow and flicked his head toward the smoke rising above the tree line. A woman rounded the corner; it was The Head in her purple suit. Her face was made up modestly, highlighting her attractive features — red lips, a yellow-gold glow on her cheeks, black around her eyes. As she neared the table, she raised her hand in greeting before bringing the same hand to her mouth, a joint held between her first two fingers. In her other hand, she carried a glass of the lilac drink. She breathed deeply, and the glowing ember at the end of her joint smoldered in response. With an open palm, Vere demonstrated that she should sit in one of the plastic chairs around the table.

"Hey, Vere," she said as she sat. "Looks like you found my fallen soldiers."

She offered Vere her joint.

"Hey, Bebe," Vere greeted her as he accepted her offering. "Couldn't take all the people?"

"Just one of them really," she answered.

She turned to Giovanni.

"Remind me your name?"

"Giovanni."

"Gio is a close friend of mine," Vere added, passing him the joint. "Gio, this is Bebe."

"How do you do, Gio?" Bebe asked.

"Fine, thanks. How are you?"

"Very well. What do you do?"

"I'm a poet," Giovanni replied.

"A poet?" she echoed.

"Yes."

"Does that pay well?"

"No."

Giovanni passed the joint to Bebe.

"Then whatever are you doing here?" she asked.

Giovanni raised an eyebrow.

"Excuse me?" he said evenly.

"I mean no disrespect," Bebe continued, "but this is not the place for a starving artist."

"How do you mean?"

She took a long drag on the joint.

"I me-e-ean," she exhaled a lungful of smoke, elongating her pronunciation of the word, "this is shameless solicitation parading as celebration."

"Well," Giovanni responded, "there's free food, so this seems like a pretty good place for a starving artist."

"Well, since you won't be funding anything, why don't you tell me a poem?" she suggested.

"I don't memorize my poems," he replied.

Bebe began giggling, snorting smoke out of her nose with each set of laughs.

"*Haha* — so, not only are you a poet — *hahaha* — but you're a poet without any — *haha* — poems? Now there's a story," she said as she passed the joint to Vere.

"I think the story about the woman who married her cousin is a bit more interesting," Giovanni muttered.

"Oh, that was just to get access to the trust," Bebe stated nonchalantly. "Granddaddy's will was very specific that his money would only go to 'his wedded progeny who can provide me with legitimate heirs.'" She began laughing again. "I don't imagine he thought we would take that first bit so literally."

"And what about the second bit?" Vere asked.

"Well, technically I'm sure we *could* produce heirs, but Bobbie never would. He's not interested in women."

"Is he gay?" Vere queried.

"No, he's not gay; he's not straight either; he's just not interested," she explained.

"Is that why he's called The Heel?" Giovanni asked, taking the joint from Vere.

"Not really. Bobbie...he was called The Heel because he gives — gave — our productions feet."

"Feet?" Vere asked.

"He made them walk, made them happen — produced them," she clarified at last. "I created many visions, but nobody would have ever seen any of them if it weren't for him — not that anybody has seen anything from us in the last ten years anyway."

"Why not?" asked Giovanni as he passed the joint back to Bebe. She took two quick puffs then passed it along to Vere.

"That's when Bobbie lost all his money in a Ponzi scheme," she said with a shrug.

Vere handed the joint to Giovanni, who took one long drag and passed it to Bebe.

"I don't understand. How did he produce the play for the festival then?" Giovanni pressed.

"The same way he's 'hosting' this party," she answered.

"How do you mean?" Giovanni asked for the second time.

"I mean this is Rex's house, and it was Rex's money that put that play on the stage."

Bebe dropped the butt of the joint into one of the glasses sitting near her elbow. The ember sizzled in a shallow pool of purple liquid then extinguished.

"And it's Rex," she continued, "who I am currently avoiding."

Vere and Giovanni smiled at Bebe's candor, but her scowl cut short their levity.

"It's exhausting. The man wants an audience, not a partner; someone to talk at, not with."

"Is that what Felicity is for?" asked Giovanni.

"Do you know how a triad works?" Bebe asked, but didn't wait for a response. "There's always a weak link. The balance is delicate. Rex can't see me as inferior to Felicity, but nor can she see me as superior to her, lest she try to undermine me with Rex. Power is a fickle mistress."

"Just ask Caesar," Giovanni replied.

"Does that make me emperor?" asked Bebe.

"Empress, I think," Vere offered.

Giovanni pressed on, raising an eyebrow to accompany his question.

"Do you love him?"

"What does that matter?" returned Bebe.

"Isn't he your husband or partner or something—"

"He's a boorish old fool."

"Excuse me?" Giovanni regarded Bebe incredulously.

It was Bebe's turn to raise an eyebrow at Giovanni's exclamation.

"Rex thinks a proud look can disguise his lying tongue. His heart devises wicked plots, and his feet hurry him to the mischief," she continued. "He's a deceitful, treacherous, manipulative little man."

"Why are you with him if you're not satisfied?" Giovanni pried.

"I said I don't love him, but love and satisfaction are not synonymous."

"How do you mean?" Giovanni asked for the third time.

"I mean you won't find satisfaction in other people," replied Bebe.

"Nor in the bottom of a glass or the butt of a joint," Vere added.

Vere looked as though he had more to say, but just then Felicity stomped around the edge of the row of trees — a feat of sorts in her stiletto high heels. She looked at each of Bebe, Vere, and Giovanni in turn before her eyes settled on the champagne flute with the bloated, purple remains of the joint lying half submerged in the last sip of liquid. She sniffed pointedly as she turned back to Bebe.

"You said you were going to wait for me," Felicity hissed.

"Yeah, but you took a re-e-eally long time," Bebe answered, widening her reddened eyes to emphasize her elongated pronunciation.

"I had to babysit our husband while he tried to sneak off with that whore!" Felicity argued. "Meanwhile, you smoked all our weed without me!"

"There's more inside," Bebe stated.

"That's not the point!" Felicity insisted.

"Calm down," Giovanni interjected. "It's not the end of the—"

"Who the hell is this?" Felicity cut him off, then sized him up with her eyes. "Never mind, I remember you," she smiled maliciously. "Have you been wearing the same clothes all weekend?"

"Pretty much," he replied.

"Oh my," Felicity snickered into her hand, "how embarrassing."

"For whom?" Giovanni responded.

"For you, obviously," Felicity shot back. "Look around you; you're surrounded by the best people in this town and you're dressed like you've just been paroled. Who even invited you?"

Felicity continued yelling while Giovanni looked on with unfocused eyes. He thought of Hermes sneaking around Atlantis and laughed.

"This is funny to you?" Felicity shrieked at him.

Giovanni brought his eyes back into focus. Felicity, Bebe, and Vere were all watching him. A small backdrop of spectators had formed behind Felicity.

"Huh?" Giovanni managed.

"I said—"

Felicity began to answer, but Giovanni wasn't interested in hearing her repeat whatever she had said. He stood and brushed unseen dust from his knees then gulped down the remains of his lilac drink. Felicity was still ranting, but she stopped mid-sentence, still mouthing her last syllable, as Giovanni tossed his glass high into the air above his head. Felicity lunged forward and cupped her hands together to catch the falling glass. She would have succeeded too, except she had forgotten about her own glass. The falling glass collided with the one in Felicity's cupped left hand, and both shattered, raining lilac-stained shards of glass onto the gravel.

"Goddamnit!" Felicity shrieked. She looked from Vere to Bebe, still seated at the plastic table, then turned her venomous stare to Giovanni. He, however, had brusquely walked away from the scene as soon as he tossed the glass into the air, and was already making his way out of the exterior door of the gatehouse when Felicity looked to where he had been standing.

Giovanni smiled at Felicity's vulgar outburst as he jogged past the wrought-iron gate. No attendant was present when he got to the valet's podium, so he opened the metal key box and removed his keys from the slot marked *27*. He stuffed a crumpled bill from his pocket into the tip jar then resumed jogging toward the herringbone pattern of parked cars that lined the street beyond the roundabout with the domineering obelisk. He read the names of his compatriots as he went — Ferrari, Lamborghini, Maserati. He recognized his own car a few paces away, just past a miniature golden angel hood ornament — or, at least, a woman whose arms were thrown back in such a way to appear as wings. He rounded the angel, unlocked his doors, and jumped into his car. As he did, the wrought-iron gate to Rex's estate split at the middle and the two halves opened outwards. A black golf cart exploded out of the narrow gap. It careened around the roundabout — nearly tipping over and spilling its sole occupant — and sped toward the cars that lined the street.

Giovanni saw the golf cart in his rearview mirror as he reversed out of his parking spot. He laughed softly to himself as he shifted into drive, but stopped laughing when he realized that the golf cart was somehow gaining on him. Giovanni accelerated down the road on the opposite side of the pond as he had on his way into the property, the huntress maintaining her aim as the black and white car raced past her. A heartbeat later, the black metal gate at the entrance to the property began to slide open.

As he neared the expanding gap in the gate, Giovanni noticed three things simultaneously: first, that the man piloting the golf cart with a maniacal look on his face was none other than his erstwhile host, Rex; second, that Rex had his rose gold pistol held in his free hand; and third, that a hulking, black truck rumbled in neutral on the other side of the gate. Giovanni downshifted and steered his car head on toward the truck. The truck flashed its headlights. Giovanni accelerated. The truck honked — once, twice, then a continuous bleating. Giovanni pressed the gas pedal against the floor. Just before colliding with the colossal truck, he jerked the steering wheel to the left and zipped though the meager space allowed by the fence post. An outraged face in the truck's passenger seat window flashed by, but Giovanni was already past before he could register a response. He yanked the steering wheel back to the right and whipped his car around the bed of the truck and onto the main street.

Bang!

A sound like a gunshot rent through the air. Glancing out his passenger window as he drove past the gate, Giovanni saw Rex hunched over the steering wheel of the golf cart. The sound had come from the cart crashing full bore into the front corner of the truck. Giovanni turned down a side street, circumnavigated Rex's neighborhood, and headed east. He rolled down his windows and spun the radio's volume dial until it reached its maximum volume: "*Bienvenido de nuevo a* W-A-K-E, The Wake! *Yo soy* DJ LP, and I've got some bad news for you, Floaters: the end is nigh. That's right; the weekend is almost over! But I've got one more track for you before I sign off. *Todos ustedes saben esto: es 'El Día de los Muertos' de Las Vírgenes del Sol!*"

Mictecacihuatl
nosotros adoramos
su la difunta
difunta Catrina

Los Muertos
caminan con nosotros
los muertos caminan
el día de los, el día de los muertos

Antes de honrar a
sus santos honramos
a nuestra propria
los padres de neustros padres

Los Muertos
caminan con nosotros
los muertos caminan
el día de los, el día de los muertos

Several songs later, Giovanni turned onto the access road to the beach. Cars still crowded the way even this late in the year, parked on either side of the single lane road; Giovanni drove along the coast until he found an empty space among them. He pulled into the spot and pressed the trunk release, then got out of his car, timing his exit to the rhythm of traffic. He pulled a pair of swim shorts, stiff with salt, from the trunk, and quickly changed into them, then grabbed his bag from the passenger seat and set off toward the beach. Despite the multitude of vehicles, Giovanni didn't see any other people on the sidewalk. He walked along, heated by the midday sun — even his shadow seemed to hide from the fury of the glowing orb at its zenith.

Giovanni ascended a flight of stairs made of rough wood planks. The stairs leveled out to form a landing after just a few steps. Past the steps, scrub grass and gnarled pines gave way to the dull glow of tan sand. He stepped off the landing and wiggled his toes as his feet sunk into the beach's warm, golden carpet. Once his feet grew accustomed to the heat, he began the laborious walk up the coast, surveying the scene around him as he went: men, women, and children in bright swim clothes sat on similarly vivid towels or nylon folding chairs; dozens of dogs of every size and color played along the shoreline — digging up esoteric sites, snapping at shadows of birds, rolling onto their backs, or spinning in circles; behind it all, the sun glinted off the surface of the water, reflecting and refracting in the gentle ripples of the calm surf.

Stopping in a relatively uninhabited area, Giovanni dropped his bag, plopped down in the sand, closed his eyes, and focused on the wind blowing softly across his face. Breathing deeply, he counted slowly to ten.

Uno, due, tre, quattro, cinque, sei, sette, otto, nove, dieci.

He exhaled and opened his eyes, squinting against the brightness of the day and the strain of his distressed eyes. He cast his gaze northward, but the lighthouse wasn't there. Or, rather, it was hidden by the coast that curved away from its apex and folded the beach behind its curtain.

Something bumped softly against his back. He looked behind him and saw a battered, white volleyball resting on his towel. Turning toward the source of the interruption, he watched a young woman hustle over to retrieve the ball. Her bikini had rainbow polka dots. Giovanni tossed the ball over to her. She caught it and smiled at him.

"Thanks," she called. "Wanna join? We need one more for five-a-side."

"Maybe later," he smiled back at her.

She shrugged and jogged to rejoin her friends. Giovanni turned back to face the ocean. He dug his black, banded notebook out of his tan canvas bag, slipped the elastic band off the cover, flipped the notebook open to the last remaining pair of pages, and set the notebook on his knees. He wrote on the right hand page, opposite his poem from the previous night.

Every day,
To myself I say,
'Will I ever love again?'

My heart says, 'No,'
My head says, 'Yes,
If you give up on revenge.'

In Fiamme

Come un prigioniero di Plato
Chi era finalmente liberato,
Cosí lui esce della grotta,
E vede é stato un'idiota,
Quindi ride a crepapelle
Quando lui vede le stelle.

John Carney was born and raised in Jupiter, Florida. He joined the military once he graduated high school, and served as a paratrooper and drone operator in the 4th Brigade Combat Team, 25th Infantry Division. After his honorable discharge, John returned to south Florida, where he graduated from university and began teaching Humanities.